# THEY WERE TRYING TO BURY HIM ALIVE

One of the giant red ants poked its head through the pit wall halfway between Geronimo and the top of the crater.

Geronimo wheeled, raising the Marlin, realizing he'd been outflanked, outmaneuvered by the crafty devils! They'd dug a new tunnel, circumventing the bodies, bypassing the dead ants and emerging from the pit wall.

Behind him, there was renewed commotion as the ants tore into the bodies, working frantically to force an exit.

He was trapped!

Ants behind him and ants in front of him!

They had him right where they wanted him.

# DAVID ROBBINS

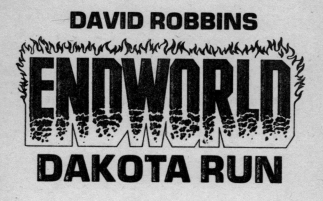

# ENDWORLD

# DAKOTA RUN

LEISURE BOOKS 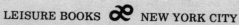 NEW YORK CITY

Dedicated to:
Judy and Joshua, of course. And
King Kong,
Godzilla,
Gorgo,
The Thing, H.G. Wells, Gordon Douglas,
George Worthing Yates,
Ted Sherdeman
and the rest of THEM. . . .

A LEISURE BOOK

Published by

Dorchester Publishing Co., Inc.
6 East 39th Street
New York, NY 10016

Printed in the United States of America

# 1

Was that a scream, or were his ears playing tricks on him?

The man paused, twenty yards below the crest of the sloping hill he was slowly climbing, and listened intently, his black hair blowing in the wind, his keen brown eyes scanning the surrounding terrain.

Who would be screaming way out here in the middle of nowhere?

He cautiously continued his ascent, his green shirt and pants blending in perfectly with the tall grass. His stocky body was tense, his senses alert, as his moccasined feet forged ahead.

There it was again!

The scream was faint and fluctuated, rising and falling in volume, apparently affected by the gusting wind. Still, he was able to pinpoint the direction.

It was coming from the other side of the hill.

The man hurried now, the Arminius .357 Magnum in its shoulder holster under his right arm bouncing as he ran. A tomahawk was tucked under his deerskin belt, and a Marlin 45-70 was draped across his back, suspended from a leather cord angled from his right shoulder to his left hip. A bandoleer, filled with cartridges for the Marlin, crossed his wide chest in the opposite direction.

The distant sound of a gunshot carried on the breeze.

He unslung his 45-70 as he reached the crest of the hill and stopped to get his bearings.

A narrow valley passed the base of his hill and, bordered by another hill to the east and a smaller one to the west, it followed a meandering course until it reached a verdant stand of trees half a mile away. Much closer, maybe a thousand yards or so, was the source of the screams.

A terrified woman, running for all she was worth in his general direction.

The man stared beyond her and discovered the reason for her panic.

Eight horsemen were on her trail, approaching at full gallop, some of them laughing and shouting and waving their arms, evidently enjoying themselves and their pursuit of the hapless female. One of them fired a rifle he was holding, pointing the barrel straight up.

The shot caused the fleeing woman to try to run even faster.

Fun and games. The man in green frowned, debating his course of action. Ordinarly, he would assist the woman without any hesitation. But after his recent experiences in Montana, after being betrayed by a woman he thought he could trust, after being almost killed, he wondered if he were justified in interfering. For all he knew, the woman might deserve whatever these men had planned for her.

The woman was tiring, her pace flagging. She nearly stumbled, recovering her footing at the last instant, and lunged forward.

Cheering wildly, the horsemen bore down on their prey. One of them pulled ahead of his companions, a lariat in his left hand.

The woman glanced over her right shoulder and screamed again, her lengthy black tresses flying.

The man on the hill bent over at the waist and ran toward the woman, keeping his body hidden below the chest-high grass and weeds, his sturdy legs pumping. He couldn't just idly stand by and watch the horsemen harm the woman, if that was what they intended to do. If he could get close enough without being seen, he might learn what this was all about.

Weariness pervading her lithe body, the woman slowed, unable to maintain her frantic pace.

The lead horseman had his lariat ready, and as he closed in on the woman he began swinging the rope in a wide circle over his head. When his horse, a powerful mare, was ten yards from his victim, he released the lariat and watched with satisfaction as the loop swung out and down, encircling the woman and pinning her arms to her sides.

"Ya-hoo!" the horseman exclaimed, elated. He never missed a beat as he tightened his grip on the lariat, his mare passing the woman and racing up the valley.

"No!" the woman managed to shout, a moment before she was brutally jerked from her feet and flung to the exposed turf.

The horseman goaded his steed to greater speed, glancing over his left shoulder, laughing as the woman was dragged along the ground, bouncing and twisting, her torn and tattered form flapping at the end of the lariat.

Relishing the spectacle, the seven other horsemen had reined in and were viewing the event with unrestrained mirth. One of them, a bearded man in buckskins, was the first to glimpse the newcomer. "Look!" he shouted, pointing.

The horeman with the lariat saw his companions gesturing wildly and shouting as they goaded their mounts in his direction. For a moment he thought they were cheering him on, until he abruptly realized they weren't looking at him, but at something else. He twisted, facing front, and was completely startled to observe a man in green standing in the grass, perhaps one hundred yards off, with a rifle to his shoulder.

So much for minding his own business! No one deserved this type of sadistic treatment. The newcomer sighed and fired, the Marlin recoiling into his right shoulder.

Reacting as if a giant had slammed him in the forehead, the horseman catapulted backwards, the rear of his cranium erupting in a crimson spray of flesh, blood, and bone. He tumbled from the mare and landed on his left side, immobile. The mare slowly came to a stop, confused by the sudden loss of its master.

The man in green shifted, sighting again. Their countenances reflecting both rage and grim determination, the remaining seven horsemen were coming straight at him. Even as he aimed, the newcomer marveled at their expertise, at their superb horsemanship. They were riding bareback at breakneck speed, seemingly part of the horses they rode. Four of them were garbed in buckskins, the rest being attired in pants and shirts of various colors. Three carried rifles, one a bow and a quiver of arrows, two held handguns, and the last a gleaming lance.

The riflemen posed the deadliest danger.

Just a few yards more! He wanted to be sure, knowing he couldn't afford to waste a single shot. The Marlin only held four rounds, and he'd expended one of them on the joker with the lariat. He fired again.

A bearded horseman was forcefully propelled from his mount, falling onto the grass in a crumpled heap, his Winchester flying from his lifeless fingers.

The newcomer turned slightly, hurriedly fixing on his next target. Another thunderous report rolled across the valley as a third horseman collapsed.

Only one with a rifle left!

This one unexpectedly veered to his left and reined in, his rifle sweeping to his shoulder.

The two long guns boomed simultaneously, and the horseman jerked sideways and slumped over his mount.

Four down and four to go!

But the remaining horsemen had other ideas. They circled wide and returned to their original position. For a minute they engaged in animated conversation, then they wheeled and raced for the trees.

Good riddance!

The man in green moved toward the prone woman, reloading his Marlin as he went. If she were still alive, he had to get her out of there before the horsemen returned, possibly with reinforcements.

Moaning, the woman struggled to rise onto her hands and knees as he approached. Her waist-length hair was caked with dirt and pieces of grass, her faded blue dress was ripped to shreds, and any visible skin was covered with bruises and welts.

"Is this your idea of a normal date?"

The woman, unaware he was standing there, glanced up, alarmed. Her lively green eyes scrutinized him from head to toe. "You're not one of them," she said, more a statement than a question.

He shook his head, watching the horsemen vanish into the trees. "After what I just did, I don't think they'd let me join them for all the gold in Fort Knox."

"The what?"

He studied her, pleased she wasn't crying hysterically or wimpering in pain from her wounds. This one was tough. He liked that. "Never mind. Fort Knox is a place I read about in the Family library."

"The what?"

"I'll explain later. What's your name?"

She managed to stand, her legs still a bit unsteady. "I'm called Cynthia Morning Dove."

"Cynthia Morning Dove?" the man repeated. "Are you an Indian?"

"I am part Indian," Cynthia proudly admitted. "My father is a white, but my mother is Oglala Sioux."

The man in green laughed.

"You find this funny?" she demanded defensively.

"It's not what you think," he told her. "Once upon a time, I believed I was the last Indian on the face of the planet. Now I'm running into Indians all over the place. We're worse than rabbits!"

"You are Indian?"

"Part Blackfoot," he informed her.

"How are you known?"

"My name is Geronimo."

"I like your name," Cynthia declared. "It has a clean, strong sound to it."

"So does Cynthia Morning Dove."

There was a pause. "Where are you from?" she asked. "How did you get here?"

"My trusty feet brought me." He grinned. "I'm

glad they did."

For an instant their eyes met, conveying mutual respect and an incipient attraction.

"We'd better make tracks," Geronimo advised, glancing at the trees. "Your friends may return."

Cynthia looked over her left shoulder. "They will return," she stated, "and they will bring others."

"Feel up to riding?" he asked her.

Two of the horses were nearby. The one belonging to the deceased lariat rider was twenty yards off, contentedly munching on the grass. Fifty yards out was the last of the riflemen Geronimo killed, still slumped over his mount's neck, the horse standing quietly, evidently awaiting a command from its owner.

"I can manage," Cynthia assured him.

"Wait here," Geronimo directed. He hastily retrieved the two animals, neither of which displayed any inclination to bolt. They certainly were well trained.

"I'll take the paint," Cynthia announced as he returned with the horses in tow, referring to the mount belonging to the man responsible for dragging her over the hard ground.

"That leaves the big black for me," Geronimo commented, gripping the leather reins and swinging up onto the stallion.

Cynthia nimbly followed suit and kneed the paint forward, heading due east.

Geronimo closed in alongside her. "Do you have a specific destination in mind?" he inquired.

"Head east. The further east we go, the better," Cynthia revealed. "If we keep going, maybe ten or twenty miles, it's not very likely they'll follow us."

"Who are 'they'?" Geronimo inquired.

"The Legion."

Geronimo twisted as they reached the top of the eastern hill and eyed the treeline. Still no sign of pursuit. "Tell me about this Legion," he instructed her.

"You've never heard of them?" Cynthia demanded, sounding surprised.

"Nope."

"What about the Cavalry?"

"The Cavalry? You mean an official military unit?"

"No. Nothing like that." Cynthia shook her head, guiding the paint around a large boulder.

"Tell me about them," Geronimo urged. "Go back as far as you can, back as far as the Big Blast if possible."

"You mean the Third World War?" Cynthia stated, grinning. "How old do you think I am?"

"Well, you're certainly not one hundred years old," Geronimo conceded. "But tell me what you can. The more I learn, the better." He looked over his right shoulder as they reached the bottom of the hill, relieved the rim was clear of horsemen. If they kept the black and the paint at a fast walk, not quite a trot, they'd conserve their energy until it was needed.

"I don't know a lot of the details," Cynthia clarified, "but I do remember what my grandfather told me."

"Let me hear it." Geronimo slid the Marlin over his shoulder, his left hand on the reins. Thank the Great Spirit the Elders saw fit to teach every Family member to ride! True, the lessons weren't extensive, because the Family only owned nine horses, but the memories were coming in handy.

"Let me see. . . ." Cynthia was saying. "After the war, after the Government evacuated many people to the Civilized Zone and established a new capital in Denver, there were still people here, people who refused to be forcibly removed from their homes. One of them owned a large ranch in eastern South Dakota. I forget his name, but he organized his neighbors and others into a vigilante group called the Cavalry. They protected themselves from the scavengers and the looters and the Government troops. This rancher owned a huge herd of horses and cattle, a couple of hundred head of each, on his ranch near Redfield. . . .''

"Redfield?" Geronimo interrupted.

"A small town about sixty or seventy miles southwest of here," Cynthia detailed.

"That explains the Cavalry," Geronimo noted, "but it doesn't explain the Legion, the ones after you."

Cynthia sighed, fatigued. "The rancher died a long time ago. Another man, name of Tanner, took control of the Cavalry. He was killed, and the leadership passed to his son, a man named Brent. Brent was gunned down, and his two sons, Rolf and Rory, became joint leaders, running the Cavalry together until about ten years ago."

"Then what happened?"

"They had a falling out over a woman. . . .''

"What else?" Geronimo smirked.

Cynthia ignored the taunt. "Rolf took about three hundred of the Cavalry with him and established his headquarters in Pierre. It used to be the capital of South Dakota, before the war. It's west of here about one hundred and fifty miles. Correction. Make that southwest of here, near the Missouri River."

"So let me guess," Geronimo interjected. "This Rolf, for some obscure reason, decided to call his followers the Legion. Am I right?"

She grinned at him. "Not bad, bright boy! The

Cavalry and the Legion have been fighting ever
since, mostly small raids and skirmishes. Neither
side wants an all-out war. The Legion has around
three hundred horsemen, the original Cavalry about
four hundred, so they're pretty evenly matched. An
all-out war would be suicidal. Not to mention
stupid.''

"How so?''

"It would leave us open to attack from the
Civilized creeps, the Government troops.''

"Ahhh, yes," Geronimo nodded. "I've had the
supreme displeasure of encountering Government
troops before.''

"And you're still alive?'' she marveled. "And
free?''

"Remind me to tell you about it sometime,''
Geronimo directed. "But tell me first how you fit
into the scheme of things.''

"Well, it's like this. The Cavalry and the Legion
protect their respective territories, insuring all the
farmers and the ranchers are safe from the
scavengers, the troops, the mutations, and whatever
else comes along. My mother and father own a small
farm about twenty miles east of here. Not much, but
we get by. We're required to provide the Cavalry
with a portion of our crops, our fair share for their
protection. But they can't be everywhere at once.
Yesterday morning a Legion patrol attacked our
farm. They burned our house and barn to the ground
and abducted me. At least,'' she said slowly, "they
didn't kill my mother and father or my younger
brothers.''

"Why didn't they?''

"I really don't know,'' she shrugged. "Unless the
patrol captain had something to do with it. I think
he wants me for himself, and he probably reasoned I'd

be more ... cooperative ... if he left my folks alive.''

''So the patrol made camp for the night in that group of trees back there,'' Geronimo deduced, ''and you made a break for it today, the first chance you had.''

Cynthia beamed. ''I am impressed. You *are* a smart one! Your mother must be real proud of you.''

Geronimo's face clouded. ''My parents passed on to the higher mansions when I was quite young.'' He quickly changed the subject. ''How many horsemen were in this Legion patrol?''

''That many,'' Cynthia said, pointing behind them. ''Plus four.''

Geronimo turned, unprepared for the sight of dozens of horsemen on the crest of the hill.

''Only thirty-two,'' Cynthia elaborated as she goaded the paint into a gallop. ''Now twenty-eight.''

''Oh. Is that all?'' Geronimo urged the black stallion forward, keeping pace with Cynthia.

The riders on the hill voiced a collective shout—a loud, sustained ''*Yaa-hoooo!*''—and descended on the fleeing duo.

And to think, Geronimo reflected, all I wanted was some quiet time to myself. Peace and solitude.

So much for that bright idea!

# 2

There were three of them lined up in a row, their hands hovering near their revolvers, their concentration centered on three rusted tin cans lying on the ground twenty yards away, awaiting the command to fire.

The first was a youth of sixteen, dressed in a black shirt and black pants, his bushy brows knit as he squinted in the bright October sun. His brown eyes never left the can directly in front of him. A slight breeze stirred his brown hair. In a holster on his right hip was a Llama Comanche .357 Magnum.

The other two were women, both young and lovely, both blonde, both with green eyes—but there the similarities ended. One of the women, the one standing in the center, was taller and leaner, with a narrow waist and unusually small feet. Her cheekbones were more prominent, her forehead higher, and her lips thinner. She wore a brown blouse patched in half a dozen spots, and baggy green pants a size too big. In her holster was a Smith and Wesson .357 Combat Magnum.

The third member of the trio enjoyed a fuller figure and slightly longer hair. Her even white teeth were clenched, her rounded chin jutting outward, as she maintained her focused determination. Her slender fingers were inches from a Ruger Super Blackhawk 44 Magnum. She was attired in blue pants constructed from an old blanket and a yellow shirt so discolored from use and age it appeared almost white.

"Are you three ready?" asked the tall man in buckskins standing nearby, his left arm upraised, a matched set of pearl-handled Colt Pythons suspended around his trim waist. He sported a full blond mustache, a perfect complement to his golden hair.

"Any time, Hickok," the youth in black declared.

"Don't get cocky, Shane," advised the man. He noted their obvious intensity and suppressed an impulse to laugh. "On the count of three. One . . ."

The trio became immobile, their nerves high-strung, their muscles rigid.

"Two . . ."

Somewhere in the distance a bird was chirping.

"Three!" Hickok barked.

Shane cleared leather first, his shot striking the tin can and sending it skidding to one side. He twisted and fired twice more, each slug scoring a direct hit.

The women drew simultaneously, with the taller of the pair firing a fraction of a second sooner. The sound of the gunfire thundered in the clearing.

Both missed.

"Damn!" the taller woman exclaimed, venting her frustration.

"Not bad," Hickok commented as he walked up to them, his blue eyes twinkling.

"Bull!" the taller woman snapped. "We missed!"

"Give yourselves a break," Hickok told them. "It's the very first time you've tried the fast draw. It requires practice. Lots and lots of practice. You don't always hit what you aim at."

"You do," said the other woman. "I've never heard of you missing a shot."

"Listen, Jenny . . ." Hickok began.

"How do you do it, lover?" asked the tall blonde.

"He has natural talent, Sherry," explained Shane. "He's the best gunfighter in the history of the Family, maybe the best who ever lived."

Hickok, embarrassed by the praise from his number-one fan and star pupil, idly poked the toe of his left moccasin in the dirt. "Don't measure your ability by mine," he said quietly. "Everybody has some talent, something they can perform extremely well. It's just a question of finding it."

"So what did we do wrong?" Jenny inquired.

"You ladies were a mite too tense," Hickok stated. "Relax. Practice every day until drawing and firing becomes as natural as breathing or loving."

Sherry winked at Jenny and leaned in closer to Hickok. "If you're leaving it up to me, I'd much rather practice our loving."

The Family's preeminent gunman actually blushed.

Sherry and Jenny laughed.

"Hey!" Shane broke in, annoyed the conversation was straying from the original subject. "What about me?"

"What about you?" Hickok reiterated.

"I didn't miss," the youth boasted. "All three of my shots were right on target."

"That's right, pard," Hickok concurred. He stepped over to Shane, nodding his head, his hands behind his back. "You did hit the can, didn't you?"

"Sure did," Shane beamed.

"Yep," Hickok said, nodding one more time. His

right hand swept upward and smacked Shane on the forehead.

Shane recoiled in surprise, not really hurt. "What did you do that for?" he demanded.

"It took you three shots to kill one little ol' tin can!" Hickok rejoined. "That's two shots too many."

"But all three hit . . ." Shane started to protest.

"I don't care if you had fired six shots into it," Hickok said, cutting him off. "Then you would have wasted five shots. Why do you think I'm always advocating going for the head? For the same reason I believe it should be one shot per customer. If you hit someone anywhere else but in the head, then you risk being taken down yourself because your first shot wasn't immediately fatal. By the same token, if you're facing five enemies and you put three slugs into one of them, you've wasted two shots and given your opponents time to waste you."

Shane was staring thoughtfully at the tin can.

"Remember our fire fight with the Moles?" Hickok reminded him.

"Of course," Shane admitted sheepishly.

"There we were," Hickok said, shaking his head and frowning, "surrounded by Moles," outnumbered better than two to one, and when the shooting commenced you fired three shots into one of them. Just like you did with the can."

"But I wanted to be sure," Shane objected.

"Can't fault you there," Hickok conceded. He sighed and gazed up at the blue morning sky. "Shane, you want to become a Warrior. You asked me to sponsor you, and I reluctantly agreed. You're young, and I don't hold that against you because I was young once too, but you're also inexperienced and that could be fatal. You must appreciate what being a Warrior really means."

"I do know what it means," Shane commented.

"Do you?" Hickok scrutinized his prodigy. "I think you see being a Warrior, serving as a protector of the Family and a defender of the Home, as an exciting adventure, providing a welcome break in the montony of daily living. You better wake up to something else real fast." Hickok reached out and squeezed Shane's left shoulder with his right hand. "When you're a Warrior, you're a killer. Plain and simple. When you get right down to it, it's you or the other guy. Or beast. Or thing. Whatever, kill or be killed is the name of the game. You'd better become the best killer you can possibly be, or you won't last long in our line of work. You've got to realize this, for your own sake."

Shane carefully considered Hickok's sage advice.

Sherry suddenly squealed in delight and clapped her hands. "Did you hear him?" she asked, glancing at Jenny. "Did you hear my hunk?"

"That I did," Jenny confirmed, grinning.

"There is a brain somewhere between those ears, after all!" Sherry continued. "You see! I knew those rumors weren't true."

"What rumors?" Hickok inquired, taking the bait.

"That you have rocks for brains," Sherry responded, giggling.

"And where did you hear this rumor?" Hickok played along.

"From Geronimo."

Hickok laughed, reflecting on one of his best friends in all the world. Where *was* that miserable Injun?

"Where is Geronimo, anyway?" Shane questioned. "I haven't seen him in a while."

"He's been gone almost two weeks," Hickok said, concern etched on his rugged features. "Said he had to get away for a while. He wanted time to think over his experiences in Kalispell."

"I was there when he requested a temporary leave of absence from Plato," Jenny chimed in. "I thought Plato was going to refuse the request, but instead he okayed it."

"I almost wish Plato hadn't," Hickok said wistfully, staring at the brick wall forty yards away, the twenty-foot-high wall completely surrounding the thirty-acre plot known as the Home.

"Well, do we keep practicing or what?" Shane wanted to know.

"We keep practicing," Hickok answered, glad for the diversion, for a reason to suspend his worry about Geronimo. He moved off to one side and raised his arm again. "Are you ready?"

All three nodded.

"Good. Then when I count to three, we go again. Get set."

They didn't appear as nevous this time around.

"One . . ."

Shane was even smiling.

"Two . . ."

"Is this a private party or can anyone join?" interjected a new, deep voice.

Jenny spun, catching sight of the bronzed, muscular man with his brawny hands on his hips, his black hair hanging over his forehead, and his gray eyes surveying the firing range. He wore a black leather vest, fatigue pants, and moccasins, but the singularly distinctive aspect of his attire were the twin Bowies hanging in scabbards on both hips.

"Blade!" Jenny ran to her fiance and threw her

arms around his neck.

"There goes the lesson for today," Hickok muttered.

Blade kissed Jenny and they strolled toward the other three arm-in-arm.

"Did you see that?" Sherry ribbed Hickok. "Some men don't turn into a beet every time they display affection in public. It won't kill you, you know."

"My personal life is none of anyone else's business," Hickok groused. "I reckon you'd prefer it if we stuck a bed outside one night and charged admission."

"Sounds like fun!" Sherry grinned. "I'm not ashamed of anything I do."

"Have you been to the library lately?" Hickok inquired.

Sherry, mystified by the query, shook her head. "No. Why?"

"The next time we're there," Hickok casually commented, "remind me to show you the meaning of the word 'modesty' in the dictionary. It promises to be one of the major revelations of your life."

Blade and Jenny reached them.

"What's going on here?" Blade demanded, eyeing Hickok.

"Why are you looking at me?" Hickok asked innocently.

"Because you have a natural knack for getting yourself into trouble," Blade replied. "If something is going on here, I assume you're the mastermind."

"That's a bad habit, Blade," Sherry mentioned.

"What is?"

"Assuming," she told him.

"Oh? Why?"

"Haven't you heard?" Sherry inquired.

"Heard what?" Blade responded impatiently.

"When you assume something," Sherry detailed, "you make an ass of you and me. Get it? Ass-you-me. Assume."

"I got it," Blade assured her. "But no one has told me what's going on here yet?"

"It was my idea," Jenny revealed.

"Yours?" Blade stared at her, genuinely surprised. His beloved was one of the Family Healers, a woman devoted to easing pain in the service of her brothers and sisters. "Why would you want to take shooting lessons? Is it time for your annual certification?"

Every Family member was required to take yearly firearms refresher and safety courses. If the Home were ever subjected to a full-scale assault, its preservation might well depend on the Family's ability to wield its arsenal. The Warriors, naturally, practiced their deadly skills more frequently. Only a few of them, though, practiced as often as Hickok: every chance he got.

"It's not for my certification," Jenny said to Blade. Her man was the leader of the Family Warriors, the man responsible for insuring the Home was guarded and secure at all times. She knew he partially blamed himself for the successful Troll attack some months ago.

"Then why?" he gently pressed her.

"I thought it might come in handy," Jenny reasoned. "After the Troll fiasco in Fox, after the horrible loss of Angela, I realized I'm woefully incapable of defending myself. I want to be ready in case I ever find myself in a similar situation again."

"What about me?" Blade questioned. "You know I'd protect you with my dying breath."

"That's just it!" Jenny said in an angry tone. "I can't rely on you all the time." She saw Blade move his mouth to object, and she quickly continued, cutting him short. "That's not meant as an insult or anything! I know you love me, and I've seen what you will do to protect me. But let's face facts. You've been gone from the Home a lot lately, what with running errands all over the countryside for Plato. What if I were attacked while you were gone? Who would save me? Hickok? He's usually with you. Geronimo? The same. Rikki? He's in charge of the Warriors in your absence and he has the entire Family to think about, not just me. No." She paused, searching his eyes for understanding and support. "This isn't a reflection on your ability as a Warrior. It simply means I realize we can't be together one hundred percent of the time, and I must be prepared to protect myself during the times we're apart. Are you upset with me?"

"A little," Blade confessed, miffed.

"Because I'm learning to stand on my own two feet?"

"No," Blade replied.

"What, then?"

"Because you went to Hickok for lessons instead of coming to me," Blade revealed.

"Touchy! Touchy! Touchy!" Hickok cracked in a falsetto whine.

"There are two reasons I went to Nathan first," Jenny explained, using the original name bestowed on Hickok at birth by his parents, the one he had opted to change at his Naming.

The Founder of the Home had instituted a special ceremony for each Family member's sixteenth birthday, a practice designated the Naming. Each member selected the name he or she wanted to be known by for the rest of his or her earthly existence. Members were encouraged to pick a name from some period before the Third World War, possibly the name of a hero or heroine or anyone they admired. This way, the Founder hoped, the Family would be compelled to remain in touch with its historical antecedents. Without a solid education and a thorough comprehension of history, the Family might tend to forget the suicidal course mankind had pursued before the war. It might neglect to learn from the folly and stupidity of its ancestors. On his sixteenth birthday, Nathan had picked the name of the man he considered the greatest gunfighter who ever lived: James Butler Hickok. Sixteen-year-old Lone Elk had become Geronimo. Young Michael had opted for a name predicated on his affinity for bladed weapons.

"What two reasons?" Blade said, prodding Jenny.

"The first reason should be obvious," Hickok said, interrupting, coming to Jenny's defense. "I'm a better shot than you are."

"You're definitely more modest," Blade rejoined.

"He's right," Jenny spoke up. "Hickok is the best shot in the Family, and I might as well learn from the best." She reached out and tenderly stroked Blade's right forearm. "You're the best knife fighter, sure, but what good would it do me to learn knife fighting? It wouldn't help me much if I was attacked by a mutate, would it? I need a weapon I can use at a distance, and guns have it over knives in that respect. So that's one of the reasons I went to Nathan without consulting you."

"What's the other?"

"Actually," Jenny said, grinning, "I was hoping to keep it as a surprise until your return from your next trip to the Twin Cities. I was planning to shock your shorts with my deadly prowess!"

Blade smiled, recognizing the validity of her

reasoning. If the affair with the Trolls had taught the Family anything, it was one paramount fact: complacency could be fatal.

"You see my point?" Jenny asked.

Blade nodded.

"No hard feelings, pard?" Hickok inquired.

"Why should there be?" Blade demanded. He looked at Sherry, eager to drop the topic. "What about you? You learning to protect yourself too?"

"Nope," Sherry responded. "I'm practicing to become a Warrior."

"*What*?" Blade and Hickok cried in unison.

Blade glanced at Hickok, noting the gunman's slack jaw and shocked expression. Sherry wasn't a Family member; she'd been rescued by Hickok from the Trolls, and the two, rumor had it—although Hickok would not confirm the report—were an item. Did Sherry know, Blade wondered, about Hickok's last love, a Warrior woman named Joan? Joan had been savagely killed in front of Hickok's eyes, and Blade knew his friend still wasn't fully recovered from that profound tragedy. How would Hickok react to this development?

"Like hell you are!" the gunfighter snapped, answering Blade's query.

"What's wrong?" Sherry demanded, perplexed by the hurt expression on Hickok's face. "I thought you'd be proud of me if I could qualify to become a Warrior."

"You thought wrong," Hickok growled.

"Don't the Elders allow women to become Warriors?" Sherry questioned him.

"There have been a few," Hickok stated, his features clouding.

"Then why don't you like the idea?" Sherry goaded him. "Is it because I'm not one of the

Family? Is that it?"

"No," Hickok snapped.

"Then what?" Sherry asked, confused. "You don't think I'm good enough to qualify?"

"That's not it either," Hickok said harshly.

"Then what?" Sherry asked, annoyed, stamping her left foot in frustration.

"Yeah," Shane interjected. "What's so wrong . . ." He stopped, startled when Hickok spun on him, the gunman's visage contorted in rage.

"When I want your opinion in a personal matter," Hickok warned, his voice low and menacing, "I'll ask for it." He looked at Sherry a moment, muttered something about "damn contrary females" under his breath, whirled, and stalked off into the trees.

"Whew!" Shane said, letting out his breath. "For a second there I thought he was going to draw on me."

"He'd never do that and you know it," Blade stated.

"What's wrong with him?" Sherry inquired of no one in particular. "What did I say to get him so mad?"

"You don't know?" Jenny questioned.

"Know what?" Sherry's eyes were rimmed with tears.

"You'd better come with me," Jenny said, placing her left arm around Sherry's shoulders. "We're going to have a girl-to-girl talk."

"You know why he's acting this way?" Sherry asked hopefully.

"I've a pretty good idea," Jenny confirmed. "Let's go find a spot where we can be alone." She blew a kiss at Blade and led Sherry from the firing range.

"So much for practice today," Shane mumbled.

"Hickok was right."

"We could practice knife fighting," Blade offered, patting his Bowie handles.

Shane gazed at the Bowies in evident distaste. "Thanks, Blade, but I'll pass. Think I'll go talk to my folks." He smiled and walked away.

Blade surveyed the now empty clearing. "What is it?" he soliloquized aloud. "My breath?" He chuckled at his own joke, mentally debating whether he should requisition a firearm from the armory and get in some drill while the range was free.

The firing range was a large clearing located in the southeastern corner of the Home, situated as far as possible from the areas normally utilized by the Family to insure greater safety for all concerned. Because the Family congregated its activities in the western half of the thirty-acre Home, reserving the eastern half for agricultural endeavors and natural embellishment, the possibility of a stray bullet striking someone, or of a child stumbling across the range while it was being used, was extremely remote.

Blade stretched, contemplating the expanse of scenery in front of him, thankful the Founder of the Home, a wealthy filmmaker named Kurt Carpenter, had had the foresight to construct it with space to spare. The thirty acres were surrounded by the twenty-foot-high brick wall, and the wall was topped with barbed wire as an added security measure. A stream was diverted into the northwestern corner of the Home, serving as a moat at the base of the wall, another precaution against attack, and channeled out of the Home under the southeastern corner of the wall.

What was that? Blade detected movement to his

left and turned, spotting one of the Warriors on guard duty on top of the wall making his rounds along the rampart. After the successful Troll assault, the Warriors had increased the frequency of their patrols, vowing they would never fail the Family again.

The Warriors. Blade sighed. As their chief, he would need to make his decision, his selections, soon. Plato and the Elders were awaiting his recommendations, his choice of the candidates for Warrior status. Four Warrior positions needed to be filled, one in an existing Triad and the other three for a brand new Triad. The Family Warriors were divided into four groups comprised of three Warriors apiece. Their code names were Alpha, Beta, Gamma, and Omega. Gamma required a replacement for a recent loss, and the Elders desired to add a new Triad, Zulu, as a guarantee that the Warrior ranks would be sufficient to adequately safeguard the Home.

His reverie was interrupted by the sound of feet pounding on the ground. Someone was in a hurry, coming from the direction of the Blocks.

Blade placed his hands on his Bowies.

A tall man with short blond hair and brilliant blue eyes burst into the clearing. He wore buckskin pants and a brown shirt sewn together from discarded pillowcases. A long broadsword dangled from a leather belt at his waist.

"Blade . . ." the man began, breathless, his brow sweating, indicating the distance he'd covered to convey his message.

"Report, Spartacus," Blade directed him.

Spartacus was a member of Gamma Triad, and one of the most trustworthy Warriors in the Family. "We've received the signal," he hastily explained. "Rikki, Teucer, and Yama are in position. Your orders?''

Rikki, Teucer, and Yama constituted Beta Triad. ''Follow me,'' Blade ordered, and took off at a brisk run.

So! The trap was set to be sprung! All he had to do was give the word.

''You planning to take any of them alive?'' Spartacus inquired.

''That decision will be up to Rikki,'' Blade replied.

Spartacus grinned. ''Then they're dead meat!''

''Better them than us,'' Blade said.

''You sound so grim,'' Spartacus noted. ''Lighten up. What can these bozos do to us anyway?''

Blade glanced at Spartacus, realizing his companion was completely unaware of the gravity of the situation. ''They could destroy the Home.''

''Destroy the Home?'' Spartacus responded skeptically. ''They have that much power?''

''They have that much power,'' Blade assured him.

The two Warriors ran in silence for a minute, passing fields of recently harvested crops. They reached a line of cabins centered in the middle of the Home, located between the eastern, agricultural half and the western, occupied section. The cabins were the homes for married couples and their families.

''I still say,'' Spartacus stubbornly persisted, waving to a nearby couple as he went by them, ''Rikki will slice them up into little pieces.''

''Let's pray to the Spirit you're right,'' was all that Blade would say. Spartacus hadn't been with Alpha Triad on its previous runs; he just didn't know what their enemies were capable of. Well, he was about to find out.

# 3

"We're gaining on them!" Cynthia happily yelled over her right shoulder, her black hair flying behind her as the paint galloped up yet another hill.

Geronimo, keeping the big black right on her heels, looked over his left shoulder to verify her assessment. She was correct; they were putting more distance between the Legion patrol and themselves. With one notable exception. The majority of the patrol was three-fourths of a mile to their rear, but a single rider, a man on a golden Palomino, was considerably closer, perhaps five hundred yards away and not losing any ground.

"We're not gaining on *him*," Geronimo shouted, nodding his head in the direction of the Palomino rider.

Cynthia smiled. "He's the one I told you about," she called out, "the captain. I think he's warm for my form!"

Geronimo grinned. What kind of woman was this Cynthia that she could make jokes at a time like this?

They were rapidly approaching the crest of the hill, a barren jumble of large boulders obscuring their view of the other side.

If we can get beyond those boulders, Geronimo

told himself, we can cut to the right and swing around in a circle. They might be able to shake the Legion patrol.

Cynthia entered the rocks first, expertly dodging her mount between the boulders, its hooves clattering on the stone underneath.

Geronimo gamely followed her, cautiously swerving and weaving the black, amazed at the consummate ease with which his steed negotiated the often narrow passageways.

A stretch of green was visible ahead.

Cynthia emerged from the boulder first, the paint darting into the open and beginning to pour on the speed again, when it abruptly tried to stop, its hind legs digging into the turf as it slewed sideways, terror stricken by the sight in front of it.

Geronimo barely avoided a collision, jerking on the black's reins and twisting the horse to one side, wondering what in the world had startled Cynthia's mount, fearing that some of the Legion patrol might have been able to get ahead of them and cut off their escape.

The paint whinnied in abject fear and scrambled to regain its footing, Cynthia clinging to the reins and the mane, striving to stay on, her slim legs clasping the animal's heaving sides.

Geronimo, concentrating on Cynthia's predicament, neglected to see the thing in front of them until it was almost upon them. He heard a thunderous bellow and whirled, momentarily shocked by his discovery.

It couldn't be!

Not now!

But it was.

A mutate.

The dreaded scourge of the post-nuclear age,

mutates overran the land. No one knew what caused them, whether it was attributable to the long-term effects of intense radiation or the consequence of the widespread use of chemical agents during the war. Plato once speculated they might be the result of a combination of the two. Whatever, the Family did know mutates were former mammals, reptiles, or amphibians converted by a mysterious process into rampaging, insatiable demons. The creature's skin would become dry and cracked, turning a brownish color, and it would be covered with large blistering sores, oozing pus everywhere. Green mucus would pour from the ears, and its teeth would turn yellow and rot away. Mutates displayed one primary purpose in life; to kill anyone and anything in their paths, to rend and destroy, to consume every living thing they encountered, even one another.

This one, Geronimo knew, had once been a bison. Its hair was gone, replaced by the pus-covered skin. Even its shaggy mane and beard had disappeared. The buffalo stood six feet high at the shoulder and weighed in the neighborhood of fifteen hundred pounds. Its horns were still attached, and they were aimed at the paint as it snorted and charged.

"Cynthia!" Geronimo shouted, reaching for his rifle, knowing he would be unable to prevent the mutate from reaching her before he could fire.

The paint managed to surge upright an instant before the mutate slammed into it, the horns ripping into the side of the horse and tearing it open, blood and guts spilling from the cavity. The paint started to go down as the mutate braced for another on-slaught.

"Cynthia!" Geronimo had the Marlin to his shoulder.

Cynthia released the reins and pushed herself free

of the plunging horse, rolling as she struck the ground. She rose to her hands and knees, keeping her eyes on the mutate.

It was well she did.

The mutate turned, forgetting the paint, focusing on this new target, pawing the grass as it prepared to attack.

Only a second to spare!

Geronimo hurriedly sighted and pulled the trigger, rushing his shot, unwilling to permit the monstrosity to get any closer to Cynthia.

The 45-70 boomed, the slug smashing into the mutate above its right eye and exiting below its left nostril, the bison's face erupting in a geyser of discolored flesh, blood, and pus. Enraged by the pain, the buffalo spun and launched its massive bulk at the floundering paint, the keen horns gouging a ghastly gash in the paint's flank. The horse was bowled over by the tremendous force of the blow.

Geronimo levered another round into the chamber and aimed for another head shot, confident he would kill the freak this time.

He didn't count on two things.

First, the big black reared, reacting to the proximity of the deformed bison.

Secondly, Cynthia rose and ran, managing to cover five yards before her right foot caught in an unseen hole and she stumbled and fell flat on her stomach. The mutate detected the motion and faced her, ignoring the thrashing paint.

Geronimo frantically attempted to bring the big black under control, his left hand clutching the reins while he gripped the Marlin with his right. The black landed on all fours, still skittish, shying away from the former buffalo.

Cynthia tried to stand, agony lanching her right

ankle. She saw the mutate lower its head and charge, and she involuntarily screamed and extended her arms in front of her in a vain endeavor to avert imminent death.

No!

Geronimo held the rifle in his right hand, the barrel pointed in the general direction of the mutate's stomach as the black bucked, and fired, the recoil almost wrenching the 45-70 from his grasp.

Seared by the slug as it tore through its innards, the bison staggered, recovered, and turned, catching sight of the black for the first time.

Geronimo released the reins as the mutate came directly at him. He raised the Marlin, hoping the pressure of his knees against the black would suffice to prevent him from falling, and levered his third round into the rifle.

The mutate bellowed as it advanced, its bloody horns glistening in the sunlight.

Eat this, sucker!

Geronimo let the bison have it again, right between the eyes. Without hesitating, he ejected the spent shell and replaced it with his fourth and final shot.

The mutate had slowed and was shaking its head, disoriented, a gaping hole in its forehead.

Once more for good luck!

Geronimo carefully aimed and fired, the fourth slug penetrating the bison an inch from the third.

This one finally did the job. The mutate quivered violently, threw its head back, seemed to gasp for air, and then collapsed. Its body shook twice before sagging into an inert heap.

Geronimo slid from the black and ran to Cynthia. "Are you all right?" he asked as he knelt by her side.

"No," she replied, rubbing her injured ankle.

"Is it broken?" he solicitously inquired.

"The ankle? It's okay. Sprained a bit, I think."

"But you said . . ." Geronimo began.

"Did you hear me?" Cynthia demanded in a disgusted tone. "I wimped out! I screamed! Did you hear me?"

"Yes, but . . ."

"I did it earlier too." She frowned and shook her head. "When the Legion men were after me. Funny. I never thought of myself as a coward."

"You're not a . . ."

"Well, I can tell you one thing," she promised him. "I'm not going to turn chicken again."

"You're not a . . ."

"Yes, sir," she went on, oblivious to his attempts to respond. "You'll never hear me scream again."

"You can't blame yourself," Geronimo said, about to elaborate when Cynthia's eyes suddenly widened and she gaped in dread at something over his right shoulder.

She screamed.

Had the bison revived? Geronimo tossed the empty Marlin aside and whirled, going for the Arminius under his right arm. He saw the deceased mutate, the prone, quavering paint, and the nearby black.

What . . . ?

Something chittered, something at ground level, and Geronimo glanced down.

A mutated prairie dog was perched on the rim of the hole Cynthia had tripped in.

Even as he spied the rodent, it launched its sixteen-inch body toward them. In sheer reflex, Geronimo snapped off a shot, surprised when it struck the prairie dog in the head and toppled it head over heels to the grass.

"Nice shot," Cynthia commented, her composure regained.

"Just don't ask me to do it again," Geronimo said, watching the rodent for any signs of life.

"I may have to," Cynthia remarked, an edge to her voice.

"What? Why?" Geronimo looked at her, puzzled by her tone.

"Didn't you know?" Cynthia asked. "Prairie dogs live in colonies. Look!" She raised her left hand and pointed.

Another mutated rodent was just emerging from a burrow twelve feet away.

Geronimo shot it in the head.

"There's another!" Cynthia squealed, pushing to her feet.

He sighted and fired, downing it with four feet to spare.

"We better get out of here," Cynthia suggested, limping toward the black.

"Look out!" Geronimo shoved her aside and shot another prairie dog emerging only inches from her feet.

The black was moving away from them, its ears laid back, spooked by the gunfire and the activity.

"We can't let him get away!" Cynthia cried.

Geronimo paused, wondering if he should reload the Arminius. He had two shots left in the cylinder. What if more prairie dogs appeared? His mind drifted, recalling his schooling days at the Home and his studies of the mammals of North America. He remembered learning they were part of the squirrel family. The lived in towns or colonies and were highly gregarious. But it didn't make any sense! If all the prairie dogs in this particular town were mutated, they should be attacking one another in a feeding frenzy. These seemed to be working in concert.

Impossible.

"Geronimo!" Cynthia yelled in alarm, shattering his recollections.

Three prairie dogs were issuing forth from three different burrows, all within twenty feet of the Warrior and his frightened friend.

"Kill them!" Cynthia urged, backing toward him.

He tried his best.

The first shot took out the nearest rodent. His second blast caught a mutated dog as it leaped at Cynthia, saliva dripping from its open mouth, pus covering its putrid form.

That left one prairie dog . . . and the Arminius was empty.

Geronimo dropped the Magnum and whipped his tomahawk from under his leather belt. He would only have one chance! If he missed, if the mutate punctured their skin and some of the pus entered their bloodstream, they wouldn't live longer than a few days.

The prairie dog was ten feet away and closing, its normally placid features transformed by feral lust.

Geronimo raised the tomahawk, gauging the distance, waiting for the instant the prairie dog would jump. While in midair the rodent would be unable to change direction, to duck or dodge the tomahawk. It would be his best bet, a fleeting twinkling of vulnerability.

The prairie dog screeched and launched itself into the air, but instead of arrowing toward Geronimo it zeroed in on Cynthia.

Geronimo swung the tomahawk, slightly off balance, the edge of the weapon slicing into the mutate's left side. The blow deflected the prairie dog, but it didn't stop the horrific deviate.

The rodent caught Cynthia on her right foot as it descended, its razor-sharp incisors lacerating an inch of skin near her big toe. She was wearing sandals, and the straps were composed of thin, durable strips of deer hide.

The mutate landed and twirled, about to pounce again.

Geronimo buried his tomahawk in the mutate's cranium, the skull splitting like a rotten cantaloupe.

Cynthia had collapsed on the ground and was staring at her injured foot in utter amazement.

Geronimo wrenched the tomahawk free and knelt beside her.

"I'm dead," Cynthia said, shocked. "I'm as good as dead!"

"Maybe not." Geronimo leaned over the foot and examined the wound. "Maybe none of the pus got into your blood."

"The way my luck has been running today," Cynthia remarked, "I wouldn't count on it."

"There don't seem to be any more prairie dogs," Geronimo commented, glancing at the nearest visible burrows. "Maybe your luck has changed."

"I wouldn't count on it," interjected a husky male voice.

Geronimo and Cynthia turned as one, registering their astonishment as they suddenly realized they were completely surrounded by a circle of horsemen quietly sitting on their mounts twenty-five yards away.

One of the riders, a handsome man in buckskins on a golden Palomino, was only ten yards off, a Winchester 94 Lever Action Carbine cradled in his big hands and pointed at the hapless duo.

"This just isn't my day," Cynthia said, sadly shaking her head.

"There still may be a way out," Geronimo stated, grinning.

The Palomino rider overheard the statement. "A way out?" he repeated. "How?"

Geronimo indicated the encircling patrol with a toss of his head. "I could always ask you to surrender."

The Legion captain cocked the hammer on the Winchester.

# 4

The western half of the Home was extensively used by the Family for various purposes. Kurt Carpenter had located the six main structures, the reinforced concrete buildings known as Blocks, in a triangular formation centered in the western section. The Block furthest south was A Block, the Family armory, personally stocked by Carpenter with every conceivable weapon. One hundred yards to the northwest was B Block, the sleeping quarters for single Family members. Another hundred yards in a northwesterly line was C Block, the infirmary. One hundred yards due east of C Block was D Block, serving as the Family's carpentry shop and all-purpose construction facility. Another hundred yards further was E Block, the library Carpenter had filled with hundreds of thousands of volumes on every imaginable subject. In a southwesterly direction, one hundred yards along, was F Block, serving as the work area for the Tillers, the building they used for storing their farm supplies and for preserving and preparing food. Finally, an additional one hundred yards to the southwest was A Block, completing the triangle.

The large area between the Blocks was the Family's primary area for socializing. Outdoor meetings were held there, worship services were conducted there, and the children often played their games there. More Family members could be found there at any given time of the day than anywhere else in the Home.

Dozens of Family members were engaged in varied activities as Blade and Spartacus jogged past them, making for the stairs leading up to the rampart above the drawbridge in the middle of the western wall. The drawbridge was the only means of entering and leaving the Home.

"We seem to be attracting attention," Spartacus noted as they neared the wooden steps.

"It can't be helped," Blade replied. While they might be curious, the members of the Family knew better than to interfere with the Warriors when they were performing official duties.

Blade reached the stairs and glanced up at the rampart above the drawbridge. Plato, the Family's wizened Leader, was awaiting his arrival, his long gray hair blowing in the wind. He wore a green tunic and pants made by his loving wife, Nadine. Beside Plato stood Joshua, one of the Family Empaths, an individual with exceptional spiritual ability. His shoulder-length brown hair and neatly trimmed beard mached his brown shirt and pants. A large Latin cross, an adornment he was seldom without, hung from his neck.

Spartacus was standing behind Blade, gazing upward. "I'm sorry to say it, Blade," he admitted, "but he gives me the creeps."

Blade knew whom Spartacus referred to, the thin gray creature looming above them, leaning against the stair railing.

Gremlin. Blade had brought him back from the trip to Kalispell, Montana. Initially enemies, Blade and Gremlin had become friends after a series of incidents involving troops from the Civilized Zone. Gremlin's skin was light gray and leathery. His features were hawkish, his nose narrow and pointed, his mouth a narrow slit. A hairless head, combined with mere ringlets of flesh for ears and bizarre eyes with bright red pupils, conspired to produce a decidedly unnerving visual impact. Gremlin was attired in a leather loincloth.

Blade took the steps three at a time, Spartacus right behind him.

"Blade!" Gremlin greeted him as he reached the top. "Good to see you, yes? Your trap has worked, no?"

"So I hear," Blade replied, moving to the edge of the rampart, carefully avoiding the coiled barbed wire placed on top of the wall.

"We received the signal," Plato stated.

"So Spartacus said." Blade peered at the cleared field beyond the wall. Past the field was the forest. Three hundred yards from the drawbridge rose a sparsely covered hillock. It would be there, he knew.

"Should we alert the other Warriors?" Spartacus wanted to know.

Blade mentally debated the question. Geronimo was off somewhere getting his head together. Hickok was in the compound, but he was in one of his blue funks. No sense in calling him. That meant assembling Alpha Triad was impractical. Beta Triad, led by Rikki-Tikki-Tavi, was out on that hillock, about to engage in mortal combat. Gamma Triad was missing a member, leaving Spartacus and Seiko.

"Where's Seiko?" Blade asked.

"He has guard duty on the east wall," Spartacus answered.

Blade thoughtfully bit his lower lip. It wouldn't be wise to recall Seiko from the east wall, leaving their eastern flank exposed. That, he bitterly remembered, was how the Trolls had managed to enter the Home months before. "What about Omega Triad?" Blade queried.

"They're asleep," Spartacus detailed. "They had night watch."

"Doesn't leave us many Warriors to work with, does it?" Blade casually mentioned.

"Now you can fully appreciate the reason I've insisted we add another Triad," Plato said in his kindly voice. "Three more Warriors are critical if we're to insure the Family's safety."

"You get no argument here," Blade reminded him.

"I can't believe they're really out there," Joshua chimed in, nodding at the hillock. "The Watchers must not know we're on to them."

No, they didn't. Blade's mind flashed over his recent experiences during the extended trip to Kalispell, Montana. Plato had sent Alpha Triad, minus Hickok, to ascertain the veracity of a report concerning a hospital in Kalispell. This hospital, so they had been told, had been left unscathed by the scavengers and the looters, its equipment intact and hopefully operative. The Family had needed certain scientific and medical supplies and instruments from the hospital. A particularly severe form of premature senility was affecting some of the older Family members. If the Family couldn't isolate the source of the senility and then treat it, Plato projected that within several generations no Family member would live past the age of thirty-five.

While at Kalispell, after being captured and held prisoner, Blade had gleaned considerable information concerning the former United States of America. He had learned that the Government had evacuated thousands upon thousands of people into an area in the Midwest and Rocky Mountain area immediately prior to, and during, the Third World War. This occupied expanse had become known as the Civilized Zone, and had been governed by the Secretary of Health, Education, and Welfare, a man named Samuel Hyde, the only Cabinet member to survive the war. Congress and the Supreme Court had been obliterated in a preemptive nuclear strike on Washington D.C. Hyde had declared martial law and become, to all intents and purposes, dictator of the Civilized Zone. When Samuel had passed on, his son had succeeded him, becoming known as Samuel the Second. He now ruled the Civilized Zone with an iron fist, and apparently entertained the notion of reconquering the rest of the former United States. The Civilized Zone now embraced the former states of Nebraska, Kansas, and Colorado, the southern half of Wyoming, eastern Arizona, all of New Mexico, and the northern half of Texas.

Samuel the Second planned to take control of Montana, North and South Dakota, and Minnesota first because they were the least populated and would offer the least resistance. His troops, the former military forces of the United States, had been entrusted with the task of discovering and monitoring all inhabited centers in the four states slated for reoccupation. These troops had become known as the Watchers to the people in the Twin Cities, and some of the Family referred to them by that name as well.

During his trip to Montana, Blade had discovered that the army of Samuel had already attacked and defeated the Flathead Indians. He had learned that troops were periodically sent to eavesdrop on the Family. They would set up their parabolic microphones and other sensitive detection equipment and position themselves in the woods surrounding the Home, in northwestern Minnesota near what had been Lake Bronson State Park.

"Shouldn't you send Rikki the signal?" Plato inquired, intruding on Blade's reflection.

Blade sighed. And that's what Beta Triad was doing on that hillock. Before he left, Geronimo had scoured the vicinity of the Home and discovered a small clearing on the hillock used frequently by a dozen or so men. Geronimo was the Family's best tracker, and he had detected footprints and equipment imprints in the soil. Blade had decided to intermittently post Warriors at the clearing in the hope of capturing some of Samuel's troops. Now, his plan was about to reach fruition, and he was worried that the Civilized Zone troops might defeat Beta Triad. The troops were well armed, their standard issue including M-16's and automatic pistols. They were also well trained. Blade appreciated from bitter experience how very deadly they could be. Twice before Alpha Triad had fought the Watchers, and both times the Warriors had narrowly escaped with their lives.

Would Beta Triad fare any better?

There was only one way to find out.

"Where's the mirror?" Blade asked, extending his right hand.

"Here you go," Spartacus answered, placing a circular mirror four inches in diameter in Blade's palm.

Blade studied the sun, noting the blazing orb was suspended in the eastern sky. He would need to angle the mirror if Rikki were to observe the signal.

"I pray the Spirit will protect them," Joshua stated.

"They're Warriors," Spartacus said proudly. "They can take care of themselves."

"If only this constant warfare weren't necessary," Joshua went on. "If only we could live on this planet in spiritual harmony."

"Dream on, brother!" Spartacus snorted.

"Are you having second thoughts?" Plato asked Blade, detecting his hesitation.

Blade glanced at Plato. "It's not easy giving others orders and knowing it could cause their deaths."

"Think of the greater good," Plato advised. "Think about the benefits to the Family, about the valuable information we could acquire."

Blade nodded. There was no avoiding it. He held the mirror at chest height and slanted it to catch the brilliant rays of the sun. Satisfied he had the inclination correct, he slowly passed his left hand over the face of the mirror. Once. A second time.

That did it.

The rest was up to Rikki, Teucer, and Yama.

He recalled a quote from Ecclesiastes: "For every thing there is a season, and a time to every purpose under the heaven: a time to be born, and a time to die."

Had he just sealed Beta Triad's death warrant?

# 5

"I must admit," the captain said in genuine respect, "I was really impressed by the way you handled yourself back there. I've never seen one person take on so many mutants at the same time and live to tell about it."

They were heading in a southwesterly direction. Geronimo was on the big black. Cynthia was behind the captain on the Palomino. The remainder of the Legion patrol clustered around them. Two Legion riders were a quarter of a mile ahead, serving as point guards.

"We call them mutates," Geronimo told the captain, "and as far as the bison and the prairie dogs are concerned, the Great Spirit saw fit to watch over me."

The captain eyed his captive. "Who is this 'we' you've mentioned a couple of times?" His eyes were clear blue, his hair a light brown tinged with gray streaks.

"Oh, Garfield and Snoopy and myself," Geronimo replied, grinning.

"Garfield and Snoopy? Are they skilled fighters like you?" the captain queried.

"Just ask any pan of lasagna and the Red Baron," Geronimo said, enjoying the confused expression on the captain's face. The good captain had no way of knowing about the huge Family library, about the five hundred thousand books stocked by Kurt Carpenter. Survival books. Hunting and fishing books. Woodworking, herbal medicine, metal-smithing, gardening, and hundreds of other how-to books. History and geography books. Volumes on military tactics and the martial arts. Reference books by the thousands. There was even a section on humorous books, one of Geronimo's favorites, containing funny books popular before the war, before mankind committed the ultimate ironic joke on itself and erased centuries of progress and striving in a demented blaze of glory. The Family's library was one of its major sources of enter-tainment, in addition to preserving the wisdom and knowledge of the ages. Every Family member read avidly, spending countless hours perusing the books for information or pleasure. The photographic books were especially prized, providing as they did an insight into prewar culture.

"I take it you're not going to give us any information on who you are and where you came from?" the captain asked him.

"I might cooperate a bit more if I knew more about you," Geronimo countered. "For starters, what's your name?"

"I'm called Kilrane," the captain revealed.

"And he has quite a reputation," Cynthia interjected.

"He does?" Geronimo said in a mocking tone. "Strange. I've never heard the name before."

"He's Rolf's right-hand man," Cynthia continued.

"Do tell," Geronimo commented, observing the captain's amused smile.

"And he's fast with his gun," Cynthia detailed.

"Real fast. Some say he's the fastest man alive."

Geronimo stared at the ivory-handled Mitchell Single Action revolver on Kilrane's right hip. "Is that right? Are you fast with that thing?"

Kilrane confidently locked eyes with Geronimo. "That's what everyone says."

"I have a friend by the name of Hickok," Geronimo mentioned. "Since he's the fastest man alive, that makes you the second fastest."

"You think this friend of yours could beat me?" Kilrane asked, chuckling.

"There's no doubt in my mind," Geronimo informed him.

"You still haven't told me your name," Kilrane stated.

"Geronimo."

"Pleased to meet you, Geronimo. Maybe some day you'll introduce me to this Hickok," Kilrane proposed.

"You mean I'll live that long?" Geronimo rejoined.

"How long you live isn't up to me," Kilrane explained. "Rolf will make that decision."

"And you're taking us to Rolf now?" Geronimo inquired.

"You got it," Kilrane confirmed. "He's in Pierre right now. That's where we're headed."

"How long will it take to get there?" Geronimo needed to know.

"Oh, about four or five days, depending on whether we push the horses or not," Kilrane replied. "Why?"

"I've been gone too long as it is," Geronimo said, frowning. "My Family is going to start worrying about me."

"Good," Kilrane said, smiling. "Maybe they'll

send someone looking for you. Maybe this Hickok."

Geronimo fell silent, contemplating the mess he was in. Kilrane had made a valid point; Plato probably would send someone after him, most likely Hickok. Why hadn't he stayed at the Home where he belonged? Why did he leave the others and go off by himself? Now he was endangering not only his life, but the life of whomever Plato would send. Then again, how would they know where to find him? One of the Empaths might be able to home in on him. Otherwise, there was no way they would be able to track him after being gone nearly two weeks.

"Hey! Why so grim?" Cynthia asked, misinterpreting his expression. "They're not going to kill you, at least not right away."

Geronimo smiled reassuringly at her. How could he tell Cynthia about Montana? How could he possibly relate the devastation he'd felt after being betrayed by a Flathead Indian woman? He'd trusted that woman, and she'd rewarded his faith in her by trying to kill him. To make matters worse, she'd almost convinced him to abandon the Family and reside with the Flatheads. Were his loyalties that shallow? How could he have fallowed his dedication and love for the Family to be so easily influenced?

"Rolf might even let you live," Kilrane was saying. "He's not as vicious as that bastard Rory."

Geronimo studied the captain, assessing him as a man of character, a natural leader, the type others would gladly follow. His men had displayed a remarkable willingness to obey his commands. Kilrane had had one of his men confiscate Geronimo's weapons while he personally inspected Cynthia's injured foot. His examination had tended to confirm Geronimo's opinion; none of the deadly pus had entered Cynthia's bloodstream. Unfortunately, they wouldn't know for sure for at least three or four days. If Cynthia remained sympton free during that period, then she was safe. If not, then . . .

Kilrane had been in a hurry to depart. He'd ordered Geronimo onto the black and hauled Cynthia up behind him on the Palomino. It wasn't difficult for Geronimo to deduce Kilrane's motivation for haste. Cynthia's farm was located in Cavalry territory. Kilrane was concerned some of the Cavalry riders might have heard the gunshots during Geronimo's battle with the mutations. He evidently wanted to return to the Legion region before his raiding patrol was confronted by a hostile force larger than his own.

"I take it the two brothers aren't very fond of one another," Geronimo said, fishing for information.

"Fond?" Kilrane laughed bitterly. "They hate each other's guts!"

"Rather unusual for brothers, isn't it?" Geronimo asked.

Kilrane stared at Geronimo, his face a study in suppressed rage. "What would you do if your own brother raped the woman you loved?"

Geronimo and Cynthia exchanged surprised glances. This revelation was news to her, too.

"Rory raped Rolf's woman?" Geronimo inquired.

Kilrane nodded. "About ten years ago."

"Why didn't Rolf kill Rory on the spot?" Geronimo prodded.

"That's what I would have done," Kilrane stated harshly. "Hell, I offered to kill Rory for Rolf! Even promised to let the prick go for his gun first. But Rolf wouldn't hear of it! He's too damn decent for his own good."

"Rolf couldn't bring himself to kill his own brother?" Geronimo asked.

"You've got to understand how it was," Kilrane explained. "Rory always was a troublemaker. It wasn't so bad when their dad, Brent, was alive. Brent was able to keep Rory in line. But after Brent was shot in the back, Rory grew worse and worse. He resented having to share leadership of the Cavalry with Rolf. He caused trouble whenever he could. Rolf just took it all in stride, certain Rory would come around some day. Well, he was wrong! Rolf fell in love with a woman named Adrian. Rory decided he wanted her for himself. The son of a bitch raped her!"

"What happened then?" Cynthia asked.

Kilrane's features clouded with the memories. "I was there when the three of them had it out. I was the only one there, and afterwards Rory made me promise never to tell any of the Cavalry what had happened."

"I'm not Cavalry," Geronimo said. "You can tell me." He sensed Kilrane wanted to tell someone, that it had been eating at his insides for a long, long time.

Kilrane glanced around, insuring none of the patrol riders were close enough to overhear. The nearest was ten feet away.

"Rory taunted Rolf," Kilrane detailed, speaking in a low voice. "Dared him to go for his gun. Rolf wanted to. I could see it in his eyes. But Adrian intervened. You see, she didn't tell Rolf right after the rape happened. No, she waited until she discovered she was pregnant with Rory's child. She said she hadn't told him because she didn't want to cause trouble between them. She didn't want their blood on her hands. Adrian is a sweet woman, you understand. The kind who wouldn't kill a fly. But she's missing a few marbles, if you ask me." Kilrane paused, frowning. "Still, Rolf loves her, and he's an honorable man. After Adrian pleaded with him to spare Rory's life, he backed down. Never saw him do that before. He decided he was going to leave and made an announcement in front of everybody, although he didn't tell them his reason. He's well liked. A lot of the Cavalry went with him and formed the Legion."

"Cynthia told me a little about it," Geronimo admitted. "What happened to Adrian? Did she go with Rolf?"

Kilrane's hands clenched and unclenched. "No! She said she loved Rolf too much to ask him to raise Rory's child. So she stayed with the bastard! Can you imagine it! Now she has a ten-year-old son called Calhoun. He's almost ten, anyway."

"And Rolf?" Geronimo queried him.

Kilrane looked at Geronimo and shook his head. "Pitiful. Just pitiful. The man is a shadow of his former self. Oh, he looks the same on the outside, but he's not half the man he used to be."

"And the brothers haven't seen each other in a decade?" Geronimo questioned.

"Nope."

"Who's the oldest?" Geronimo casually inquired.

"Neither," Kilrane answered.

"I don't follow you," Geronimo admitted.

"Didn't I tell you? They're twins," Kilrane explained.

One of the other riders, a small man with a wisp of a moutache and a scruffy beard, wearing faded brown pants and a green shirt, rode closer to Kilrane.

Geronimo remembered this one; he was carrying the Marlin and had the Arminius and the tomahawk stuck through his belt. The man's own Winchester was slung over his back.

"What is it, Hamlin?" Kilrane demanded.

"Aren't we getting pretty close to the Dead Zone?" Hamlin asked, nervously glancing to the northwest.

"We are," Kilrane verified.

The left corner of Hamlin's mouth twisted downward. "Listen, don't get me wrong," he said to Kilrane. "I'm not questioning your judgment or anything, but aren't we taking a big chance?"

"I know we are," Kilrane agreed. "But I figure the Cavalry patrols won't come this close. We should be able to return to our own territory undetected."

"I hope you're right," Hamlin stated.

"What's the Dead Zone?" Geronimo interrupted.

"You've never seen it?" Cynthia queried.

Geronimo shook his head, shrugging at the same time.

"Actually, there's more than one," Kilrane mentioned. "But this one is special."

"Why special?" Geronimo pressed him.

"Dead Zones are areas devoid of life," Cynthia said.

"My Family calls them Hot Spots," Geronimo revealed. "They were areas impacted by a nuclear weapon during the Big Blast. We haven't entered any of them because we have no way of knowing what the level of radioactivity might be."

"Sounds like the same thing," Cynthia confirmed.

"But you still haven't told me why this one Dead Zone is so unique," Geronimo reminded them.

It was Hamlin who responded. "This one has life in it, if the reports are true."

"What reports?" Geronimo quizzed them.

"Only one person we know of ever returned from

this Dead Zone," Kilrane elaborated. "He told fantastic tales of bloodthirsty monsters before he died. That was years and years ago. Some curious types have ventured into the area in recent years, but not one of them ever came back."

"Can I ask about something else?" Geronimo inquired.

"What is it?" Kilrane replied.

"You can read, can't you?"

Kilrane's surprise registered. "Yeah. My parents taught me. So what?"

"I can read too," Cynthia stated with a trace of pride. "My family owns a primer and a dozen other books." She paused. "At least we did until this dimwit burned everything!" She whacked Kilrane on his right shoulder.

Amazing behavior for a captive! Geronimo considered the information revealed during the course of their conversation. "How do the two sides feel about the conflict?" he questioned Kilrane.

"They don't much like it," Kilrane answered. "They never did understand the real reason Rory and Rolf had their falling out. Most of them want the two factions to reunite. Whole families were divided by the breakup. Brother against brother. Cousin against cousin. Can you imagine what it's been like?" He stopped, reflecting a moment. "Many of us feel the Cavalry will be whole again after Rolf or Rory die. Some of us have even been discussing how to accomplish it, if you get my meaning."

"I understand," Geronimo said.

"Hey," Hamlin interjected, looking at Geromino. "Why'd you ask about the reading? I can't read. What's the big deal over a bunch of stupid books?"

"My Family are readers," Geronimo divulged. "I would imagine the citizens of the Civilized Zone can read too. But it's not that way elsewhere. Reading and education are lost arts.''

"So what's the big deal?'' Hamlin reiterated.

"Readers are thinkers, Hamlin,'' Geronimo told him.

"So who needs to think?'' Hamlin wanted to know.

Their discussion was abruptly punctuated by the sharp retort of gunfire ahead.

Kilrane reined in and the remainder of the patrol did likewise.

The two point men were approaching at a gallop. Behind them rose a spreading dust cloud.

"Three guesses what that is,'' Hamlin remarked nervously.

Geronimo knew what he meant, even before the point men arrived.

"It's a Cavalry unit!'' one of the point riders shouted. "About three dozen.''

"They took some shots at us,'' the second point man yelled, "but they were too far off.''

"We'll head southeast,'' Kilrane ordered. "Maybe we can swing around them.''

The patrol wheeled.

"Look!'' someone cried. "There's more of them!''

Geronimo estimated another three or four dozen were fast approaching from the southeast. With the first group coming in from the west, Kilrane wasn't left with many options. If he attempted to travel south, his patrol would be caught between the two larger Cavalry units. There was only one viable alternative.

"We go north!'' Kilrane directed, waving his right arm over his head.

"We can't!'' Hamlin exclaimed, alarmed. "Look!''

More Cavalry riders were coming at them from the north.

"We're boxed in!" a Legionnaire voiced the obvious.

"No, we're not!" Kilrane declared, and indicated the northwest.

Many of the men exchanged anxious looks.

"The Dead Zone," Hamlin said in a subdued tone.

"What if you just surrender?" Geronimo asked.

"Rory would have us shot," Kilrane replied. "No, there's only one way out of this, and I'd bet they planned it this way."

"They're trying to force you into the Dead Zone?"

Kilrane nodded, his blue eyes glaring at the Cavalry riders. "What else? They outnumber us, sure, but why waste men and ammunition when they can let the Dead Zone do their dirty work for them?"

"Maybe we could make a stand here?" Hamlin feebly suggested.

Kilrane motioned with his arm and urged the Palomino forward, bearing northwest.

After a moment's hesitation, his men followed his example.

Geronimo stayed alongside Kilrane, reluctant to allow Cynthia out of his sight. She was visibly pale, evidently quite frightened. Who could blame her? What was it Kilrane had said? Fantastic tales of bloodthirsty monsters?

Great!

Just great!

The next time I want to be alone with my thoughts, Geronimo promised himself, I'll simply dig a hole somewhere in the Home and meditate in it until I'm ready to come out again.

Someone should have warned him.

Introspection could be hazardous to your health!

Maybe Hamlin had the right idea after all.

Who needs to think?

# 6

Rikki-Tikki-Tavi was concerned. The diminutive, wiry leader of Beta Triad counted eleven uniformed soldiers in front of him, meaning his Triad was out-numbered by almost four to one. Not the best of odds. Ultimately, though, the amount of their opponents was irrelevant. Orders were orders. There could be twenty-five soldiers and it wouldn't negate their instructions. Blade's directive had been explicit: "We can't permit them to return to their headquarters with more information concerning the Family. Take them out. If possible, a prisoner or two would be nice. But beyond that, there must be no survivors. Understood?" All three members of Beta Triad had acknowledged their comprehension.

Their moment of truth was upon them.

Rikki was crouched behind a boulder on the western edge of the hillock. He wore his usual baggy black pants and shirt and ankle-high moccasins. His black hair and brown eyes matched the serious, intense expression on his angular face. Clutched in his left hand was a long black scabbard containing his prized katana, the only genuine Japanese sword the Family owned. It was his by virtue of his amazing skill in the martial arts, exactly as Hickok possessed the Colt Pythons and Blade his cherished

Bowies; they were the best with those particular
weapons. Every Warrior took lessons in unarmed
combat, taught by an Elder, a former Warrior.
These lessons were called simply Tegner, because
the manuals of instruction were dozens of books
written by a man named Bruce Tegner. Kurt
Carpenter had placed every book Tegner ever wrote
in the Family library: illustrated, step-by-step
volumes on kung fu, savate, karate, jujitsu, judo,
and other styles of martial combat. Rikki-Tikki-
Tavi was the Family's premier martial artist.

Rikki glanced to his left and spotted Teucer
behind a tree, his compound bow in his hands, an
arrow already notched on the string. A full quiver
was attached to his belt and slanted across his right
hip. His green pants and shirt provided perfect
camouflage. A six-inch strip of leather secured his
shoulder-length blond hair at the base of his neck,
suspending his blond locks in a ponytail. His blond
beard was trimmed so that it jutted forward on his
chin, presenting a decidedly medieval appearance.
As he had several times before, Rikki wondered why
the bowman had selected the name Teucer instead of
Robin Hood or William Tell at his Naming. It was
probably for the same reason Rikki had picked his
own name; Teucer was as ardent a fan of Homer as
Rikki was of Kipling.

The final member of Beta Triad was lying behind
the fallen trunk of a former giant of the forest, off to
Rikki's right. Rikki could see his motionless,
muscular form prone on the ground. Of all the
Warriors in the Family, only one came anywhere
close to matching Blade's awesome physique and
deadly ability with knives; of all the Warriors, just
one could approximate Hickok's incredible skill
with handguns; and when it came to the martial

arts, this same man was able to hold his own against Rikki and Seiko in competition. While not necessarily outstanding with any one weapon, or extremely exceptional in any lethal art, he was recognized as the best all-around Warrior the Family currently had, the one man capable of doing all things well. Rikki was grateful Plato had assigned him to Beta Triad. He just wished the man had chosen a more conventional name. Who in their right mind would want to be named after the Hindu god of death? And who else would have asked the Weavers to create a seamless dark-blue garment with the ebony silhouette of a skull on the back?

Only Yama.

There was another essential difference between Yama and the other Warriors. Although all of the Warriors were proficient in the use of various firearms and other weaponry, most evinced a predilection for a particular favorite: Blade, his Bowies; Hickok, his Pythons; Geronimo, his tomahawk; Teucer, his bow; and Rikki his katana. Yama displayed a small preference for a carved scimitar, but he tended to utilize a vast variety of arms, far more than any of the other Warriors. For this occasion he was armed to the proverbial teeth. He carried his scimitar in a sheath attached to his belt above his left hip. On his right hip was a fifteen-inch survival knife. In a shoulder holster under his right arm was a Browning Hi-Power 9 millimeter Automatic Pistol. Under his left arm he sported a Smith and Wesson Model 586 Distinguished Combat Magnum. Today he also had a Wilkinson "Terry" Carbine, converted to full automatic by the Family Gunsmiths and adapted to hold a fifty-shot magazine instead of the standard thirty.

Yes, sir, it definitely was wiser to have Yama on

your side than against you.

Rikki admired the discipline Yama exhibited. The man might be petrified for all the movement he showed. The only incongruity about him was his cropped silver hair and drooping silver moustache.

Bright light suddenly flashed from the direction of the Home, arresting Rikki's attention. He counted the times the light flicked out. One. Two. And the light was back. Now it was gone.

So.

It was time.

Rikki studied the Civilized Zone troops in front of him, the men belonging to the Army of Samuel, the ones called the Watchers. They were busily engaged in erecting their monitoring equipment. Rikki was unsure of its function, but he knew that with it they were able to overhear Family conversations at great distances and to take photographs like the ones in the books in the Family library. There was a unit on a tripod, a large bowl-like affair with the convex end toward Rikki and a long metal stick pointed at the Home. A soldier was squatting beside this unit, headphones over his ears, adjusting the dials on a square metal case affixed to the base of the bowl. Another soldier was alongside the first, holding a pen and pad in his hands. Nearby two other soldiers were fiddling with what looked like a huge camera with a telescopic lens. Three more of the troopers were clustered around a portable radio placed on a flat rock. The rest of the troopers were idly standing around, relaxed, apparently not expecting any trouble. Why should they? According to Blade, the Watchers regularly engaged in this spying and had been doing so for years. They were unaware Blade knew about the clandestine operation; to them, this was simply business as usual.

Yama had heard them approaching first. Within moments, Beta Triad had been hidden from view. Rikki, using a small mirror he carried in his right front pocket, had signaled the Home. The soldiers had congregated in this relatively barren section of the hillock, Beta Triad had assumed its positions, and Rikki had awaited the cue from Blade.

Now, he had gotten it.

"What's the hold up?" one of the soldiers near the radio demanded, looking at the pair preparing the big dish.

Rikki recalled Blade mentioning this thing. He'd heard about it in Montana and researched it after returning to the Home. What was it . . .

"It's a bit fuzzy, sir," the soldier with the headphones replied. "There's static from somewhere, distorting the microphone."

That was it! Rikki remembered. It was a parabolic microphone.

"Clear it," the first trooper commanded. He, evidently, was their officer. None of the others wore little gold bars pinned to their collars.

The soldier responsible for handling the radio glanced up at the officer. "I have Colonel Jarvis on the other end, Lieutenant Putnam."

Lieutenant Putnam took the radio's microphone from the operator and raised it to his lips. "Lieutenant Putnam reporting as ordered, sir." He hastily donned a headphone set.

Rikki, only twelve feet from the officer, clearly heard every word.

"No, sir. No problems."

There was a pause while Putnam listened to Jarvis on the headset.

"We're just about set up now, sir."

Pause.

"Twenty-four hours. Yes, sir."

Pause.

"We have ample cassettes, sir. Anything in particular?"

There was an extended wait while Colonel Jarvis dictated his instructions.

"Yes, sir. Anything dealing with why Blade was in Montana shall be immediately brought to your attention. Likewise, any information pertaining to their efforts at reversing the senility."

The premature senility. What did these Watchers know about the dreaded affliction?

". . . thought it was impossible," Lieutenant Putnam was saying. "The Doktor must be furious! I agree. Anything the Doktor wants, the Doktor gets. Any references to the G.R.D. will be relayed to you as soon as possible."

Rikki entertained an inkling of the subject of Putnam's conversation. The G.R.D. was the creature called Gremlin. Blade had supplied the essential information.

The capital of the remnant of the United States of America was currently located in Denver, Colorado. But Denver was not the only city still intact in the Civilized Zone. One city, once known as Cheyenne, Wyoming, was now called the Cheyenne Citadel. A contingent of the Army of Samuel was based at the Citadel. Also conducting operations from Cheyenne was the mysterious man known only as the Doktor. The mere mention of the Doktor would suffice to arouse fear in the ordinary army troops. The precise nature of the Doktor's work and status in the new Government was unknown, although Blade had discovered the Doktor was very close to Samuel II. Blade had also learned that the Doktor operated something called the Genetic Research Division, the unit Gremlin had belonged to before deserting the Doktor and joining the Family.

"The jeeps?" Putnam said, still talking to the colonel. "We left them at the usual spot. No mechanical problems enroute. Yes, sir, will do. Over and out."

So they had arrived by jeep? Rikki grinned. The Family could use additional modes of transportation. It only owned nine horses and the SEAL.

Lieutenant Putnam handed the microphone and the headset to the radio operator and turned toward the two men beside the parabolic microphone. "Is it clear yet?"

"Yes, sir," the trooper handling the cassette recorder at the base of the microphone replied.

"Good. Then proceed. Be sure your transcript of the tape is legible," Putnam ordered.

"Will do, sir."

Rikki glanced at Teucer and Yama, still holding their positions and awaiting his command. The soldiers were engaged in their respective tasks, oblivious to the three Warriors only yards away.

Perfect, Rikki thought. They'd be able to neutralize this patrol with a minimum of difficulty. Surprise was totally on their side. The setup couldn't be better if he'd personally planned it this way. It didn't seem likely that anything could go wrong now.

As if to prove him wrong, a tremendous racket commenced in a tree near Yama.

Rikki-Tikki-Tavi looked up into the branches above Yama's head and pinpointed the source of the hubbub.

Dear Spirit! Not now!

A blue jay was perched on a limb twenty feet above Yama. The bird had spotted the intruder at the base of his tree and was letting the world know there was danger in the area.

Would the soldiers pay any attention? Were any of them sufficiently versed in wood lore to recognize the traditional warning cry of the jay?

One of the troopers, a lean soldier holding an M-16 and idly standing on guard about six feet from Yama, glanced up at the noisy bird, his brow furrowed.

Rikki tensed. What would he do? Would he investigate, or decide it was just a loud-mouthed blue jay?

The guard shuffled several steps toward the tree.

Yama was still invisible behind the log at the bottom of the tree.

The blue jay was screaming bloody murder.

Shut up! Rikki's right hand closed on the hilt of his katana.

The soldier had spied the prancing jay and was watching it, smiling at its antics.

Good! Now just turn around, like a nice little boy, and return to your post! Rikki started to slide the katana from its scabbard.

Shaking his head, the trooper began to turn. Apparently, he finally realized the jay was excited about something at the base of the tree. The man hesitated.

Rikki imagined he could read the trooper's mind. Should I take a peek or not? the man was probably thinking.

Don't do it!

Leave it alone!

The guard lowered the barrel of his M-16 and advanced on the log, not really expecting trouble.

Rikki's katana was clear of the scabbard.

Teucer had raised his bow and was sighting at a target.

Yama was still immobile on the ground.

The blue jay was squawking to high heaven.

Another soldier noticed the first moving toward the tree and turned to watch.

I never did much like blue jays, Rikki told himself.

The guard reached the fallen tree and peered over the top of the log.

Rikki could only imagine the shocked expression on his face.

With a startled curse, the guard leaned forward, aiming his M-16.

# 7

"There you are! I've been looking all over for you."
She found him sitting beside the moat in the northeastern corner of the Home, as far from the mainstream of Family activity as he could get.

"I'd prefer to be alone," he grumbled, his buckskin-clad form hunched over, his hands on his knees. His handsome face was a study in sorrow, a rare emotional display for him.

"We need to talk," she persisted, staring at the reflection of herself in the water, her long blonde hair stirring in the breeze.

"We have nothing to talk about," he groused.

"Give me a break!" She sat down next to him, examining his rugged, troubled features. "Never thought I'd see you like this. I'd heard the great Hickok never let anything affect him. Well, almost never, anyway."

Hickok actually glared at her.

"Oooooh! Aren't we pissed!"

"Leave me alone, Sherry," Hickok told her gruffly.

"And what if I don't?" Sherry retorted. "Are you going to whip out your famous Pythons and blow me away?"

Hickok studied her. "Why are you doing this to me?"

"I refuse to let you sit out here feeling sorry for yourself," Sherry replied.

"If you knew why . . ." he began.

"I know," she informed him. "Jenny just told me all about Joan. How you loved her. How she was killed. And how you're not over her yet, not by a long shot."

Hickok didn't say anything.

Sherry tenderly placed her left hand on his shoulder. "I didn't know about Joan when I proposed becoming a Warrior, but it wouldn't have changed my mind even if I had known."

Hickok started to speak, but she placed a finger over his lips.

"Hear me out, lover. This is important." Sherry paused, gathering her thoughts. "I think I've already told you my life in Canada, before the Trolls kidnapped me, was pretty dull. Boring, in fact. I never liked it. I always wanted something more, some excitement in my life. And then you came along."

Hickok was attentive to her every word.

"You rescued me from those miserable bastards. My own Prince Charming to my rescue! It was marvelous. I didn't want to go back to Canada and a monotonous routine, so I persuaded you to bring me here to the Home. I want to stay here, Nathan. I thoroughly enjoy it here. But I wouldn't feel right about it if I didn't contribute to the Family. Everyone here has a specific job to do. Where would I fit in? As a Tiller? Don't make me laugh. As a Weaver? It'd be duller than Canada. As an Empath? I don't have the talent."

"But why a Warrior?" he interjected.

"It's the obvious choice," Sherry explained. "I can learn to handle a handgun. You know I'm already a good shot with a rifle. Aren't I?"

"You are," Hickok reluctantly admitted.

"So there! Becoming a Warrior is the logical choice."

"There's more to being a Warrior than just being competent with firearms," Hickok stated.

"I can learn the martial arts too," Sherry said confidently.

"It's not that," Hickok said. "It's a state of mind you must have if you're to succeed as a Warrior. Without it you wouldn't last five minutes in the field."

"What state of mind?" she asked.

"You must constantly be prepared to kill or be killed. The fancy talk about preserving the Home and protecting the Family is well and good, but when you get down to it, to the bare facts, being a Warrior is synonymous with being a killer."

Sherry inexplicably began laughing.

"What's so funny?"

"I just realized you haven't used your usual Wild West talk once this whole conversation."

"I thought we were having a serious talk here," Hickok snapped. "Blasted contrary females!"

"I'm sorry," Sherry apologized.

"I'll bet."

"Listen," Sherry quickly continued, "maybe I'm not a natural killer like you, maybe I'm not cut out to be a Warrior. But I won't know unless I try, will I?"

"You could be dead before you learn the answer," Hickok rejoined, expecting her to ignore the remark. She did.

"Well, what's so bad about being a killer? You're one, right? And Blade and Geronimo and Rikki and the other Warriors. You don't seem to mind your profession. How come it's so bad for me?''

"You don't understand," Hickok mumbled.

"No, I'm afraid I don't," Sherry said. "Why don't you enlighten me.''

Hickok sighed and gazed into the distance. "I just don't want it to happen again," he stated quietly.

"Are you afraid you'll lose me the same way you lost Joan?" Sherry asked. "Is that it?''

Hickok's reply was inaudible.

"I can't hear you," she prompted him.

Hickok whirled, his face contorted in anger. "*Yes!*" he exploded. "I don't want to lose you! Satisfied now?''

Sherry clearly perceived the profound depth of his affection for the first time, and the staggering intensity of it shocked her. "I'm sorry," she whispered. "I had no idea. . . .''

Hickok was ripping handfuls of grass from the earth in unrestrained annoyance.

"If you don't want me to be a Warrior, I won't," Sherry offered.

"It's your life. Do whatever you want!''

Sherry eased her body closer to his and pressed against him. "I don't ever want to do anything to hurt you, Nathan. You mean more to me than anyone else in the world.''

Hickok ceased his assault on the turf and looked into her green eyes.

"I'm serious," Sherry said, conveying her innermost feelings, baring her soul. "I love you, you big lug! You know that. If it means so much to you, if it's going to rip you apart, I won't become a Warrior.''

"You'd give it up for me?" Hickok questioned her.

"Of course.''

The gunman nodded thoughtfully. "Then it's

settled," he announced.

"You want me to give it up?" Sherry inquired dispiritedly.

"Sure don't, ma'am," Hickok answered, grinning. "I reckon I couldn't live with myself if I forced you to do that. You're going to become the best damn female Warrior this here Family has ever seen!"

Sherry squealed with delight and hugged him. "I knew you'd come around, you adorable dummy!"

"Just don't tell anyone else I'm such a softie," Hickok admonished her. "It'd ruin my image."

"You certainly changed your mind pretty fast," Sherry observed, running her fingers through his yellow hair.

"Not really," Hickok disagreed. "I was sitting here thinking about my behavior before you showed up. I realized I was being a mite selfish. It's your life, after all. I may not be too fond of the idea, but if you really want to become a Warrior, then I won't stand in your way."

"I appreciate that," she said sincerely.

"But you're going to learn from the best," Hickok went on. "I'll teach you handguns, Blade will instruct you in knife fighting, Geronimo in tracking, Rikki in the martial arts, and the others in whatever they're tops at." He smiled. "By the time we're through with you, you'll be a lean, mean, fightin' machine!"

"Better not mess with me then," Sherry joked in mock seriousness.

Hickok suddenly grimaced.

"What's the matter?" she asked.

"It just occurred to me!" Hickok exclaimed.

"What?" Sherry queried, concerned.

"I may go to romancing you one night, and you might have a headache or something, and if I don't take no for an answer you just might wallop the tar out of me!'' Hickok feigned terror at the prospect.

Sherry snuggled against him. ''No need to worry about that, lover!'' She giggled. ''And I don't have a headache right now.''

''Do tell.''

They embraced, Sherry passionately pressing her warm form into his hard body, their lips locked together, their tongues entwining.

''Mmmmmmm,'' Sherry moaned after they finally broke the kiss. ''That was *real* nice! Do that again!''

''Anything you . . .'' Hickok abruptly sat up, alert.

''What's wrong?'' Sherry questioned, gazing around them. ''Did you see something?''

''Listen.''

''What?''

''Quiet! Listen!'' Hickok released her and stood, his hands on his Colts.

''I don't . . .'' she began, then stopped, hearing the distant sounds.

Popping noises.

''It's gunfire,'' Hickok stated, facing toward the west.

''Some of the Warriors practicing?'' she suggested.

''Nope.'' Hickok shook his head. ''Too far off. What could it be? No one's sounded the alarm.''

''One of the Family out hunting?'' Sherry opined.

''Too many shots. It's still . . .'' Hickok started a sentence, then snapped his fingers. ''Of course! It has to be!''

''Of course what?'' Sherry rose to her feet.

''Come on!'' Hickok was running off.

''Wait for me!'' She ran in pursuit.

Hickok slowed to allow her to catch up. ''Looks

like I'll need a rain check on some heavy breathing.''

"Just don't make a habit of it," Sherry warned him. "My hormones couldn't take the stress!"

# 8

The Dead Zone certainly lived up to its reputation.

In all his travels, in all his experience, Geronimo had never encountered any terrain as devoid of life, any geographical area so utterly barren and destitute.

It was uncanny, almost as if he'd been transported to a landscape on another planet.

Vegetation was completely absent. Wildlife was nonexistent. Even the breeze seemed sluggish and abnormally warm. The earth was a reddish color and unnaturally fine.

How could anything live in such a sterile habitat?

The Legion patrol was gathered on top of a large hill, the riders allowing their weary mounts a brief rest.

"I don't see any sign of pursuit," Hamlin noted. "Do you?" he asked Kilrane.

Kilrane was studying the plain below them. "None," he agreed.

"They must have given up!" Hamlin elated. "They knew they couldn't catch us!"

"Or they had accomplished their purpose and wisely withdrew," Kilrane stated.

"What do you mean?" Hamlin inquired.

"They may figure we're far enough into the Dead Zone to accomplish their goal," Kilrane elaborated. "We must be a good fifteen miles into this wasteland."

"So what now?" Cynthia queried.

Geronimo was wondering about the same subject. He mentally attempted to envision their approximate location. He knew the Cavalry and the Legion occupied the eastern half of South Dakota, dividing it between them with the Cavalry controlling the eastern section and the Legion the western part. They were still in Cavalry territory, somewhere in the northern portion. He tried to recall the map of South Dakota he'd seen while paging through the atlas on the trip to Montana. Strange. He couldn't remember any important military or civilian targets in this region. Why had it sustained a direct hit from a nuclear weapon? Maybe it was another miss. From records and journals kept immediately after the war, and from the data acquired since commencing Alpha Triad's extended travels, the Family knew many primary military and civilian targets had been spared direct hits during the Third World War. Other areas, lacking any major significance, had been struck. A peculiar paradox, explained away by one of the Family Elders who suggested that the incoming missiles hadn't been as accurate as the other side had boasted. It was entirely feasible that a missile aimed at, say, a missile silo in North Dakota might have strayed a few hundred miles and instead obliterated a grazing herd of pronghorn antelope in South Dakota. When dealing in distances of thousands and thousands of miles, any slight deviation in the missile's trajectory would negate a direct hit and result in a miss of gigantic proportions. The history books in the Family library also mentioned a disturbing number of disastrous high-technology-related accidents in the years before the war, clearly indicating that humankind's vaunted ingenuity had been an infinitesimal speck compared to its exaggerated ego.

"Maybe we should head southwest," Hamlin was suggesting. "We'd get to Pierre a lot faster if we made a beeline for it."

"I was thinking along the same lines," Kilrane said. "The Cavalry might anticipate our move and attempt to cut us off, but it can't be helped. We can't remain in the Dead Zone. The sooner we're out of here, the better."

"Do you see that?" one of the other riders asked, pointing to the west.

Geronimo swiveled, surprised at the sight.

A mile or two distant towered a huge conical mound, rearing up several hundred feet from the ground. The mound was massive, staggering the senses. Some low clouds seemed to be brushing the top of the cone.

"What the hell is that?" Hamlin inquired in awe.

"Maybe it's where the missile or bomb struck?" Cynthia suggested.

"No," Geronimo mentioned. "They left gaping holes, not the other way around. Some force pushed that mound up from within."

"Could it be a . . ." Hamlin paused, searching for the right word.

"Volcano?" Geronimo guessed, and Hamlin nodded. Geronimo shook his head. "I never heard of any volcanoes in South Dakota."

"Look!" Cynthia cried. "At the top of the mound!"

Geronimo saw it, and his skin suddenly tingled,

goosebumps all over his arms.

Some . . . thing . . . was moving along the rim of the cone. Details were indistinct because of the great range involved, but whatever the creature was, it appeared large and oddly menacing.

"L . . . L . . . Let's get out of here!" Hamlin stuttered, his fright readily apparent.

"Let's go!" Kilrane barked, sweeping his left arm toward the southwest.

Geronimo kept the big black close to the Palomino as they descended the hill and galloped across the plain, great clouds of red dust billowing behind them.

What *was* that thing? Geronimo's mind drifted as he rode, pondering the drastically altered nature of the environment and the ecology since the Big Blast. The so-called experts had failed to accurately predict the devastating consequences mega-doses of radiation and toxic chemicals would wreak on the organisms affected. Diligent research had proven radiation induced bizarre mutations. Combined with the unknown chemical elements, it was no wonder the land was crawling with deviate life forms. There were mutates everywhere. Deadly opaque green clouds proliferated; one such cloud had killed the Founder of the Home, Kurt Carpenter. And to top it off, the Family had fought other recurrent horrors, including rare cases of giantism restricted to insects or their close kin. Who knew what else lurked out there? As Plato had once noted, all it would take would be two similar mutations mating and the world could see the rise of a new species unheralded in its ferocity and adaptability. If this ever happened, it could well signal the death knell for the human race on planet earth.

Geronimo's attention was arrested by an

enormous hole off to the right, measuring at least thirty feet in diameter.

There was movement in the center of the hole.

Geronimo tried to focus on the gaping cavity, finding the task difficult with the big black running all out. There seemed to be two stick-like affairs waving wildly in the middle of the aperture. They displayed a pale reddish color, the same as the big object seen on the mound.

What in the world was it?

Geronimo noticed Kilrane watching the sticks. "Do you see them?" Geronimo called.

Kilrane nodded.

"Any idea what they are?"

Kilrane shook his head.

Cynthia was also staring at the hole, her face markedly pale, her slim hands clinging to Kilrane's broad shoulders.

I wish he'd placed her up behind me, Geronimo mused, feeling slightly jealous. He found himself experiencing a strong attraction toward Cynthia and resented this forced intrusion on their budding relationship.

A series of low hills rose ahead of the racing patrol. Kilrane led them up one side and down the other, the horses flying, the dust clouds rising behind their passage.

Another hole lomed directly in front of them.

Kilrane turned the Palomino to the left, opting to circumvent the crater. The majority of the patrol cued on his lead.

Except for two.

This duo was at the rear of the column. The choking, blinding dust raised by the others obscured their vision, preventing them from realizing the main body of the patrol had veered to the left until it was too late.

Geronimo heard screams and shouts and looked over his right shoulder in time to observe the two riders plunge over the lip of the crater and vanish from view.

Kilrane missed seeing the duo drop into the hole, but he did hear the piercing shrieks of agony and terror that immediately followed. He brought the sweaty Palomino to an abrupt stop. "What was that?" he demanded, surveying the area.

Geronimo pointed at the shadowy cavity. "Two of your men just fell in."

"What?" Kilrane goaded the Palomino toward the hole, the strapping stallion seemingly reluctant to comply. The horse tossed its head, its ears laid flat, and balked, forcing Kilrane to forcefully exhort his mount to achieve obedience.

Geronimo, despite an overpowering premonition of impending danger, stayed with Kilrane. Hamlin, visibly scared, stayed a few feet behind them. The remainder of the patrol hung back, some of them experiencing difficulty controlling their plunging steeds.

"Where the hell are they?" Kilrane asked, poised at the edge of the opening.

Geronimo examined the crater, more mystified than ever. This hole, like the first, was approximately thirty feet in diameter at the top. The cavity tapered toward the center and ended with a dark hole, about ten feet in circumference, at the bottom of the pit. The sides of the crater were smooth, evincing a neatly excavated appearance.

There was no sign of the two Legionnaires.

"I don't get it," Hamlin said. "What'd they do? Fall in . . ." He paused, petrified.

A pair of red-hued rods rose from the black depths

of the pit and began swaying back and forth.

"I don't like this," Kilrane hissed between clenched teeth. "I have a gut feeling we'd better make tracks, and pronto!"

"Hold it!" Geronimo barked, keeping his eyes peeled on those red rods.

Kilrane, about to turn the Palomino, quizzically gazed at Geronimo.

"My weapons," Geronimo stated.

"Your what?" Hamlin snapped. "Who do you think you are? In case you hadn't noticed, you're our prisoner, fool!"

Kilrane glanced at the ominous hole. The red rods had disappeared. "Give him his arms," he ordered.

"Do what?" Hamlin objected, peeved. "Since when do we allow prisoners to have their weapons?"

"Since I just said so," Kilrane countered, his tone low and threatening. "I don't have time to argue, my friend. Give them to him now!"

Hamlin, anger creasing his features, tossed the Marlin to Geronimo and handed him the Arminius and the tomahawk.

"Thank you," Geronimo said, feeling a surge of confidence. If they were attacked now, at least he'd have a chance to defend himself and protect Cynthia. He looked into Kilrane's blue eyes. "I owe you one."

"I hope I live long enough to collect," Kilrane muttered. He pressed his legs against the Palomino's sides and rapidly brought the horse to a gallop.

The men in Kilrane's patrol closed in around him, packing together in a dense mass, their flagging morale bolstered by their proximity to their leader.

Geronimo was watching Cynthia. Her ordeal was catching up with her. She was slumped against

Kilrane, fatigued to the point of exhaustion.

Another mile along and they encountered a third crater.

Kilrane gave this one a wide berth, swinging his patrol to the left again, always bearing to the southwest.

"You know," Hamlin announced after they passed the third hole, "this ain't so bad. Not too much longer and we'll be rid of this damn place!"

Geronimo, staring ahead, realized the small man had spoken too soon.

"Look!" someone shouted. "Up ahead!"

The entire patrol slowed, then halted, stunned by the sight in front of them.

Not now! Geronimo wanted to scream. Not now!

A quarter of a mile away, completely blocking their escape route, filling the sky and obscuring the ground with its raging intensity, was a titanic dust storm. It was turning the very air red with the tons of dust particles borne into the atmosphere.

Kilrane shouted, bearing to the west, hoping they could outrace the storm.

He was wrong.

The Legion patrol managed to cover a thousand yards before the dust storm surged into them. The air promptly became almost unbreatheable, the hot wind searing their skin, the swirling dust stinging horse and rider alike. They were caught in the open, exposed and vulnerable, the nearest cover a good mile off.

Geronimo could barely see Kilrane and Cynthia only yards in front of him. He held his left arm over his mouth and nose to prevent the dust from entering. His eyelids were burning from the dust, and his body felt like hundreds of tiny critters were trying to prick him to death.

"Stay together!" Kilrane shouted. "We can't afford to stop! Get a fix on my voice!"

Easier said than done. Geronimo could discern several moving shapes nearby, but he had no idea where the rest of the patrol was. Maybe, he told himself, maybe the storm would end soon.

Instead, its violence increased.

Geronimo focused his entire attention on Kilrane and the Palomino, unwilling to lose sight of Cynthia, even for a moment. The whistle of the wind attained a shrill pitch.

How much longer could this storm continue?

The onslaught persisted, seemingly interminable, a natural temper tantrum of incalculable magnitude.

Once, Geronimo felt the big black falter and recover, and he marveled at the animal's endurance. The horse must be suffering greatly, but it never quit, it never surrendered to the elements.

Could he do any less?

Geronimo formulated a plan. Timing would be critical, but if successful he would be rid of the Legion patrol and Cynthia would be free of their clutches.

It all depended on the dust storm.

Eventually the storm would abate, and if he waited for the right moment, for the interval between the initial slackening of the storm and the time it stopped, he would have a few precious minutes when the visibility would improve enough to maneuver and the Legionnaires would be off-guard, not expecting any trouble.

It had to be then.

Geronimo waited impatiently, fingering the trigger on the Marlin. He recognized his own nervousness and willed his mind and body to relax.

Oh Great Spirit, he prayed, guide your son and servant in this enterprise! Preserve your children that we may honor and worship you all the days of our lives in this world and in the mansions on high! We are children of peace thrust into times of conflict, and we would live your will in this as in all other matters!

The storm slackened, the wind decreasing, the air slowly beginning to clear.

Geronimo could see Kilrane and Cynthia off to his left, about five yards separating them from him.

*Now!*

Geronimo surged the black forward, the reins and his Marlin clasped in his right hand. He deliberately rode the black into the Palomino, staggering Kilrane's mount, even as his left arm encircled Cynthia and yanked her off the Palomino. In another instant, he was clear of the Palomino and racing eastward.

"Geronimo, stop!" Kilrane shouted behind him.

Geronimo ignored the command, knowing the rest of the patrol would be unaware of the escape in progress, eager to take advantage of the element of surprise.

"Stop!" Kilrane yelled again.

Cynthia was clutching Geronimo with all her strength. "You're losing him!" she cried.

The dust storm, while continuing to diminish, was still stirring the dirt and posing a navigational problem, preventing Geronimo from seeing more than ten yards in front of the black.

"Geronimo!" Kilrane called a final time, sounding distant.

It was working!

Geronimo risked a glance over his right shoulder, elated to discover none of the Legion patrol was in sight. If the black could pour on the speed for another mile, their getaway would be assured.

Cynthia's grip on him suddenly tightened, her nails digging into his shoulder. *"Look out!"* she screamed in frantic warning.

Geronimo, alarmed, twisted forward, his senses thrown off kilter when the black abruptly catapulted downward, seeming to float for several seconds before smashing into an earthen wall. The brutal impact wrenched Cynthia from Geronimo's grasp and tumbled him from the horse. He felt his body tossed head over heels before he landed with a painful, jarring collision on the ground.

"Geronimo!" Cynthia shrieked somewhere nearby.

Geronimo struggled to rise, trying to assess their situation and locate Cynthia in the gloom. What had happened? Where were they?

There was a patch of light above his head, a wide circle about thirty yards in diameter.

Circle?

Thirty yards!

Geronimo, shocked by the realization, deduced where they were even as a shuffling noise sounded to his rear. He tried to turn, to confront whatever was lurking in back of him, but he was too slow.

A hard object struck the Warrior's head with a resounding crack.

Geronimo toppled to the ground, striving to maintain consciousness. Red dirt filled his slack mouth as he landed with a dull thud. His thoughts swirled, tenuous and distressing.

From the proverbial frying pan into the fire!

So sorry, Cynthia!

Being captives of the Legion was a breeze compared to their present predicament. In all the confusion and excitement of their mad dash for freedom, he'd managed to commit the folly of all follies! Blunders, in matters of life and death, were inexcusable and invariably fatal. Simple mistakes could cost you your life. Things like failing to keep your guns loaded. Or hurrying a shot at an opponent. Or turning your back on an avowed enemy.

Or plunging into a large hole in the Dead Zone.

Geronimo strained to rise, aware of a clammy, trickling sensation near his left ear. Blood. He managed to reach his hands and knees before a suffocating wave of vertigo overwhelmed him and he collapsed in a heap.

"Geronimo!" Cynthia screamed.

Unfortunately, he couldn't hear her.

# 9

The inexperienced guard really should have shot first and cursed later.

A burst from the Wilkinson tore through his forehead, blowing the rear of his cranium completely away.

Yama's shots precipitated immediate mayhem on the hillock. He leaped to his feet and fired again, this time catching the second guard in the midsection and doubling him over, his abdomen ruptured and leaking blood like a sieve.

One of the troopers, reacting in reflex, snapped a shot from his M-16 at the silver-haired intruder.

Yama dove for cover behind the log.

A soldier on the far side of the clearing was unslinging his M-16 when an arrow penetrated his head from behind, the three-bladed hunting point emerging from between his eyes. The trooper jerked spasmodically as he fell.

Rikki-Tikki-Tavi was already in motion, the scabbard lying behind the boulder, his katana upraised as he ran from hiding and made for the soldiers near the radio. One of the Watchers was grabbing for his automatic pistol as Rikki, thankful none of the troopers wore helmets, swept the razor-edged blade downward, burying the katana in the man's forehead and splitting it open with the same ease a sharp knife might cut a melon.

The remaining soldiers were galvanizing into action, several of them firing at the log Yama was behind. Others were shooting wildly at the trees to the north of the clearing, trying to nail the bowman.

The second radio man had his pistol out and aimed.

Rikki sidestepped as the gun boomed, his left side wracked with a burning sensation, knowing he'd been creased, but ignoring the pain as he savagely wrenched the katana sideways, the gleaming, bloody blade slicing through the second man's wrist and severing his hand from his arm.

The soldier wailed and held the crimson-covered stump aloft, gaping at it in abject horror.

Rikki finished him with a tsuki thrust, the point of the katana lancing into the soldier's throat.

The last trooper near the radio was Lieutenant Putnam. Initially shocked by the carnage, he recovered as the swordsman faced him. Instead of drawing his automatic, or retrieving his M-16 on the grass near the radio, he leaped at the swordsman, his arms held wide.

Rikki allowed Putnam to tackle him, releasing the katana as they tumbled to the ground. Putnam landed on top, pinning him.

Putnam, outweighing the swordsman by at least forty pounds and towering over him by a good two feet, was confident he could subdue this little man and take him prisoner.

Rikki-Tikki-Tavi grinned as he brutally jammed his forehead into Putnam's nose. He could feel the nasal cartilage break as fresh warm blood gushed over his face.

Putnam squealed in agony and released the

swordsman, attempting to roll to his feet.

Rikki struck again, a hiji blow to Putnam's jaw from the side.

Lieutenant Putnam weaved as he rose to his knees, his mouth and jaw coated with his own blood.

Rikki followed the elbow strike with the coup d'etat: a tega-tana-naka-uchi, a cross-body chop of the hand to the Lieutenant's temple, downing Putnam instantly.

The battle elsewhere was still raging.

Rikki, still on his back, glanced up. He saw another trooper on the ground with an arrow imbedded in his chest. Seven downed and four to go. One was to his left, raking the trees with automatic fire while crouched behind a small boulder. Three more were to his right, advancing on the log, holding their fire and waiting for Yama to appear.

Yama did.

A blue form suddenly hurtled from the underbrush twenty feet from the log, the Wilkinson chattering. One of the Watchers was ripped from his crotch to his throat. The other two hit the dirt, firing as they did. The dust around Yama's feet swirled upward as he leaped into a shallow depression.

Rikki began to rise, to aid his fellow Warriors, when the trooper on his left turned, having spotted Yama out of the corner of his eye. The soldier had a clear shot and he hastily raised his M-16, forgetting, for the moment, the bowman in the trees.

Unerring as ever, Teucer's arrow took the Watcher in the neck. The trooper gurgled and gasped as he slid to the ground.

Only two of the soldiers were still standing.

One of them, throwing caution to the wind, recklessly charged Yama's position, blasting at the depression with his M-16. He was ten feet from

Yama when he expended the final rounds in his clip. Pausing, he urgently endeavored to reload.

Yama was up and running at the trooper, gambling he could reach the Watcher before the soldier succeeded.

Rikki jumped to his feet and reclaimed his katana, prepared to assist his fellow Warrior if necessary.

But his aid wasn't needed.

Yama's incredible speed was equal to the occasion. He slammed the butt of the Wilkinson into the trooper's head just as the soldier was bringing the M-16 into play.

The final Watcher bolted, tearing into the trees, bearing to the south.

Rikki-Tikki-Tavi started in pursuit. He looked over his left shoulder and spied Teucer emerging from his vantage point. "You two mop up!" he ordered, then dove into the undergrowth on the trail of the last soldier.

More than likely the trooper was making for the jeeps. Rikki realized he must prevent the Watcher from escaping at all costs. If word of this ambush managed to reach Samuel II, the dictator might opt to launch a full-scale assault on the Home. The Family was well armed, and the Home adequately fortified, but there was no way the Family could fend off a determined attack by a vastly superior force.

From somewhere up ahead came the noisy sounds of someone crashing pell-mell through the forest.

Good.

It made his task easier.

Rikki focused on the snapping and crackling sounds generated by the Watcher's passage. He judged the trooper to be about twenty yards in front of him, and slightly to his left. How far from the hillock would the soldiers have parked their jeeps? Not too distant, because they had to lug all that equipment. Yet not too close either, for fear the Family might hear the engines and come to investigate.

The Watcher abruptly altered direction and was now heading due west.

Rikki slowed, debating his next move. Was the soldier lost and uncertain of where they left the vehicles? Was he aware he was being chased and attempting to elude his pursuer? Or, even more likely, had the man fled south in his initial panic and was now compensating and correcting his escape path?

Whatever, the move placed the Watcher at a disadvantage.

Rikki accelerated, angling toward the southwest, running as rapidly as he could and as silently as possible. If he pushed himself, he might be able to outdistance the soldier and pounce on the Watcher unexpectedly from concealment.

The hillock was far behind them, at least half a mile, when the woods tapered into a large field.

Rikki stopped at the border of the field. What should he do? If he went into the open, the Watcher would spot him instantly. But if he stayed in the forest, the soldier would be . . .

The matter was abruptly rendered moot.

The Watcher burst from the tree line fifteen yards south of Rikki's position, his youthful face caked with sweat and his green uniform in disarray. Without missing a beat, he continued his breakneck pace, his brown eyes alighting on the far side of the field, a satisfied smile creasing his features.

Rikki followed the trooper's line of vision and promptly darted on his heels.

Four jeeps were parked on the other side of the field.

Rikki found himself at least twelve yards behind the soldier. He concentrated, pushing his muscles to the utmost, his legs flying.

The trooper either heard or sensed he was being followed, because he glanced over his left shoulder, his eyes widening at the sight of the black-garbed Warrior after him. His exertions intensified and he pulled slightly ahead.

Rikki-Tikki-Tavi was calculating probabilities. Fifty yards separated the Watcher from the jeeps. The soldier enjoyed a longer stride and his flight was fueled by the impetus of stark fear. It would be impossible for Rikki to overtake the trooper before he reached the vehicles. The Watcher might be able to start a jeep and drive away before Rikki reached him. Or the soldier might decide to try to get Rikki with the M-16. If the trooper reached the vehicle first, Rikki would have ten yards of open space, minimum, to cover before he could engage the Watcher. Plenty of time for a competent marksman to nail a moving target.

Rikki was compelled to try a long shot.

So to speak.

The Warrior slowed as he reached behind his back and unsnapped the flap on the leather pouch he carried attached to his black belt. His probing fingers closed on the object he required and he slipped the metal into his hand, cautiously avoiding lacerating his skin on the wicked points.

Convinced he was winning their race, the Watcher looked back again confidently.

Rikki was now fifteen yards behind the fleeing trooper with his mind centered on the soldier's head.

Nine yards separated the Watcher from the

nearest vehicle.

Rikki held his ace in the hole in his right hand, his katana in his left.

Seven yards.

The soldier was gripping his M-16 in both hands.

Five yards.

Rikki stopped and raised his right arm over his head, his elbow bent, his hand clasping one of the points.

Three yards.

Rikki-Tikki-Tavi tensed his shoulders and arms, judging the trajectory and determining the angle for a perfect throw.

Two.

One.

The elated Watcher reached the first jeep and whirled, the M-16 up and ready, his finger tightening on the trigger, a self-satisfied look on his face.

Rikki threw, all the power of his steely frame unleashed along his right arm, his technique honed during hours and hours of practice. The sunlight glittered on the four-pointed shuriken as it sped from Rikki's hand and flashed across the intervening space to penetrate the soldier's forehead.

The Watcher's eyes comically crossed as he endeavored to pinpoint the object buried in his forehead. His hold on the M-16 relaxed, his fingers going limp, and the weapon dropped to the ground. Feebly, the trooper tried to speak, to no avail. His mouth opened and closed several times, his body stiffened, and he toppled to the grass and lay there, quivering.

Rikki carefully approached the vehicles, surprised there wasn't a guard posted.

Birds twittered and a squirrel chattered, the normal forest sounds, indicating all was well.

The jeeps displayed evidence of advanced age; some of the tires were bald, a few of the seat covers were ripped and in need of repair, one of the vehicles had a cracked windshield, and all four were filthy with dirt. Still, they would make a welcome addition to the Family's sole means of mechanical transport, the SEAL.

Rikki searched the jeeps for their keys, but could find none. The Watchers undoubtedly carried the keys on their persons. It would be easy to check the bodies and find which ones had them.

The forest suddenly went deathly silent.

Rikki spun, his katana at the ready, scanning the vegetation. What was out there? A mutate? He waited and watched, his ears straining, alert for anything out of the ordinary.

Nothing.

The woods gradually filled with wildlife calls and cries again: birds in the trees, crickets in the grass, and somewhere to the south the croak of a frog.

Rikki decided to return to the hillock, but first he bent over the dead soldier and extracted his shuriken from the trooper's forehead. He wiped his crimson fingers and the gory shuriken on the green grass at his feet.

Not a bad day's work! Plato and Blade would be immensely pleased at the outcome of the conflict. From Lieutenant Putnam and the other captured Watcher, the Family might be able to learn considerable information concerning the Civilized Zone and Samuel II. Every tidbit of new data they could glean would be crucial. The more they could learn about their enemies, the better.

Rikki-Tikki-Tavi slowly traversed the field and

disappeared in the trees.

Mere moments later, two grotesque creatures stepped from the forest near the jeeps and glanced at one another.

"We should have finished him when we had the chance," the taller of the creatures stated. It stood over seven feet in height and weighed over four hundred pounds. Except for a deerskin loincloth, the being was naked. Its skin was light blue and had a scaly aspect. Blazing red eyes peered at the world from under a sloping forehead. Its wild shock of hair and prominent eyebrows were colored black. A pointed nose and a cruel slit of a mouth completed the picture.

"Oh, sure," the smaller of the duo retorted, its voice raspy and low. "And arouse their suspicions! Great idea, Ox!"

"Are you making fun of me, Ferret?" the giant demanded.

The second creature chuckled. This one only reached four feet in height and attained sixty pounds in weight. Brown hair, on the average about three inches long, covered its entire form. Like the first being, this one wore a loincloth. Its head was outsized for the body, its nose long and tapered, its beady eyes always shifting as it scanned the surrounding terrain. "I wouldn't think of making fun of you, Ox," Ferret replied.

"Well, you better not!" Ox threatened.

"Did you see the way he took Private Murray out?" Ferret said, changing the subject and nodding at the deceased soldier.

"These Warriors are very skilled," Ox admitted.

"Which is precisely the reason we didn't kill the Warrior with the sword," Ferret explained. "The Doktor gave us explicit orders. If we fail to follow them to the letter we're as good as dead. You know that!''

Ox visibly shuddered. "The Doktor! Ox forgot! We must do exactly what the Doktor says."

Ferret reached up and touched the metal collar around his neck. A small indicator light was placed in the center of the collar. "We have no other option," Ferret stated.

"We must be good!" Ox reiterated. "We must not make the Doktor mad!"

"We won't," Ferret promised. "We'll surreptitiously enter their Home tonight and kill him as ordered. We'll be in and out before they know what hit them!"

"Can I terminate?" Ox beseeched his companion. "You know how I love to snap their puny necks!"

"Be my guest," Ferret said.

Ox walked over to the fallen Watcher, grasped the man's left arm in his brawny right hand, and effortlessly tore the arm from its shoulder.

"What are you doing?" Ferret demanded.

Ox held the arm under his nose, sniffing at the torn flesh and the dripping blood. "Ox needs a snack." He extended the arm toward Ferret, smiling. "How about you? Would you like a bite?"

"I'm not hungry," Ferret replied.

"Suit yourself," the giant shrugged. "But there's nothing like fresh munchies." Ox stripped the sleeve from the arm and hungrily tore a chunk of flesh off, exposing a row of wickedly pointed teeth. He greedily gulped the mouthful, grinning broadly.

"UmmmMmmm, good!"

# 10

There were ninety of them in all, camped on the plain to the southwest of the Dead Zone. Most of them were sound asleep at this late hour. A dozen were on guard duty, patrolling the perimeter. Others tended the many fires intended to discourage any aggressive animals, or worse, in the area. A few were gazing up at the star-filled sky in silent contemplation. And two of the ninety were standing by themselves in the middle of the encampment, engaged in antagonistic conversation.

"I still say we should have headed back for Redfield," one of them was saying. "We're wasting our time staying here."

"You're not thinking of countermanding my order, are you?" asked the second man in a flat, vaguely menacing way.

"You know better, Rory," replied the first man.

"Do I, Boone?" Rory rejoined. "Do I really?"

Boone sighed and stared at the heavens, his mind uneasy, his hands resting on the 44 Magnum Hombre single-action revolvers in matching holsters on both hips. He was a tall man, over six feet, with broad shoulders and a narrow waist, attired in the typical frontier garb of the post-war plains: buckskins. His shoulder-length brown hair was stirred by the night wind.

Rory was staring at Boone's hands and the Magnums. He was shorter than Boone, a squat, muscular, powerhouse of a man with a blond crew cut and green eyes. His brown pants and shirt, tailor made by his wife, Adrian, could scarcely conceal his impressive bulk. He too wore twin guns, but in his case they were Star BM automatic pistols. "You two were good friends once, weren't you?" he asked Boone.

Boone's brown eyes narrowed as he faced Rory.

"I know it for a fact," Rory continued. "Admit it."

"What if we were?" Boone countered testily.

"No need to get all bent out of shape," Rory said quickly. "I only mention it to show I can understand how you feel. I'd feel the same way if it was one of my friends."

Boone turned his back on Rory and resumed gazing at the sky. "Yeah. Kilrane and I were real close before the split. So what?"

Rory's hands drifted toward his automatics. For several seconds he wavered, debating whether to shoot Boone in the back and fabricate a pretext later. He no longer trusted his second in command, sensing Boone was unhappy with the status quo. Rory knew many of his men were tired of the rift and wanted the two sides to be together again. Well, that would never happen! Not as long as Rolf was alive! There was only room for one top dog, and Rory was determined the head man of the Cavalry would be him!

Boone still had his back to him.

Rory's fingers clenched and unclenched mere inches from his pistols. Boone posed a threat to his leadership. Of all the men in the Cavalry, Boone was the most universally respected. Rory was undoubtedly the most feared, but he recognized respect could conquer fear in the long run. If enough of his men wanted to unite the feuding factions, they might turn to Boone for guidance and direction.

Rory couldn't allow that.

Should he do it now? No. Two reasons dissuaded him. Boone had many friends, and some of them might seek revenge if Boone were gunned down in the back. The second reason was even more persuasive; Boone was fast with those revolvers, real fast, with a reputation almost as widespread as Kilrane's. At this range, Boone might be able to get off a few shots before Rory finished him.

Rory couldn't take the chance.

"Are you sure it was him?" Boone suddenly inquired.

"No doubt about it," Rory confirmed. "I saw him through my binoculars."

"Do you think the dust storm got them?" Boone questioned, glancing toward the Dead Zone.

"Who knows?" Rory replied. "Just thank your lucky stars it missed us! If all goes well, those things in the Dead Zone will take care of Kilrane and company."

"So if you expect those monsters in the Dead Zone to do your dirty work for you," Boone commented, facing Rory, "why are we sitting here? Why aren't we heading for home?"

"Because I need to be sure!" Rory declared. "If any of the Legion patrol survive the Dead Zone, odds are they'll come this way. We'll canvass this section for a few more days, then head for Redfield if nothing develops." Rory paused, musing. "We were lucky one of our boys spotted them shortly after they entered our territory and reported the word to us. It isn't very often we catch a Legion patrol in the act.''

''We were lucky,'' Boone conceded halfheartedly.

"Can you imagine it?'' Rory went on. ''The look on Rolf's face when he learns I've killed his pet executioner, Kilrane? My dear brother might have a heart attack!'' Rory threw back his head and laughed.

Boone stared at the Cavalry leader, barely able to suppress his contempt. He mentally castigated himself for not going with Rolf and Kilrane a decade ago. Why hadn't he? Because he'd never understood the cause of the breakup, and at the time it transpired he wasn't aware of Rory's true nature. But now he was. Now he recognized the man for the devious, spiteful, evil person he really was. What should he do about it? Gun Rory down? Challenge him to a gunfight? Would the rest of the Cavalry understand? Not many knew Rory as he did.

What to do? What to do?

"Maybe my darling brother will attempt to avenge Kilrane.'' Rory was gloating. ''Maybe he'll enter our territory to find me for Kilrane's death. Wouldn't that be great! I'd have that bastard right where I want him!''

Boone thoughtfully bit his lower lip.

"And after the Cavalry and the Legion are reunited, watch out!'' Rory raved, his brow covered with sweat, his face flushed, and his eyes wide as he watched a nearby fire. ''I have plans! Big plans! You'll see!''

Yes, sir.

Something needed to be done about Rory, and the sooner, the better.

Boone walked away from Rory and melted into

the night, contemplating the best answer to the
question of the hour. Of the decade.

But what to do?

# 11

"Geronimo? Can you hear me?"

Geronimo's mind floated in limbo, suspended between consciousness and oblivion, awash in a sea of pain.

"Geronimo? You've got to hear me!"

Someone was shaking him and he wished they'd stop. His poor head was pounding like crazy, and his stomach was on the verge of disgorging its contents.

"His eyelids moved!" the someone said. "He's alive!"

"Told you," another party chimed in.

"Geronimo! Wake up!"

Geronimo opened his eyes, and for a moment he suffered the delusion they were still closed. Where was the sun? The moon? Any light, for that matter. The world was pitch black.

"Wake up!" a woman goaded him.

Geronimo managed to move his lips, the effort causing considerable torment, his mouth responding sluggishly and his lips apparently swollen. "Where am I?"

"You're awake!" the woman squealed in delight, hugging him.

Geronimo realized he was lying on a cool granular surface. His eyes were adjusting to the subdued lighting and he was able to distinguish Cynthia kneeling beside him, his head cradled in her lap. "What happened?" he croaked. His head was pounding and he focused his thoughts with supreme difficulty.

"You fell into one of the pits," a man remarked pleasantly.

Geronimo turned his face to the right and spotted a dark form crouched six feet away. "Kilrane? Is that you?" he asked.

"None other," Kilrane replied.

"I think it's coming back to me," Geronimo stated, sitting up. "The dust storm. All those holes. And I fell into one." He swiveled and gripped Cynthia's slim shoulders. "Are you hurt?"

"I'm fine," Cynthia said. "But you took a nasty spill, and then one of the creatures struck you on the head."

"Creatures? What creatures?" Geronimo felt Cynthia tremble.

"I don't know what it was," Cynthia answered in a low voice. "It was all set to eat you! I didn't get a real good look at it."

"Eat me?" Geronimo interrupted.

". . . and Kilrane came over the edge of the hole," Cynthia resumed, "blasting away with his revolver. The thing made this terrible noise . . . you should have heard it!" She stopped, horrified by the memory.

"What happened then?" Geronimo queried her.

"The thing ran off, still screaming, making this awful racket. Kilrane found this spot before the light faded for good. We've been trapped in here for hours and hours," Cynthia finished.

"Where are we?" Geronimo questioned, glancing around. He could dimly perceive walls of some sort three feet away on either side. Kilrane was about six feet away, near a lighter-shaded space.

"We're in a crevice not far from the opening you dropped into," Kilrane answered. "We'd be dead right now if we hadn't stumbled onto this."

"Dead? Why?"

"You'll understand when you see them," Kilrane promised.

"Them?"

"You'll see," was Kilrane's response.

"Why don't we leave now?" Geronimo asked.

"Because it's the middle of the night and we can't see more than a few feet," Kilrane explained. "They, evidently, can see real well in the dark. A horde of them went past us while you were out. Thank goodness none of them spotted us in here. It wouldn't take them long to dig their way in."

Geronimo discovered he could stand, but not fully erect. His head brushed the roof of the crevice, causing some dirt to trickle over his hair and face. He moved to Kilrane's side.

"Wait for me!" Cynthia hastily joined them.

"I take it I owe you my life," Geronimo said to Kilrane. "Thanks."

"I didn't have much choice," Kilrane quipped. "If I hadn't of shot the damn thing, it would have attacked me next."

"Did you fall into the pit the same as me?" Geronimo casually inquired.

"Something like that."

"How far is this crevice from the opening?" Geronimo asked, reaching out to find the crevice exit.

"Not more than twenty yards," Kilrane revealed. "We got in here just as a bunch of them came running by, heading for the opening, apparently looking for us."

Geronimo inched forward, groping carefully. He could see the jagged rift separating the crevice from a larger tunnel.

"I wouldn't do that, if I were you," Kilrane advised.

"Why?"

"Because they might come by while you're out there, and they would tear you to pieces before you could do a thing."

Geronimo stopped four feet from the rift. "Should we be talking like this?" he questioned, concerned their voices might attract the . . . things.

"Just keep it low," Kilrane warned. "I don't think any of them are out there now. Most left at nightfall. Besides, you'll hear them when they come our way."

"Kilrane saved your rifle," Cynthia commented. "Not that it will do us much good." She picked up an object from the ground. "Here."

Geronimo took the proffered Marlin and hefted the gun in his right hand, making a fast check with his left; both the Arminius and his tomahawk were still in place. Thank the Spirit! He was still upset over losing one of his prized tomahawks in the Twin Cities a few months before.

"Either of you have any idea how we'll get out of here?" Cynthia asked them.

"I'm working on one," Kilrane answered.

"Did you bring your rifle?" Geronimo inquired of Kilrane.

"Didn't have time," Kilrane said. "I did think to bring along my lariat."

"What good is a stupid rope going to do?" Cynthia remarked derisively.

"You never know," was all Kilrane would say.

Geronimo leaned against the wall of the crevice,

resting his pounding temples. "I don't think I can wait until morning," he told the others. "Kilrane, did you see what it was that attacked me?"

"An ant," Kilrane stated.

"Come again?"

"A giant ant," Kilrane reiterated. "You had to see it to believe it!"

"I believe it," Geronimo affirmed. "I've seen some of the giants before. A few months ago some friends and I had a disagreement with a huge spider."

"What happened?" Cynthia questioned him.

"What else?" Geronimo smiled. "It killed us."

"Maybe we should try and get some rest," Kilrane proposed. "There's nothing we can do until morning."

"I couldn't sleep," Cynthia declared. "I'd be afraid to close my eyes."

"And I've already had my beauty sleep," Geronimo said. "But if you need a nap, Kilrane, you go ahead. I'll keep watch."

"I don't reckon I could sleep much," Kilrane observed.

Geronimo started laughing.

"What's so funny?" Cynthia inquired, puzzled.

"Kilrane . . ." Geronimo began, then vented another fit of mirth.

"What did I do?" Kilrane queried.

"You used the word 'reckon,'" Geronimo responded. "It reminded me of my best friend, an idiot who likes to use this ridiculous Wild West talk all the time. He uses the word 'reckon' a lot." Geronimo paused and sighed. "I miss the big dummy."

"Is this friend of yours the one you call Hickok?" Kilrane guessed.

"How'd you know?"

Kilrane chuckled. "It wasn't hard to figure. When you talk about this Hickok your tone reflects your feelings. It must be nice to have a close friend like that."

"Don't you have one?" Geronimo asked.

"Not really . . ." Kilrane said slowly.

"What about Rolf? Or Hamlin?" Geronimo could feel a damp sensation on the back of his head. Was he still bleeding?

"Rolf's the legitimate Cavalry leader and I respect him a lot," Kilrane revealed. "Hamlin's okay and a good buddy, but he looks up to me all of the time instead of treating me as an equal."

"You must have one close friend," Geronimo stated.

"There is one fella," Kilrane acknowledged. "His name is Boone."

"And where is he?"

"Boone stayed with Rory after the split," Kilrane said, and Geronimo and Cynthia could plainly detect the sadness in his voice.

"Maybe you could . . ." Geronimo began, then stopped, his ears detecting a new sound, faint, in the distance, but growing louder with each passing second.

The noise resembled an outlandish twittering.

"It's them!" Cynthia cried.

"Hurry!" Kilrane directed, his shadowy form moving toward the rear of the crevice. "Get as far from their tunnel as you can or they might detect you."

Geronimo complied, following the others until they reached the end of the crevice, fifteen feet from where the cleft fronted the tunnel.

The bizarre twittering grew louder, rising in

volume, reaching a piercing crescendo.

Cynthia placed her lips against Geronimo's left ear. "Some of the ants are returning," she whispered.

If he squinted, Geronimo could vaguely detect the passing of huge black forms scurrying past the crevice. How many ants were there? he wondered. More importantly, how in the world were they going to get past the ants and reach the surface? And even if they did manage to reach topside again, what chance did they have on foot in the Dead Zone?

Geronimo closed his eyes and started praying to the Great Spirit.

Cynthia pressed her mouth to his ear again. "They're really red," she explained for no apparent reason, interrupting his prayer. "They just look black in the dark." She straightened.

Geronimo resumed his praying.

"You know," Cynthia said, leaning close to him, "it's too bad your friend Hickok isn't here. We could use all the help we can get."

"I know," Geronimo agreed, and continued his worship.

Cynthia's lips were glued to his ear once more. "What are you doing?"

Geronimo placed his mouth near her right ear. "Praying to the Great Spirit."

"You're religious?" she inquired, sounding astonished at the prospect.

"Of course," Geronimo whispered back. "Aren't you?"

"I never really gave it much thought," she admitted. "Oh, I believe there's a God up there somewhere, but I don't attend services regularly."

"Services?"

"Yeah. We have a few spiritual people called

ministers. They hold services once a week and talk about God and all that stuff. I always found it pretty boring.'' She hesitated. "I never expected you to be the religious type."

"Why's that?" Geronimo wanted to learn.

"Oh, I don't know. I guess because you're such a good fighter and our ministers are always telling us fighting is wrong.''

"Have you ever read the Bible?" Geronimo questioned her.

"Nope," she confessed.

"Too bad. Maybe then you'd understand. The Old Testament tells us about a lot of great fighters, superb warriors, who were also deeply religious men. Samson, David, and Joshua, to name just three of the many. My Family has a number of Warriors, and all of them, to varying degrees, are religious.''

"You'll have to tell me more sometime," Cynthia suggested.

"As soon as we get out of this mess," Geronimo pledged, his thoughts straying. Her warm breath on his ear, combined with the proximity of her voluptuous body and the intoxicating fragrance of her woman scent, had agitated his equilibrium. How was he supposed to concentrate on the Great Spirit with her near-naked form so close to him?

Discipline, he told himself.

I need more discipline!

Cynthia snuggled nearer. Kilrane was three feet off, reclining against the other wall.

"I don't know if we're going to make it out," she said in a barely audible voice. "So I want to tell you this now. I like you, Geronimo. I like you a lot. I want to get to know you better. There's something about you. . . ." She paused. "How do you feel about me?"

Geronimo twisted his head to respond and suddenly found his lips mere inches from hers, her breath on his face.

The ants were still creating a racket in the tunnel.

Geronimo experienced an overpowering impulse to kiss Cynthia and he deliberately suppressed it. What kind of idiot would take the time to kiss a lovely woman while trapped in the subterranean lair of monstrous ants? With Kilrane only three feet away!

Kilrane!

Geronimo abruptly recalled that Kilrane entertained designs on Cynthia. He glanced at the captain, unable to read his expression in the gloom.

Kilrane, evidently, was able to read minds. "Don't pay any attention to me," he said to Geronimo. "I know when I'm licked, and I'm not the type to force my affections on a woman."

"Besides," Cynthia added, "he knows how I feel."

"He does?" Geronimo whispered.

"Sure. I told him while we were riding today."

"Told him what?" Geronimo asked.

"That I was interested in you," she replied.

"You just up and told him that?" Geronimo marveled.

"Of course. I knew he was attracted to me, and I didn't want to lead him on. I don't believe in beating around the bush," she stated, her lips next to his ear. Her moist tongue suddenly flicked across his lobe.

Geronimo could feel a stirring in his groin.

"What's the matter with you?" Cynthia demanded. "Can't you take a hint? Are you the bashful type or something?"

"I happen to believe there's a time and a place for

everything," Geronimo countered, "and this isn't the time or place."

"We may never have another opportunity," she reminded him.

"I'm not like my friend Hickok," he explained. "He does things on the spur of the moment. I can't. I like to think things out and I don't like surprises."

"Pretend you're Hickok," Cynthia suggested.

"What?"

"Better yet, I'll pretend I'm Hickok!"

Before Geronimo could react, she embraced him and planted her eager lips on his. He opened his mouth to speak and found her tongue entwined with his own.

Kilrane was chuckling.

Geronimo relaxed, allowing his body to respond to her passion, to the feel of her firm breasts pressed against his chest.

So much for discipline!

# 12

They entered the Home in the wee hours of the morning, well before the horizon would be tinged by the brilliance of the rising sun. Their method of entry was ingenious, a technique the Warriors hadn't considered and planned against.

Kurt Carpenter, the Founder, had provided for the Family's water supply and effectively utilized this water as a secondary means of defense. A stream entered the Home in the northwest corner, via an aqueduct, and was diverted along the base of the brick wall surrounding the entire thirty acres. The flowing water exited the Home through another aqueduct under the southeastern corner.

The pair knew the layout of the Home; their intelligence information was superb. They dove into the stream outside the wall and swam underwater through the northwestern aqueduct, emerging in the middle of the stream inside the Home completely undetected by the Warriors on guard duty. Cautiously, they clambered onto the bank and scanned the immediate vicinity for any signs of life.

The Family members were all fast asleep.

"Where do you think he is?" Ox questioned his diminutive companion.

"Beats me," Ferret answered. "We'll have to

search this entire place until we find him."

"Should we split up?"

"No. We'll stick together. My nose is better than yours and I might pick up his scent first," Ferret stated.

"Whatever you say," Ox acquiesced.

They carefully scoured the western sector of the Home, avoiding all open spaces, sticking to whatever cover was available. Fortunately, there were plenty of trees, bushes, and shrubs to facilitate their clandestine hunt. Their primary concern was the solitary Warrior stationed on the west wall, but he seldom glanced in their direction. He naturally focused his attention outside the Home, alert for potential invaders.

Over an hour elapsed.

"Where the hell is he?" Ox demanded when they stopped in a stand of trees not far from the cabins in the center of the Home.

"Beats me," Ferret replied. "I've been unable to catch his scent."

"Do you think he's left?" Ox queried.

"Doubt it," Ferret responded. "Where would he go? Back to the Civilized Zone? No way. He knows the Doktor would fry him to a crisp. The only friends he has are the people here, this Family. He'll stay here for as long as he can."

"Maybe he was never here to begin with," Ox speculated. "Maybe the Doktor was wrong."

Ferret, startled by Ox's stupidity, glanced at the collar around the giant's neck, waiting for the blue indicator light to flash and Ox to writhe on the grass in acute agony.

Nothing transpired.

Ox, belatedly, realized his blunder, a shocked expression crossing his face. "I . . . I . . . I didn't mean . . ." he stammered.

"The Doktor knows you didn't," Ferret said. "That's probably the only reason you're alive right now."

Ox's brow broke out in sweat.

"They way I see it," Ferret was reasoning aloud, "he's here, all right, but he doesn't sleep with the others. He's found someplace private, somewhere he can be alone. He won't come out until morning."

"So what do we do?" Ox queried.

Ferret stared toward the eastern half of the Home. "That part is maintained in its natural state. Lots of woods, plenty of hiding places. I say we hide out there and keep our eyes peeled. Sooner or later he'll show his ugly face, and then we do as the Doktor wants and finish the traitor off."

Ox was studying the forested eastern section. "Sounds okay to me."

"Let's go." Ferret moved nearer the cabins, listening for any indication of an early riser. If his memory served, these cabins were used by the Family's married couples as their individual homes. Once past the cabins, the pair would be safely beyond any inhabited structures.

The rear door on a nearby cabin opened.

Ferret dropped to the ground, Ox at his side.

A young girl with long black hair came forth and closed the door. She grinned and ran westward.

"She'd make a tasty treat," Ox whispered, licking his lips.

Ferret shook his head and rose, watching until the girl was out of sight. Secretly, he wished the Doktor had paired him with someone else instead of Ox. The big lummox was constantly hungry. Ox thought with his stomach instead of his brain, a troublesome weakness at best, a fatal failing at worst.

Using whatever available cover presented itself, the deadly duo successfully passed the cabins and reached a dense stretch of forest beyond.

"We'll wait here," Ferret announced when they were safely hidden from view.

"I just hope this doesn't take too long," Ox grumbled.

"Why?" Ferret inquired, already knowing the answer.

"Because," Ox began, I'm . . ."

"Who's in there?" demanded a new voice, a man, from perhaps fifteen yards off, to the north.

Son of a bitch! Ferret hastily scrambled through the underbrush until he spotted the speaker, an elderly Tiller dressed in faded, patched overalls and an old blue baseball cap. Ferret's sensitive nose detected the man's stale body aroma. His acute hearing permitted him to detect the Tiller's raspy breathing. Hidden in a thicket only six feet from the aged farmer, Ferret patiently waited, knowing the Tiller would depart soon if he didn't hear any more voices or anything unusual happened.

But something did.

Ferret, amazed, saw Ox rise from cover behind the Family member. The Tiller sensed danger and started to turn, his face contorting in horror when Ox's brawny hands clamped onto his neck and squeezed. Ferret could see the man's discolored expression as he valiantly struggled for air, kicking and thrashing to no avail. Ox grinned, his bony blue fingers slowly crushing his victim's throat, gouging into the soft flesh and splitting it apart. The Tiller gasped and gurgled as Ox lifted him bodily from the ground and, with a savage wrench, tore the head from the body. The headless form toppled to the grass, blood gushing from the severed neck vessels.

Ox grinned, raised the head to his lips, and hungrily slurped at the stump below the chin.

Enraged, Ferret rose from concealment and advanced on Ox. "You damn idiot! What the hell did you think you were doing?"

Ox, flabbergasted at the reproach, ceased his meal and lowered the grisly head. "He heard us. We couldn't let him tell the others."

"You big jerk!" Ferret fumed, his tiny ears twitching. "He just heard voices. For all he knew, it was some kids playing in the trees. If you'd left him alone, moron, he would have gone about his business none the wiser!"

Ox stared at the body, embarrassed. "Gee, Forest, I didn't think. . . ."

"You never think!" Ferret exploded, forgetting the necessity for silence. "You don't have a brain to think with! A turnip has more intelligence than you do, fool!"

"Well," Ox said, attempting to appease his small friend, "at least we have some food. . . ."

Ferret, beside himself, kicked Ox on the right shin. "Food! That's all you ever think of!"

Ox, although he scarcely felt the blow, winced. "I'm sorry, Ferret, Please don't be mad at Ox!"

Ferret glanced around, insuring they were still alone. "We must hide the body. We'll drag it into the woods and bury it. You'd best hope the Family doesn't miss him and send Warriors looking for this Tiller before we locate the one we're here to find!"

"Please don't be mad at Ox!" the blue colossus repeated.

Ferret looked up at the pitiful, pleading countenance on Ox. "How can I stay mad at someone who can't tell his right foot from his left?"

Ox, perplexed, gazed down. "What do my feet

have to do with it?"

Ferret, exasperated, sighed and shook his head. The Doktor's handiwork sometimes left a lot to be desired.

"Are you still mad?" Ox anxiously inquired.

"No," Ferret replied, lying. "I'm not still mad! But you better give me your word you won't make another move unless you consult with me first. Agreed?"

Ox eagerly nodded. "Ox won't kill another person unless he asks you first!"

"Good!" Ferret pointed at the prone form sprawled in a spreading pool of its own blood. "You snuffed him, you carry him! Come on!" He beckoned for Ox to follow and headed for the thickest cover he could find.

Ox shuffled behind him, the Tiller carelessly draped over his left shoulder, a red stain oozing down his broad back.

Ferret reached an ideal spot and nodded at the earth underfoot. "Okay. Here's a good place. Start digging."

"Whatever you want," Ox said. "Hold this for me." He tossed the Tiller's head to Ferret.

Ferret reflexively caught Ox's trophy, appalled and fascinated by the gruesome visage. The farmer's eyes were frozen wide open, the blue orbs seemingly gaping at Ferret in astonishment; his lips were almost purple and puffy; and his tongue protruded from the right corner of his mouth. Ferret suppressed an impulse to shudder. He could kill and maim with the best of them, but he didn't revel in the gore and the slaughter as some of his fellows enthusiastically did; he simply wasn't as bloodthirsty. Many of the G.R.D.'s displayed a singular purpose, namely to murder at the Doktor's bidding.

They functioned as the Doktor's personal assassin corps, obedient to his every whim. Others, like Ferret, although they dared not publicly question the Doktor's commands for fear of the lethal consequences, privately hated the Doktor and longed for an escape from his ruthless dictates.

"Is this deep enough?" Ox asked, interrupting Ferret's reflection.

Ferret blinked, collecting his thoughts. Ox had scooped a six-foot trench in the soft dirt, about two feet deep. "It's fine," Ferret stated. "Drop the body in and cover it up."

"Can I keep the head?" Ox queried expectantly.

"Why?"

"I like brains. They're my favorites!"

"All right," Ferret agreed. "But I don't want to hear another peep from you about food until the job is done. Understand?"

Ox beamed and resumed his burial detail.

Ferret removed the baseball cap from the Tiller's head. "Here. You won't be eating this." He tossed the cap into the trench.

Ferret laid the head on the grass and walked to a nearby tree. He crouched and rested his back against the trunk. If only they could complete their mission and return to the Civilized Zone! He wasn't particularly happy with the assignment; he rather admired the one they were here to terminate. It wasn't often one of the G.R.D.'s managed to slip through the Doktor's fingers. Inwardly, Ferret wished he could do likewise.

Ox was busily filling in the grave.

Still, Ferret realized, there was no way he could dispute the Doktor's orders. Either he obeyed or he died. It was as simple as that. No matter what his personal feelings might be, the outcome was inevitable:

Gremlin must die!

# 13

The sun was rising above the eastern horizon in a cloudless sky, the birds chirping and singing as they greeted a new day, when Blade walked from B Block and lazily stretched. He wore green fatigue pants and his leather vest and was armed with his Bowies in their respective sheaths on both hips. He decided he would visit C Block and check on the two prisoners. They were being held in the Family infirmary under Warrior guard. One of the captured soldiers, the officer, had sustained a broken nose. The other trooper, according to the Healers, suffered from a mild concussion. Blade was anxious to interrogate the pair, but Plato wouldn't allow any questioning until the soldiers were somewhat recovered from their ordeal.

Blade turned left, toward C Block, casually scanning the wide cleared space between the concrete bunkers. His gray eyes passed over the SEAL, then immediately returned to the vehicle, aware that something was amiss.

The SEAL was the Founder's pride and joy. Kurt Carpenter had spent millions of dollars on its development and construction, wisely foreseeing that his beloved Family would require an exceptionally durable and versatile vehicle to travel across the dramatically altered post-war terrain. SEAL was an acronym for Solar Energized Amphibious or Land Recreational Vehicle. The green van-like transport was powered by the sun, a pair of solar panels attached to the roof collecting the sunlight and a bank of six revolutionary batteries mounted under the vehicle serving to store the converted energy. The SEAL's body was an impervious plastic, its four enormous tires composed of a unique, indestructible synthetic. To the Family, the SEAL was a virtual godsend, enabling those who used it to travel vast distances protected from the numerous lethal denizens proliferating unchecked across the entire land.

Ordinarily, the SEAL was kept locked to deter a theft or worse. Two months ago a saboteur had attempted to demolish the transport with explosives, and Blade readily recalled his timely intervention and fight with the mysterious intruder. Since that disturbing incident, the Warriors were instructed to scrutinize the vehicle at every opportunity, and Plato personally verified the SEAL was secure each night before retiring. The night before, Blade had observed his mentor standing beside the transport and tugging on the driver's door handle, guaranteeing the door was fastened shut.

Now that same door hung wide open.

Was Plato up this early and working on the vehicle?

Unlikely.

Blade ran toward the SEAL, his big hands on his Bowies. Who else would be in the transport this time of the day? No one he could think of. Only Alpha Triad knew how to drive the SEAL, and Hickok was still asleep. With Geronimo absent, there wasn't anyone else authorized to be inside the vehicle.

So who was it?

Ten feet from the open door Blade reduced his speed and crept forward, prepared to draw his Bowies at the slightest hint of danger.

If it was another damn saboteur, Blade vowed, he'd gut the bastard on general principles.

Blade was five feet away when he heard the humming and relaxed, releasing his knives. What in the world was *she* doing in there?

The hummer was a young girl of twelve dressed in homemade buckskins, buckskins made by her deceased mother. She was huddled under the dashboard, her beautiful black hair obscuring her face and falling to her waist. Her name was Star and she was, so far as anyone knew, the sole survivor of the Flathead Indians of Montana. The rest of her tribe had vanished after a confrontation with the soldiers from the Cheyenne Citadel. Plato and his wife Nadine had adopted the girl and accepted her as their own and she had adapted marvelously to Family life.

Blade leaned against the SEAL, grinning. He saw Plato's keys lying on the dash and realized how Star had gotten inside.

The interior of the transport was spacious. Two bucket seats were positioned in the front with a console between them. Behind the bucket seats was a single seat running the width of the vehicle. A large storage area completed the interior design.

Silently, Blade eased toward Star until his head and shoulders were inside the SEAL.

"*Boo!*"

His shout terrified the poor girl. She involuntarily jumped, cracking the top of her head on the dashboard. Her dark eyes swung around and caught sight of Blade.

"Owwww! My head!" Star frowned, rubbing her bruise, and glared at the strapping Warrior.

Blade began laughing.

"What'd you do that for?" she demanded, annoyed. "I could have been hurt!"

"It would serve you right," Blade countered, chuckling.

"What do you mean?" Star asked.

"It would serve you right for swiping Plato's keys and sneaking into the SEAL without permission," Blade explained to her.

Star's mouth fell open. "How did you know?"

"It didn't take a genius to figure it out," Blade retorted. "The question is why."

"Why am I here?"

"You got it," he confirmed.

Star jerked her left thumb toward the dashboard. "I'm looking for clues."

"Clues?"

"Clues," she nodded. "Something that might tell us about the toggle switches."

The toggle switches! Blade's brow knit as he stared at the four switches in the center of the dash. Each was labeled with a single letter below it: M, S, F, and R. Mystery surrounded the toggle switches because their function was unknown.

Kurt Carpenter had buried the SEAL in a specially fabricated underground chamber with explicit orders that the transport was to remain untouched until a critical situation developed and the Family Leader decided the vehicle was needed. After a century, Plato had been the Leader who had finally opted to uncover the chamber and retrieve the SEAL. Inside the chamber the Family had also found detailed instructions, an Operations Manual, explaining every aspect of the vehicle with one glaring exception: the toggle switches. Plato had given specific directions to Alpha Triad, advising them to avoid even touching the switches until their purpose was discovered.

Only one person had violated Plato's edict.

Star.

While in Montana, during a battle with Government troops, she had inadvertently bumped one of the switches, the one marked with an R. Although the soldiers had seen what transpired next, unfortunately none of them had survived to tell anyone else. Blade and Star had been inside the vehicle at the time, and they vividly remembered the SEAL lurching, followed by a tremendous explosion. The Citadel troops had been destroyed in the blast.

But why?

What had caused it?

"Why are you so interested in the toggle switches?" Blade asked her.

"Curiosity," Star responded.

"What makes you think you'll find something in here?"

Star straightened and reclined against the console. "It's the logical place to look."

"How do you figure?" Blade inquired.

"Your Founder planned everything so well," Star said. "He laid out the Home and stocked all the provisions. He had this vehicle built for your future use. Carpenter left nothing to chance. There must be instructions about these toggle switches somewhere."

Blade resisted the temptation to dispute Star's logic. For a twelve year old, she was extremely bright, even by Family standards. The girl was a voracious reader; since arriving in the Home she had spent every spare minute in the Family library.

"Don't you agree?" she asked him.

"What you say makes sense," Blade concurred, "but there may be an explanation for the missing directions."

"What?"

"As you probably know," Blade began, "Carpenter was afraid someone might be tempted to steal the SEAL if he left it above ground. That's part of the reason he hid it in the underground chamber. The Family Leaders have passed on the news of its existence by word of mouth from one Leader to another. Isn't it possible one of the Leaders neglected or was unable to pass on the information about the toggle switches?"

"Hmmmmm." Star tapped on the console, eyeing the switches, her fertile mind weighing the probabilities.

Blade had to admire the young firebrand. He wondered which vocation she would choose for her career. Her natural vitality tended to exclude any of the less exciting options like Weaver or Librarian. He could easily envision her as a Warrior, or possibly she would devote her life to one of the sciences.

"I don't think so," she finally stated.

"To tell you the truth," he admitted, "I don't think so either. Carpenter obviously spent a considerable amount of money converting the SEAL, modifying it, and incorporating armament into the body. If he went to all that trouble to install the equipment, he'd want to be certain the Family knew it was there."

"And there's no mention of it in the Operations Manuel?" Star probed.

Blade spotted the Manual on the back seat. He

picked it up and tossed it to Star. "See for yourself. I've read the whole book three times and there's no mention of the toggle switches."

Star opened the Manual to the first page, the Table of Contents. Twenty-five chapters were listed, covering the solar panels, the engine, the batteries, the transmission, and everything else in the transport down to the windshield wipers. "I don't understand very much of this," Star acknowledged.

"Neither did we until Plato explained it," Blade informed her.

"Why'd you do this?" she asked, running her right index finger across the page.

"Do what?"

"Mark the page up this way." She glanced up, puzzled.

Blade, equally perplexed, extended his left hand. "What are you talking about?"

"Here," she said, offering the Manual. "See for yourself."

Blade took the Manual and examined the page. "What? It's just a list of the contents." He couldn't see anything out of the ordinary.

"Look real close," Star prompted him.

"I'm looking," Blade said, confused.

"Do you see it?"

"See what?" Blade snapped impatiently.

"Whoever heard of dotting an H?" Star inquired, mystified.

Dotting an H? What did she . . .

He suddenly saw what she meant.

"Damn!" he inadvertently exclaimed. Right in front of their faces the whole time! The first H on the page had a tiny black dot above it, so small it would be overlooked as a speck on the paper. In the next line an E was below one of the dots. Further along two different L's were dotted, as was an O in the following line. The dots were even smaller than the ones used to dot the I's and wouldn't attract attention unless you were looking for something unusual. Let's see. He mentally ticked off the first five dotted letters. H-E-L-L-O.

"Hello," he said aloud.

"Hello to you." Star grinned. "Do you think we're on to something?"

"I think if you were ten years older Jenny would have some serious competition," he told her.

Star giggled. "Don't tell Jenny. She might get jealous!"

Blade closed the Manuel and gave the book to her. "Take this to Plato right this instant."

Star started to clamber over the console toward him. "What if he's still asleep? He isn't feeling too good lately, what with having the senility and all."

Blade assisted her in exiting the transport. "Wake him up. Insist. Tell him it's important and show him the Operations Manual. He has plenty of paper and pencils in his cabin. He'll be able to decipher the message in no time."

Star stood next to him, staring at the book. "You think it will tell us about the toggle switches?"

"I'd bet on it," Blade nodded.

"But why did the Founder leave a secret note? Why do it this way?" she queried.

"My guess would be he wanted it kept a secret," Blade reasoned. "Maybe one of the early Leaders knew about it but passed on before revealing what he knew. Who can say?" He spun her around and patted her on the back. "Get going!"

Star began running.

"Wait!" Blade abruptly called.

She stopped and faced him. "What's wrong?"

Blade picked up the keys from the dash and locked the door. "We wouldn't want anyone to sneak into the SEAL, would we?" He flipped the keys to her and watched as she raced toward the cabins.

"Much excitement, yes?" shouted someone off to his left.

Blade twisted, smiling. Gremlin was standing at the entrance to the underground chamber used to store the SEAL. He walked in Gremlin's direction as the creature approached him.

"Good morning, no?" Gremlin greeted him. "Catching worms, yes?"

"Catching worms?" Blade repeated, then grinned. "You must be hanging around Hickok too much. Your jokes are getting as corny as his."

Gremlin chuckled. "Bad news, yes? It means Gremlin's brain functioning like Hickok's, no? How awful!"

The mention of a brain reminded Blade of a conversation he had had with Gremlin in Montana, one they had never satisfactorily resolved. "Gremlin, if you don't mind, I'd like to talk."

"About Hickok's brain?" Gremlin retorted. "Small subject, yes?"

"No, not about Hickok's brain," Blade said. "About you."

Gremlin's levity vanished. "We must, yes?" he asked, frowning.

"We must."

"Why?"

Blade placed his right hand on Gremlin's left shoulder. "You must see my position. I know you don't like to talk about your past, but it can't be helped or delayed any longer. I'm head of the Warriors, as you know, and I'm responsible for the

Family's security. I think you have information
critical to the welfare of the Family. I've postponed
questioning you because I was reluctant to disturb
you, but we're going to talk now. There's no one else
up yet so we can enjoy a heart-to-heart without
interruption. Is it okay?''

Gremlin sighed. "If we must, we must, yes?" His
expression saddened. "Does hurt, though."

"Then we'll begin with a painless question,"
Blade said. "Like what were you doing in the underground chamber?"

"Sleep there, no?" Gremlin responded.

"You sleep down there?" Blade's surprise showed.
"Why? You could use a bunk in B Block."

Gremlin shook his head. "Gremlin know some of
Family afraid of him, yes? Not want to upset their
sleep, no? So sleep by self."

Blade knew better than to argue. While most
members of the Family, especially the children, were
fond of Gremlin, there were a few who were uneasy
in his presence. Blade decided to change the subject.
"There's something else I've been meaning to ask
you. I shot you in Montana, remember?"

"Gremlin not forget little things like that, yes?"
he sarcastically quipped.

"You healed so quickly," Blade stated. "I know I
missed a vital organ, but your recovery was still
remarkable. And the wound on your neck where the
collar used to be also healed incredibly fast. How?"

Gremlin tapped his chest. "Accelerated repair,
yes?"

They absently began strolling as they talked,
heading on an easterly course.

"I don't understand," Blade confessed. "You'll
need to tell me everything."

"Everything?" Gremlin repeated. "Not serious,

no?''

"Completely serious," Blade assured him. "Listen. What do I know about you? Very little. I know you're from the Cheyenne Citadel, and you were in a unit called the Genetic Research Division, or G.R.D., as it's known. This G.R.D. is operated by the man they call the Doktor. You also told me you talk the way you do because part of your brain was removed by this Doktor. And you said you were once a man. Am I right? Did I get all the facts straight?''

Gremlin, downcast, nodded.

"I must know more," Blade urged him. "I believe the Family is in deadly danger from this Doktor and Samuel II. The more I can learn about them, the better." He paused, touched by regret, sorry he was distressing Gremlin. "Let's take the items one at a time. What do you mean by saying you were once a man? A man like me?''

"Almost a man, yes?" Gremlin detailed. "Would have been, no?''

Blade shook his head. "I'm afraid I don't understand.''

"Doktor . . ." Gremlin said, his expression tortured. "Doktor change human embryo, yes? Make Gremlin. Understand, no?''

"You mean," Blade stated, "the Doktor took a human embryo, a perfectly normal embryo, and somehow made you?''

Gremlin slowly nodded.

Blade's mind whirled, staggered by the implications. Tampering with an innocent embryo! The very idea was obscene! "The Doktor is capable of such an atrocity? He has the skill and the means to accomplish such a feat?''

Again Gremlin nodded. "Doktor is living evil,

yes? But very smart man. Genius, no? Scientist. Expertise in chemistry, electronics, radiology, and genetics. Much more, yes?"

"And there are others like you?" Blade inquired.

"Fifteen hundred, yes? More or less, no?"

Fifteen hundred! That tallied with the figure Blade had learned in Montana. "Were all of them created from an embryo like you?"

"No," Gremlin answered. "Some, yes? Not all, no. Others made by Doktor in his laboratory."

"What else does the Doktor do?"

"Experiments all the time, yes? Uses living subjects, no?"

Blade stopped. "He experiments on living people?"

"Yes. Especially babies. Doktor likes babies, yes?"

Blade, stunned, continued moving toward the cabins. "And he gets away with it? Why don't the people in the Civilized Zone stop him?"

"How, yes?" Gremlin gestured hopelessly, uplifting his palms and shrugging. "Doktor's lab is fortified, yes? Has personal bodyguards from his creations, no? Army also protects. Nothing people can do."

"I was told by a soldier in Montana," Blade said, "that the Doktor and Samuel II are very close. Is that true?"

"True, yes? They work together, plan together, to reconquer United States for themselves. Gremlin hopes it never happens, no?"

"We'll do our utmost to insure it doesn't," Blade pledged. "You told me before that the Doktor maintains his headquarters in the Cheyenne Citadel. How long has he been there?"

"Since right after the war, yes?" Gremlin gazed

ahead. They were abreast of the row of cabins and still bearing east.

"Right after the..." Blade repeated, then laughed. "You're pulling my leg, or else you misunderstood. I asked..."

"Gremlin know what you asked," Gremlin snapped, cutting him off. "And Gremlin gave right answer, yes? Doktor has been in Cheyenne Citadel since right after war."

"The Third World War was a century ago," Blade reminded his companion.

"Gremlin know that," Gremlin stated indignantly.

"Are you trying to tell me the Doktor is almost one hundred years old?" Blade questioned skeptically.

Gremlin shot Blade an annoyed glance. "Gremlin not trying to tell you anything, yes? Gremlin is telling you Doktor is over one hundred years old, no?"

"Impossible," Blade flatly disputed him.

"You can look at Gremlin and say that, yes?" Gremlin retorted.

Blade absently stared at the trees ahead, reflecting. Was it really possible? Could this Doktor be that old? If so, how? Life expectancies were markedly reduced since the Big Blast, an inevitable consequence of the harsh struggle for existence, an invariable result of reducing the state of society to the survival of the fittest. Gremlin must be mistaken. It simply wasn't feasible. But what about the rest of the information? The experimentation and the Genetics Research Division, the babies and removing a portion of Gremlin's brain. How did it all tie together? What was the Doktor's purpose?

Gremlin was rubbing the fingers of his left hand

over a scar on his neck. "Want to thank you again, yes? For removing the collar from Gremlin and giving me freedom. Can't thank you enough, no?"

According to the story imparted to Blade in Montana, the collars were the Doktor's effective technique of compelling compliance, of forcing his genetic deviants to obey his commands. The collars evidently contained highly sophisticated electronic gadgetry linked to an orbiting satellite. They permitted the Doktor to monitor the G.R.D.'s and, if they violated his edicts or incurred his displeasure, to electrocute them on the spot.

"Can you tell me more?" Blade asked. "I . . ." He stopped, hearing footsteps behind them.

In unison, Gremlin and Blade glanced over their respective shoulders.

Sherry, attired in a newly repaired pair of faded jeans and a clean white blouse, ran up to them. "Morning," she smiled. "I saw you out here and wanted a word with you. I'm not interrupting anything, am I?"

"Not interrupting, yes?" Gremlin replied. "Gremlin will leave."

"No need for that," Sherry said, grabbing his right wrist. "What I have to say to Blade isn't private. You can stay."

"What's up?" Blade queried.

"Have you made your decisions about the new Warriors yet?" Sherry inquired.

"Not yet," Blade told her. "But soon. Why?"

They were idly sauntering due east.

"Because Hickok and I have reached an agreement. He may not be too crazy about the idea, but he won't oppose my becoming a Warrior if that's what I really want, and it is. But we have a problem."

"What kind of problem?" Blade asked.

Sherry was watching Blade's face closely, attempting to assess his reaction. "Candidates for Warrior status usually have sponsors. Hickok previously agreed to sponsor Shane and he won't renege on his word, which leaves me high and dry. Unless you'll help."

"How can I . . ." Blade began, then saw what she was getting at.

"I want you to sponsor me before the Elders," Sherry declared.

"I don't know. . . ." Blade hedged.

"Why not?" Sherry demanded. "Have you already said you'd sponsor someone else?"

"No . . ."

"You don't believe women make good Warriors?" Sherry pressed him.

"That isn't it. . . ."

"Then what? Because I'm an outsider?"

"A Warrior from outside the Family would set a precedent," Blade admitted, "but it's not a major stumbling block."

"Then how about it?"

Blade stopped and faced her. "It's not possible."

"Why?"

"Because I'm the one who must make the final recommendations to Plato and the Elders," Blade stated. "I can't express any favoritism whatsoever. If I sponsored you, it might reflect badly on the other candidates."

Sherry's disappointment was conveyed in her quavering voice. "But I'll never have a chance if I don't have a sponsor! Hickok is going to stand up before the Elders in council and vouch for Shane. All the candidates will have sponsors except me. I'll never be picked!"

"There is a way out," Blade suggested.

"What?" Sherry eagerly inquired, her countenance lighting up.

"Find another sponsor," Blade advised her.

"Another sponsor? Who? I don't know anyone else here all that well." She frowned, her hopes prematurely dashed.

"Try Rikki."

"Rikki-Tikki-Tavi? I've only talked to him once or twice. What makes you think he'll sponsor me?" Sherry asked doubtfully.

"Trust me."

Now it was her turn to balk. "I don't know. . . ."

"Well, if you won't ask Rikki, then try Yama," Blade proposed.

"Yama? Are you nuts? He scares me!"

Blade shrugged, grinning. "It's up to you. If you want to become a Warrior badly enough, you'll ask one of them to sponsor you."

Sherry was about to comment when her gaze strayed past Blade. Her green eyes unexpectedly widened, her expression registering shock.

Blade spun, his hands on his Bowie handles.

There were two of them, standing at the edge of the trees only ten feet off. A huge blue thing and a short furry thing.

Gremlin suddenly hissed, sounding enraged. "You!"

"Yeah, Gremlin, us!" the smaller of the pair responded in an unusually low voice. "You were expecting maybe Santa Claus?"

The big one laughed. "Santa Claus! That's a good one, Ferret!"

"Who are you?" Blade demanded. "What do you want?"

"Why don't you ask your friend Gremlin?" Ferret

rejoined.

"Are those two friends of yours?" Blade asked without turning his attention from the duo.

"G.R.D.'s, yes?" Gremlin said. "Not friends now, no?"

"How did you get in here?" Blade asked. "What do you want?"

Ferret snickered disdainfully. "Your vaunted Home isn't so difficult to break into, not if you can swim. As to why we're here, Warrior, we've been asked to relay a message to Gremlin."

"What message?" Blade queried.

The one called Ferret looked up at the large blue hulk and they grinned at one another.

"What message?" Blade repeated.

"Oh, it's not very long or anything," Ferret finally replied. "It's simply this." He paused, smiling. Without warning, he snarled and crouched on the grass. "*Die!*"

The two creatures charged.

# 14

*"Die!"*

He towered above the others in the expansive chamber, this lean, brooding skeleton of a man. His broad shoulders, covered by a knee-length white smock, were set arrow straight, his delicate fingers clasped behind his back. The small speaker on the console in front of him conveyed the sounds of the conflict and he smiled, revealing two rows of tiny teeth, teeth curiously thin and pointed. His eyes were placed deep in their sockets and seemed to blaze with fiery inner light, although in reality they were an unfathomable black. The top of his sloping head was completely bald, but the sides still retained long wisps of fine white hair. His figure presented an amazing paradox; it appeared incredibly ancient and yet immensely powerful simultaneously.

A young man in a green uniform dutifully approached and stood at attention.

The eerie one in the smock slowly turned. "Yes, Captain?" he asked, his voice a resonant rumble in his chest.

The frightened captain swallowed hard. "I beg your pardon for disturbing you, sir."

"Quite all right," the tall man stated. He nodded

at the speaker. "You're not interrupting anything important."

The captain could distinctly detect the sounds of combat emanating from the speaker in the bank of electronic equipment and his eyebrows arched.

"What you hear," the first man continued, "is the end of a nuisance, the termination of a particularly troublesome thorn in my side." He stared into the captain's brown eyes. "And we both know how I deal with those who oppose me, don't we?"

The captain was too wise to reply.

"Now, what may I do for you?" demanded the one in the smock. His right hand flicked a switch on the board and the speaker went dead.

The captain cleared his throat. "I'm from Communications, sir."

"I know," affirmed the tall man. "Captain Miller, isn't it? You've been at the Citadel only two weeks, correct?"

"Yes, Doktor," Captain Miller replied. How did the fiend do it? Scuttlebutt had it the Doktor was endowed with a startlingly efficient photographic memory. Rumor also was that he read the new Personnel Report for the entire Citadel each week and memorized its contents!

"I'm waiting," the Doktor said.

The captain raised the message in his left hand.

"What have we now?" the Doktor muttered and took the message. Although the typed copy on the yellow teletype paper was twenty lines long, the Doktor read the contents in the time it took the captain to blink once.

Captain Miller felt his skin crawl. He fervently wished he were anywhere but in the freak room at the moment.

The Doktor abruptly hissed and crumpled the

message into a ball. "Damn infantile idiot!" he snapped. "He is positive proof that stupidity is genetically inherited!"

A clammy sweat broke out all over the captain's body.

The Doktor glared at the officer. "Does the fool think I make these suggestions for my health? He doesn't realize the danger!"

Mustering his courage, Captain Miller ventured to speak. "I was told to await your reply, sir."

"I'll provide you with a reply," the Doktor growled. "You will transmit a one word response to him."

"What word is that, sir?"

"*No!*" the Doktor roared.

Captain Miller recognized the symptoms. The Doktor was in one of his infamous rages, and the slightest upsetting remark, no matter how innocuous, might trigger his violent wrath.

"Are you familiar with the Family?" the Doktor unexpectedly inquired.

"I believe so, sir," Captain Miller politely answered. "I've seen dispatches on them from time to time. Aren't they the outfit in Minnesota?"

"They are indeed," the Doktor said. "And they constitute a supreme threat to the Civilized Zone."

"The Family, sir? They only have six or seven dozen members. We could crush them easily," Captain Miller commented, and instantly regretted his blundering indiscretion, appalled at the sheer fury displayed on the Doktor's visage.

"You sound exactly like that fool Samuel!" the Doktor bellowed, livid. "I can't seem to impress upon his pitiful semblance of intelligence how grave the danger is!" The Doktor checked himself, making a mighty effort to control his surging emotions.

"What is so hard to comprehend?" he asked Miller. "The threat the Family poses to our system, to the very fabric of our society, isn't predicated on their relatively few numbers. Instead, the source of the danger is their value base, their moral and spiritual orientation. Do you see it now?"

Captain Miller timidly shook his head. "I'm afraid I don't see what you mean, sir."

The Doktor sadly gazed at the cement floor, his shoulders slumping. "I'm surrounded by incompetents! Once, just once, I'd enjoy encountering a person of true intellect." He looked at Miller. "I will sum up their danger as succinctly as possible." He paused. "The Family believes in God."

"In God, sir?" Captain Miller laughed. "Everyone knows there isn't any God."

The Doktor seemed to suddenly grow in stature, to loom over the terrified officer. "You still don't see it, do you? You know there isn't any God. I realized a long, long time ago, when I was four years old, that the concept of a Supreme Being was inconsistent with observable reality. So you know it and I know it. But what about the ignorant masses? What about them?"

"The masses, sir? They know it's illegal to believe in God."

The Doktor's eyes resembled blazing coals in an inferno. "And we both know they never break laws, right, Captain?"

Captain Miller lost all moisture in his mouth.

"Laws, Captain," the Doktor declared, "maintain order in any society only so long as that society possesses the necessary military force to compel compliance. That's why the ideal state is the police state. Every aspect of daily existence for the masses, from the moment they stumble from bed in the morning until their final fleeting thoughts before retiring, must be stringently controlled. Every nuance in their culture must be censored and constructively channeled along acceptable lines. Everything, from the food they ingest to the thoughts in their heads, must be only what is allowed, only what conforms to dictated doctrine. And all of this manipulation must be performed in such a manner, using whatever deception is required, as to present the illusion to the masses of freedom. The secret to successfully governing the masses is not to let them know they are being controlled, and to convince them all laws are beneficial and enacted for the good of all the people. Do you understand this elementary civics lesson?"

"Yes, Doktor," Captain Miller promptly replied.

"Good. Now follow me on this next part. If dominating the masses depends on their doing only what we want them to do and thinking only what we want them to think, what transpires when an alien concept is thrust into the social stream?"

"Sir?"

"For instance, our culture teaches there is no God. We inculate the precepts of atheistic humanism upon our citizens, because we rightly recognize the validity of humanism and the inferiority of other philosophical and religious beliefs. We instruct our people this life is all they get. There is no afterlife, no heaven and certainly no hell. Simply seventy short years and oblivion, eternal nothingness. We arouse them to fear the idea of dying, to view death with the utmost dread. By doing so, we inspire in them an urge to comply with our every edict because they know to do otherwise is to hasten their leap into the void. Have you followed me to this point?"

"Yes, sir."

"Good. So what happens when a new idea enters the collective social consciousness? What will occur when the people begin believing in an afterlife? If they believe they will survive this life in the flesh, then they will not fear death any longer. And if they don't dread dying, why should they listen to us? If they believe they are endowed with an immortal soul, let us say, and if they exercise faith in the promise of an everlasting life, they might come to view the thousands and thousands of laws our society has enacted as unnecessary, or even evil. For example, if they don't fear dying, they won't consider the consequences of a firing squad much of a deterrent for breaking our laws, will they?"

"No, Doktor."

"Then hopefully you can begin to appreciate the threat this Family poses. Samuel can't." The Doktor frowned. "I have an important matter to attend to, Captain. Relay my response to Samuel and return with his reply. That is all."

"Yes, sir," Captain Miller said. He saluted, wheeled, and gratefully departed, mulling the Doktor's words. For all his vaunted intellect, the Doktor was worried about nothing, making a mountain out of a molehill. The Army, under Samuel's direction, was the ruling class in the Civilized Zone, and the military commanders dominated the people with an iron fist. Samuel would crush any rebellion before the rebels knew what hit them. So why worry about some jerks who believed in God?

The Doktor watched the officer leave. He frowned and shook his head. The juvenile imbecile, like that foppish Samuel, failed to comprehend the gravity of the situation. The Family must be eliminated, and the sooner the better.

"Blithering twit," the Doktor muttered, still furious with Samuel for refusing his request to send a battalion to destroy the Home and capture the Family.

Not at this time, Samuel had wired!

Can't spare the men!

Preparing for an offensive against the Cavalry and the Legion while the two sides remain separated!

The unmitigated stupidity of the man!

The Doktor pounded the equipment in front of him with his right fist. If he didn't detest the machinations of governmental office, if he didn't loathe the thousand and one nitpicking details requiring daily attention and despise the whining syncophants invariably present at all levels of a governing regime, he'd wrest control of the Civilized Zone from Samuel and attend to the Family personally. Possibly later. Right now he had a critical matter to oversee. He stared at the backs of his hands, noting the deep wrinkles and the spreading lines, twice as many as were there the day before. Time was of the essence.

But first . . .

He bent over the console and turned on the speaker, listening, waiting to learn the outcome of the confrontation.

There was only static.

What had transpired? He glanced at a cabinet to his right and spotted the blinking blue light. Three rows of bulbs below the blue light was a flashing red light.

So!

The Doktor switched the speaker off and straightened. The Family could wait a while longer.

There were more important things to do.

He looked around the room and saw one of his assistants, a young woman with serpentine features, yellow skin, and narrow lavender eyes. She stood before a table containing a rack of flasks and vials, examining a test tube, most of her body concealed by a white smock.

"Clarissa!" the Doktor called. "It's time!"

Clarissa looked up, her forehead furrowed, her oily black bangs hanging over her right eyebrow.

"That's right," the Doktor affirmed. "It's time again."

Clarissa placed the test tube on the table. "Which sex this time Doktor?" she inquired.

The Doktor reflected a moment. "Bring me a girl this time. Not more than six months old, either. One of the Flatheads should suffice nicely."

Clarissa nodded and moved toward a far door.

"And don't forget the scalpel and the blood vat," the Doktor reminded her.

"Certainly, Doktor," Clarissa replied over her shoulder.

The Doktor grinned. In a few days he would be as good as new, and then he would travel to Denver and have a long talk with that cretin Samuel.

Sooner or later, one way or another, the Family was going to be erased from the face of the earth.

The Doktor almost laughed at the prospect.

# 15

"Geronimo! Wake up! You dozed off!"

He felt her hand gently slapping his left cheek and he opened his eyes, his mind sluggish, his senses groggy.

"How's your head feel?" Cynthia questioned.

"A little better than last night," Gernonimo informed her.

"You up to a little action?" Kilrane interjected.

Geronimo glanced around, slightly dazed, wondering if he'd sustained a concussion in the fall into the pit. Kilrane was squatting against the opposite wall. They were still at the rear of the crevice, as far from the ant tunnel as they could get. "What do you have in mind?" he asked.

"A little reconnaissance," Kilrane answered, nodding toward the tunnel. "It's daylight and I haven't heard one pass by in a long time."

"Maybe they're nocturnal," Geronimo deduced, "and they hole up during the day. They were awful active last night." He gazed at the tunnel, surprised at how clear everything appeared. The bright sunlight outside the crater was flooding the tunnel and providing sufficient illumination for their eyes, long since adjusted to the murky visibility, to discern every nook and cranny in the crevice and the lighter shade of the tunnel beyond.

"Then now is our best bet to make a break for it,"
Kilrane declared. He flattened and slowly crawled
along the crevice floor, making for the ant tunnel.

Geronimo promptly followed, the Marlin in his
right hand, collecting his thoughts.

"I just hope you're right," Cynthia whispered,
falling in behind Geronimo.

Kilrane cautiously edged nearer the opening,
slowly easing his body over the lumps of dirt and
stones on the floor. He reached the rift and stopped,
waiting for the others. The crevice widened at its
junction with the tunnel, enabling the trio to huddle
side by side.

Geronimo glanced at the other two, then inched
his face to the lip of the crevice and peered out.

The ant tunnel brightened to his right, indicating
the hole to the outside was in that direction. The
industrious ants had carved a passageway about ten
feet in diameter, its sides and ceiling smooth and
unbroken, the floor littered with a jumble of
indistinguishable debris except for a few prominent,
pale white bones. The crevice started five feet from
the tunnel floor and continued up to the ceiling.

The tunnel was deserted.

"Say, Kilrane," Geronimo said softly. "Why
didn't you try to get out of the hole after we fell in,
instead of bringing us deeper into this tunnel?"

"Didn't have any choice," Kilrane replied. "Your
horse died in the fall. I might have climbed back out,
but there was no way I could tote you too. The sides
of the pit are too steep. So we hurried in here. I was
hoping I could find a side tunnel and hide for a spell.
We lucked out finding this."

"Do we make a run for it?" Cynthia inquired
nervously.

"It may only be twenty yards to the crater,"

Kilrane responded, "but we'd still have to climb out and that would take some doing. What if we're caught on the sides of the hole and an ant shows up?"

"Good point," Geronimo remarked, debating their next move. What *should* they do? Kilrane was right; if they tried to scale the pit, they'd be exposed and prime prey for the ants. On the other hand, if they didn't make their bid for freedom while they still had the light, they'd be forced to remain in the crevice another night and increase the likelihood of being discovered by the ants. Neither proposition was particularly appealing.

"Listen!" Cynthia warned them.

Geronimo heard the high-pitched twittering coming from the direction of the crater. An ant was returning!

They froze, holding their breaths.

Despite being forewarned of their immense size, despite having encountered giants before, Geronimo was stunned when the gargantuan insect passed the crevice opening, unprepared for the sheer, overpowering enormity of the creature.

The red behemoth passed the crevice at a leisurely pace, its six legs moving in instinctive precision, its elbowed antennae waving in the air as it walked. This particular ant was at least seven feet in height and twelve feet long. Its compound eyes seemed to be focused on the tunnel ahead as it carried a large object in its huge jaws, the object dwarfed by the insect's five-foot-wide head.

What was the ant carrying? Geronimo wondered. Whatever it was, the thing was twitching. Where would the ants find food in the Dead Zone? He marveled at the insect's flawless symmetry, noting the exceptionally elongated head with the massive jaws, the relatively narrow waist between the two large body segments, and the lustrous sheen to the entire form. He recalled his schooling days at the Home and his intensive studies of the flora and fauna of the region. Courses were taught on the mammals, reptiles, amphibians, birds, and insects likely to be encountered in the vicinity of the Home. He remembered receiving instructions concerning ants, but the years since the lesson had tarnished his memory.

What exactly did he know about ants, anyway?

They were likely social and lived in colonies in the ground or in dead wood. These colonies were called nests, and Geronimo speculated the mountainous mound spotted earlier was the main nest for this colony. If true, it meant they were trapped in a subsidiary tunnel, which worked in their favor. The ants were apt to increase in number the closer to the mound you went. In one of their secondary tunnels, therefore, there would be fewer ants!

What else did he recollect about ants?

Their bodies were comprised of the head, the abdomen, and the thorax, but he forgot which was the abdomen and which the thorax. Many species included different types within the colony: workers, soldiers, and queen ants. The queens would be secreted in an inner chamber in the nest, but the workers and the soldiers would emerge on a regular basis to conduct their business, whether it be foraging for sustenance or fighting an enemy.

How could you tell a worker from a soldier?

Geronimo couldn't recall, and the information might be crucial. Worker ants might not be much of a threat, but the deadly soldiers were another matter.

The ant with the food in its jaws disappeared

around a far turn in the tunnel.

"Whew!" Cynthia whispered in relief. "I thought for a second there the thing saw us."

"I don't see any more coming," Kilrane observed, staring in the direction of the hole. "Should we make our break for it now?"

"I see no reason to wait," Geronimo replied. "Besides, I never expected to end my days on this planet as ant fricassee."

"But even if we do make it out," Cynthia mentioned, "where will we go? Without the horses we wouldn't last very long."

"Care to place a bet on how much longer we'd last down here?" Geronimo queried.

Cynthia shook her head.

"Still no sign of any ants," Kilrane commented.

"May the Great Spirit be with us," Geronimo said, and slipped over the edge of the crevice.

The tunnel remained empty.

Geronimo crouched, the Marlin ready, and motioned for the others to follow him with his left hand.

Kilrane came next, his lariat in his right hand.

Cynthia took a deep breath and jumped to the floor of the tunnel.

"It must have taken considerable effort to get me up to that crack in the wall while unconscious," Geronimo stated, looking at Kilrane.

"It was tough," Kilrane admitted, grinning. "Maybe you should go on a diet in case we ever need to go through this again."

"You can barely see the crevice from the crater," Cynthia interjected. "If we . . ."

A distant twittering carried to their ears.

"An ant!" Cynthia exclaimed.

"It's coming from down there," Geronimo

declared, pointing down the tunnel shaft.

"Do we go for it or climb back up?" Kilrane demanded.

"Go!" Geronimo suggested, already in motion, running for the exit opening twenty yards off.

Cynthia and Kilrane were on his heels as they raced along the tunnel and reached the bottom of the pit. The rim of the crater appeared impossibly far off, and the smooth sides presented an almost insurmountable challenge.

"You two start," Geronimo directed, waving them on. "I'll hold the fort until you reach the top."

"Why you?" Kilrane argued.

"You don't have a rifle," Geronimo reasoned, "and this baby would stop a charging elephant."

"What's an elephant?" Kilrane inquired.

"You've never heard of an elephant?"

"No. Why?"

Geronimo grinned. He kept forgetting others did not enjoy the same access he did to the invaluable wealth of information in the Family library.

"What's an elephant?" Kilrane repeated.

"Just think of it as an ant with a whopper of a nose," Geronimo said. "Now get going!"

Cynthia was already striving to climb the pit, her feet slipping and sliding in the fine, loose dirt.

"I won't leave you," Kilrane balked.

Geronimo stared into the bigger man's blue eyes. "I appreciate the thought, but you've got to go. I'll cover for you as long as I can."

"I've never deserted a friend in my life," Kilrane said defiantly, "and I'm not about to start now."

Geronimo noticed the compliment. "Please, Kilrane. Get Cynthia out of here. For me, as a personal favor."

Kilrane glanced at the struggling woman,

frowned, and nodded. "All right," he reluctantly growled, "but I'm coming back for you."

For a moment, their eyes locked in silent understanding, and then Geronimo swung around, facing the tunnel. Cynthia had been right; he could just distinguish the rift they'd used as their refuge. He heard Kilrane attempting to negotiate the steep sides of the crater, but he steeled himself and locked his eyes on the fissure. If he glanced behind him to ascertain their progress in navigating the hole, his attention would be distracted from the tunnel for an instant, providing the ants with a momentary edge.

An experienced Warrior never gave an opponent the edge.

Geronimo's mind wandered, his thoughts drifting to the Family and the Home. And Hickok. His best friend. It was funny, sometimes, how you never truly valued someone until deprived of his presence. All those years of brotherhood with Hickok, sharing the sweet and the bitter, the laughs and the tears, had resulted in an ingrained bond of affection, a mutual affinity predicated on a thorough understanding of one another. He fondly remembered the time Hickok tried driving the SEAL and nearly succeeded in planting a tree in the driver's seat. Grinning, he recalled another time when Hickok was caught with his pants down, so to speak, about to take a leak when a mutate popped up.

Would he ever see Hickok again?

Or Blade?

Or Plato?

Or . . .

What was that?

There was vague movement near the crevice.

Geronimo dropped to his right knee and sighted

along the Marlin. He could still hear Kilrane and Cynthia doing their utmost to reach the lip of the hole.

A pair of antennae became visible, swaying in the air.

Geronimo patiently waited, his finger on the trigger.

The head of an ant appeared, the insect hesitating, apparently endeavoring to identify the commotion in the hole.

Good.

Take your time, gruesome!

How long could he hold them off? Geronimo speculated. The Marlin might be able to down a few, but if they surged through the tunnel in any great number, all at once, there was no way he could keep them back.

The front section of the ant was now clearly in sight.

Geronimo suddenly had an idea. What if he was able to kill a couple of the things? Maybe, just maybe, their bodies might block the tunnel for awhile. At least, long enough for Cynthia and Kilrane to make good their escape.

Would it work, though?

There was only one way to find out.

Geronimo aimed between the two antennae, held his breath, and fired. The blast of the Marlin was deafening in the confines of the tunnel, and Geronimo was aware of a ringing in his ears as he levered his second round into the chamber.

The ant staggered with that first shot, then plowed ahead, emanating a high-pitched screeching as it attacked.

Geronimo fired again, this slug ripping into the ant's right eye and tearing through its head.

The ant almost stumbled, but it recovered and lurched forward, its jaw working frantically.

So!

The head was a weak spot!

Geronimo quickly shot a third time, aiming between the antennae again.

The ant dropped to the floor of the tunnel, its antennae flapping overhead, twitching and quivering.

Geronimo, elated, hastily reloaded the three spent shells from his bandoleer.

The Marlin was effective against the creatures! It meant he could buy Kilrane and Cynthia more time, if his ammunition held out. He could . . .

Something was moving in the tunnel behind the dead ant.

Geronimo squinted, peering into the passageway. So soon?

A second ant was pushing the body of the first aside as it struggled to squeeze past, twittering like crazy.

The ants must possess a remarkable communications system. Reinforcements were probably on their way, rushing to repel the intruders. How many? Ten? A hundred?

Did it matter?

Geronimo sent three shots into the head of the second ant. This one thrashed and clutched at the sides of the tunnel before collapsing alongside the first.

This isn't so hard, Geronimo thought. Like shooting ducks on a pond from a blind.

A third red ant started to climb over the dead duo.

Geronimo sighted and fired, the recoil slamming the Marlin's heavy stock into his shoulder.

The third ant reared and snapped at the ceiling.

Geronimo reloaded, keeping his eyes fixed on the ant.

The third ant was struggling to press past its fallen comrades.

Geronimo shot again, aiming above the insect's left eye.

The ant abruptly collapsed onto the deceased pair, kicking spasmodically.

No time to lose!

Geronimo ejected the spent round and replaced it. He couldn't afford to be caught empty when the big rush came.

What was going on now?

There was a bustle of activity immediately to the rear of the three dead ants.

Were they trying to extract the bodies from the corridor?

Geronimo leaned forward, puzzled. Was it his imagination, or were those dead ants moving? They were! They were actually creeping toward him! But how?

The ants must be pushing from the other side, using their former mates as a shield, protecting themselves from the rifle.

Was it possible?

Were ants that smart?

The bodies were about twelve yards away and slowly inching nearer. The live soldier ants were making an incredible racket.

What should he do? There weren't any clear targets yet, and he refused to waste a bullet. All he could do was wait, the sweat pouring from his pores, and strive to calm his nerves.

The makeshift barricade was ten yards away.

Had Kilrane and Cynthia made it yet? Geronimo

wanted to take a peek, but the glance could prove fatal.

Eight yards.

Geronimo sighted on a head visible above the pile of bodies and fired. His shot was rewarded with a piercing squeal and the head vanished from view.

Six yards.

Geronimo's fingers flew as he replaced the round. It wouldn't be long before the ants made their bid.

The tunnel suddenly went quiet.

Geronimo shifted to his left knee. Where were they? What were they up to?

Something chattered and the prone body on top of the pile was hastily hauled backward, out of sight. Another ant, a live one, quickly filled the gap, scrambling over the dead pair still blocking the tunnel.

Geronimo let him have two shots in the forehead, delighted when the ant froze and slumped on top of the other dead forms.

So far, so good!

Geronimo could see ants moving behind the dead ones blocking the tunnel.

What were they up to now?

A spray of dust settled around Geronimo's shoulders and he coughed, clearing his dry throat. Kilrane and Cynthia had probably dislodged some dirt near the top of the pit.

The ants congregated on the other side of the bodies suddenly started making a veritable din.

They're up to something, Geronimo told himself.

More dust fell from above, covering Geronimo's shoulders.

What were they trying to do, bury him alive?

The ants still in the tunnel sounded like they were

throwing the party of the millennium.

A third deluge of dirt and dust descended on Geronimo and caked his clothes with a fine reddish film.

What in the world were they doing? Didn't they see him at the bottom of the pit?

Geronimo risked a quick glance overhead, intending to discover the culprit.

And he did.

But it wasn't Kilrane or Cynthia.

It was an ant, its head poking through the pit wall halfway between Geronimo and the top of the crater, just to his right.

Geronimo wheeled, raising the Marlin, realizing he'd been outflanked, outmaneuvered by the crafty devils! They'd dug a new tunnel, circumventing the bodies, bypassing the deceased ants and emerging from the pit wall.

Behind him, there was renewed commotion as the ants tore into the bodies, working frantically to force an exit.

He was trapped!

Ants behind him and ants in front of him!

They had him right where they wanted him.

It looked like he'd never get to see Hickok's ugly white puss again.

Geronimo aimed the rifle, prepared to acquit himself honorably. He saw Kilrane and Cynthia, to his left, near the top.

The ant above him finally detected its prey and shrieked in triumph.

# 16

Blade whipped his Bowies from their sheaths as the blue G.R.D. charged him. The scaly skin, the fiery red eyes, and the unruly black hair presented a disconcerting aspect, enhanced by the creature's maniacal countenance. Its bulk alone was intimidating, and Blade knew if he was caught in those massive arms he'd be crushed to a pulp as easily as he could squash a moldy mushroom.

He wasn't about to give the thing the opportunity.

The blue monster lunged at Blade with outstretched hands, its tapered teeth white in the morning sun.

Blade ducked under the G.R.D.'s arms and pivoted, driving his left Bowie up and in, feeling the point penetrate the chest of his opponent. The Bowie was buried to the hilt before the thing could arrest its momentum, and it savagely wrenched the knife from Blade's grasp as it spun, clipping the Warrior's head with the back of its left hand.

Staggered by the glancing blow, Blade stumbled for a few feet, then recovered. He saw Gremlin and the one called Ferret grappling on the grass and Sherry standing nearby with her mouth open in astonishment.

Big help she was!

The blue creature was glaring at Blade, ignoring the knife in its chest, its bony fingers clenched into claws.

"Ox want you bad," the G.R.D. hissed. "You hurt Ox!"

"So your name's Ox?" Blade rejoined, grinning. "The Doktor obviously didn't name you for your brains!"

Ox, livid at the slur, roared and leaped, hurtling through the air and striking Blade around the mid-section, bearing him to the ground.

Blade stabbed Ox's back as he fell, three times in rapid succession, planting the second knife between Ox's shoulder blades. His breath was caught short as they crashed on the grass, Ox on top, the thing's forehead in his stomach.

Ox gripped the second Bowie in his right hand and tore it free of Blade's grip. "See how you do without little pin," he sarcastically cracked, tossing the knife aside.

Blade surged against the G.R.D.'s heavier mass, striving to flip the thing over.

Ox, straddling the Warrior, laughed. "Try again, puny man! You can't hurt Ox!"

Blade, twisting and thrashing, spotted Gremlin and Ferret still locked in combat. Ferret appeared to have the upper hand. It looked as though Gremlin had tripped over a log, and Ferret was on top, flailing away with all his strength.

Sherry suddenly recovered her voice. She faced the cabins, cupped her hands to her mouth, and stretched her vocal chords to the limit.

"*Hhhheeeellllpppp!*"

Ox glanced up, distracted.

"Shut her up!" Ferret barked, still pummeling Gremlin.

Sherry took a few steps toward the cabins.

"*Hhhhheeeellllpppp!* Help us! Over here! Hurry!"

"Damn it!" Ferret fumed. "Shut her up *now!*"

Ox immediately obeyed, forgetting Blade, hastily standing and running at Sherry.

Blade rolled to his feet. "Sherry! Look out!"

She heard him and turned, her initial panic gone, replaced by grim determination.

Blade ran toward them, fearing for her life. She was unarmed, untrained, and the G.R.D. outweighed her by a good three hundred pounds. What could she possibly do against the hulking deviate?

Sherry was in motion, racing toward Ox instead of in the other direction.

The G.R.D. slowed, perplexed by this unexpected development, its dull wit encumbering its exceptional reflexes.

Sherry was only two feet from the creature when she abruptly dropped to the grass, tumbling, her body striking the blue thing across the shins and causing it to lose its balance.

Ox attempted to stay erect, but his impetus prevented him from stopping completely. Before he could recover, he lost his footing and fell, his knees inadvertently striking Sherry on the left temple as she tried to dodge aside, stunning her.

Blade, intent on Sherry's dilemma, failed to notice Ferret coming at him until it was too late. He was bowled over, and before he could regain his feet, in a flurry of brutal punches and jabs, the diminutive G.R.D. dazed him, almost rendering him unconscious.

Ferret spun on Ox, still on his hands and knees next to Sherry. "Can't you do anything right?" He pointed at the Warrior. "Bring him and I'll carry Gremlin!"

"Ox thought we were going to kill them," Ox stated, crossing to Blade and easily lifting the muscular Warrior in his brawny arms.

Ferret knelt and hefted Gremlin over his left shoulder. "We are," he told Ox. He rose and began moving toward the trees. "But that woman's big mouth has alerted the Family and they'll come to investigate. The Warriors will come. We can't be here when they arrive."

"Ox isn't scared of the stupid Warriors," Ox declared.

Voices were being raised in alarm from the direction of the cabins.

"Move your ass!" Ferret barked, leading the way.

They entered the woods and headed due east, skirting the fields, sticking to the heavier under-brush, and listening for any sounds of pursuit.

There were none.

"Ox still don't see why we didn't just kill them," Ox protested.

"Because," Ferret said over his right shoulder, "the Doktor told us to terminate Gremlin a certain way. Remember?"

Ox grinned at the memory. "Yes. Doktor wants us to make an example of Gremlin."

"That's right. The Doktor doesn't like it when one of his little charges goes traipsing off on its own. It makes the Doktor look bad and the Doktor doesn't like that."

"No, Doktor doesn't," Ox snickered.

They covered over five hundred yards before Ferret was satisfied they were temporarily safe.

"Drop him here," Ferret directed when they reached a small clearing. "This will do."

Blade and Gremlin were deposited side by side on the grass.

"Now?" Ox asked eagerly, licking his lips.

"No, not yet," Ferret replied. He leaned over Gremlin and slapped him three times across the face.

Gremlin came awake, still woozy. "You!" He attempted to rise, but Ferret shoved him onto his back.

"Stay put, traitor!" Ferret ordered. "Enjoy the few precious moments of life left to you."

"Now?" Ox inquired again.

Ferret glared at his companion. "Let me guess. You're hungry again!"

"Of course," Ox responded. "Ox is always hungry."

Ferret looked at Gremlin. "I'm sorry about this, but orders are orders. It's nothing personal, you understand."

"Gremlin understand, all right, yes?" Gremlin answered, nodding. "Gremlin knew Doktor would send someone, no? But why you?"

"The Doktor created you," Ferret said sadly, "and me. He knows us, our limitations and our capabilities, better than we know ourselves. He knows how fast you are, and he knew my speed is superior to yours. I may be smaller, but I'm equally as strong as you. He sent the lummox here," and Ferret jerked his right thumb toward Ox, "as added insurance."

"What's a lummox?" Ox wanted to know.

"Doktor must be monitoring us right now, yes?" Gremlin said, staring at the collar around Ferret's hairy neck.

"Undoubtedly," Ferret agreed, studying the scar on Gremlin's throat. "It's amazing you were able to discard yours," he said in a low voice, a tinge of admiration in his tone.

"A miracle, yes?" Gremlin acknowledged, glancing at Blade. "Gremlin owe it to him."

Ferret gazed into Gremlin's eyes. "How? How was it done? You know what happens to us if we try to remove the collars. How were you able to do it?"

"Gremlin not sure," Gremlin admitted. "Blade and Gremlin were fighting, yes? In Flathead Lake in Montana, no? Possible water shorted circuit."

"I'm seeing it," Ferret said, fingering his own metal collar, "and I still can't believe one of us is free."

"Why all this damn talk?" Ox demanded. "The Doktor said we must kill him. Let's do it before someone comes!"

"How are you to kill Gremlin, yes?" Gremlin questioned.

Ferret frowned. "The Doktor said he wanted an appropriate example made of you. A fate to match the crime, as he put it."

"What fate, yes?" Gremlin goaded him.

Ferret's face reflected his loathing as he looked at Ox. "I'm to hold you down while Ox here eats you alive."

"Eats alive, yes?" Gremlin repeated, shocked.

"And Ox is ready," Ox announced, coming closer. "I'll start with your soft belly and work my way up," he said excitedly.

"Just think, Ferret, yes?" Gremlin remarked. "This could be you someday, too?"

Ferret pondered the prospect, his low brow knit in thought.

"Let's get on with it," Ox stated impatiently.

Ferret slowly nodded, his eyes conveying his regret. "I'm really sorry," he said to Gremlin. "I have no choice."

Ox stood next to Gremlin, towering over him, leering and drooling.

Gremlin nodded once, then attacked, lashing out with his right foot and striking Ferret in the loincloth. Ferret gurgled and fell to one side. Gremlin rolled to his left, away from Ox, hoping to make a break for it and return with the Warriors.

Ox was on Gremlin before he took two steps, gripping Gremlin from behind and pinning his arms to his sides. "Going somewhere?" Ox taunted. "I don't like to see my meals running off like this!"

Gremlin, try as he might, couldn't break free.

"Have a seat," Ox advised, and followed his words with action. He savagely slammed Gremlin to the ground, knocking the wind out of him and causing a searing pain in both legs.

Gremlin contorted into a ball, clutching his injured legs, the pain agonizing.

"Now maybe you'll stay put for Ox," Ox said, grinning.

"Maybe he will," someone else interjected, "but I sure as hell won't!"

Ox whirled.

Blade was in midair. He was astounded to see his Bowie still buried in the G.R.D.'s chest, and he grabbed for the hilt with his right hand as he collided with Ox, the force of his lunge staggering the creature but not downing him.

Ox growled as he clung to Blade's arms and endeavored to pull the Warrior toward his fangs.

Blade, stymied in his efforts to bring the Bowie into play, instead slammed his forehead up and inward, smashing it against Ox's nostrils. The nasal passages caved in, blood gushing from the shattered cavities.

Ox bellowed in torment and flung the Warrior aside, pressing his left hand against his nose in a futile attempt to stop the bleeding.

Gremlin was lying on the ground, his features twisted in misery.

Ferret was on his knees, holding his groin and groaning.

"*You bastard!*" Ox roared, and lunged at the rising Warrior.

Blade sidestepped and spun, watching as Ox checked his plunge and turned to confront him again. The G.R.D. was in the grip of sheer fury, reacting on a basic bestial level. It snarled and came at him, and Blade nimbly ducked under the groping arms and stabbed his Bowie into the creature's left thigh, pulling the knife clear as Ox passed by.

Undeterred, Ox twirled and managed to grip Blade's left wrist with his right hand.

Blade immediately buried the Bowie in the hand holding him.

Ox snarled and released Blade's wrist, yanking his arm back and causing the knife to rip through half of his hand, tearing the flesh open from his knuckles to his wrist. Disregarding the injury, Ox swept his left leg up and caught the Warrior in the midsection, doubling him over.

"Blade!" Gremlin cried. He was trying to crawl to Blade's assistance.

Ox used his massive left fist and clubbed the Warrior to the ground.

Ferret was finally recovered and on his feet. "Nice going," he complimented Ox. "Now let's get this over with. I want to get the hell out of here."

Gremlin, despite excruciating torment in both

legs, endeavored to stand.

"No problem," Ox said. "This will only take a minute." He walked over to Gremlin and kicked him in the head.

Gremlin collapsed into a senseless heap.

Ox flicked his thick tongue over his lips, tasting his own blood and relishing the flavor.

"Get on with it," Ferret snapped, disgusted.

"Don't worry," Ox said, grinning. He bent over Gremlin, his mouth only inches from his victim's exposed stomach. "This will be a piece of cake." He opened wide, prepared to rip a large chunk of flesh from Gremlin's abdomen.

The new voice intruded on his concentration.

"Did someone call my name?"

# 17

Geronimo frantically backpedaled, putting distance between himself and the ant emerging from the pit wall. He aimed and fired, the ant shuddering at the impact of the heavy slug, but it kept coming, pushing through the wall. Geronimo shot again, and this time the insect slumped in the opening, motionless.

Another ant appeared, shoving the first ant completely through the hole it had made. The dead ant tumbled down the crater wall and disappeared in the tunnel.

Bull's-eye! Geronimo grinned. He'd love to have that ant on his dart team!

The second ant was perched at the lip of the new hole in the wall, its antennae waving wildly.

Hold that pose, beautiful! Geronimo sighted and pulled the trigger, the big gun booming in his ears.

The ant recoiled as it was torn by the slug. It rebounded and exited the hole, hastening down the slope, coming toward the human on the other wall.

Toward Geronimo.

It was too bad the Great Spirit didn't provide mortals with wings, Geronimo mused, as his legs churned and he tried to run up the far side of the crater.

No go.

Murphy strikes again!

Geronimo turned, aiming the Marlin.

The ant was at the bottom of the pit, only ten yards away, about to begin its ascent.

Geronimo held his breath, steadying the rifle, and pulled the trigger again.

Nothing happened!

What the . . . ?

Geronimo worked the lever, ejecting an empty shell from the chamber. The rifle was empty? But that was impossible! He'd kept track of his . . .

Damn!

He'd neglected to reload after shooting twice at that last ant inside the tunnel, the one trying to bulldoze past the bodies blocking the passage!

Idiot!

The latest threat was now five yards off, its jaws clicking together as they worked back and forth in anticipation.

So much for the Marlin!

Geronimo heaved the rifle at the ant, his throw true, the Marlin smacking the ant across the head and causing it to momentarily halt.

Try eating that, sucker!

Geronimo whirled, clawing at the earthen wall, pumping his legs, attempting to climb to the top of the crater.

It was impossible!

It was worse than running on wet, slippery grass.

A premonition of impending danger compelled him to cast a glance over his left shoulder.

The ant was stalking him again, only four yards away.

Geronimo turned and flattened, drawing the Arminius. The Magnum was a powerful handgun against mortal foes, but how would it fare against this gigantic insect?

Only one way to find out.

Geronimo fired twice, to no noticeable affect.

Uh-oh!

The ant stopped, only two yards separating them, the insect towering over Geronimo and seeming to reach the clouds themselves. Its jaws never ceased working.

Geronimo emptied the Arminius into the ant's head, then quickly rolled aside, putting distance between them just in case.

It was well he did.

The ant uttered a peculiar high-pitched squeal, shuddered, and toppled over, sliding down the side of the crater. Its body came to rest near the tunnel.

Geronimo replaced the Arminius in its holster, eyeing the tunnel and the hole in the opposite wall.

No more ants in sight.

Time to make tracks!

Geronimo rose and started up the slope. There was no sign of Cynthia or Kilrane anywhere in the pit. Good! They must have escaped while the insects were occupied. His left foot slipped and he glanced down, righting himself, his attention diverted for the briefest instant.

But it was enough.

Something twittered directly in front of him, and Geronimo looked up, startled.

An ant was at the top of the crater, directly in front of him. In a burst of speed, before the man could wheel and run, it slid over the edge and pounced. Its huge jaws closed around Geronimo's waist and lifted him from the ground.

Great Spirit, no!

Geronimo struggled, his arms still free. He

grabbed the tomahawk in his right hand, raised it over his head, and plunged the sharp blade into the ant's left jaw.

It was like hacking at a petrified tree.

The curved mandibles were impenetrable, bone-like in substance.

Geronimo decided to strike at the ant's head. If his bullets could inflict fatal wounds in that area, his tomahawk might do likewise. He hesitated, wondering why the ant wasn't crushing him to a pulp.

The ant was simply standing there, holding him in its jaws, its tremendous head tilting from side to side, evidently examining the being it held.

What was it waiting for?

Geronimo checked his swing, confused. If the ant wasn't intending to rend him to pieces, perhaps wisdom dictated he shouldn't do anything to provoke it.

But why?

His thoughts raced, his mind seeking a logical explanation. Was this ant a worker instead of a soldier? Would that explain its behavior? Were worker ants natural killers like the soldiers, or was their function merely to build, dig, and forage? More to the point, how could you tell a worker from a soldier?

Geronimo tensed, waiting for the ant to make a move.

Any move.

The jaws weren't hurting him. Yet. But the slightest additional pressure could have lethal consequences.

Come on! Geronimo wanted to scream.

Do something!

Anything!

His skin was tingling, a reaction to the supremely uncomfortable feeling, the sensation of expectant imminent doom.

The ant finally did do something.

It unexpectedly moved toward the tunnel.

No!

Geronimo reared up and brought the tomahawk down, planting it as near to one of the eyes as he could. The blade penetrated the face next to the left eye, biting deep, creating a large gash oozing with a slimy, colorless liquid.

The insect responded violently, jerking backwards, instinctively releasing the source of its anguish. The jaws opened and discarded their cargo.

Geronimo dropped to his knees, overwhelmed with relief. He looked up at the underside of the ant's head and swung the tomahawk again, ripping a two-foot tear in the insect.

The ant twisted to one side, then attacked.

Geronimo made a diving leap, landing in the dirt under the charging insect. He found himself on his left side, lying under the soft abdomen, and he spun, swinging the tomahawk. A smelly, sticky mess spattered all over him as the ant passed overhead and turned, running toward the tunnel.

He could take a hint!

Geronimo leaped to his feet and did his utmost to reach the peak of the crater before another ant appeared.

He failed.

Two ants emerged simultaneously, one from the tunnel and the other from the new hole in the opposite wall. They converged at the bottom of the pit and made toward the struggling human near the top.

Geronimo's fingers were only a foot away from the

edge of the crater, grasping for the rim, extending his arms until his shoulders hurt. His moccasins were slipping and sliding on the steep slope, unable to find adequate traction in the fine soil. In a desperate gambit for freedom, he lunged, hoping to grab hold of the top of the pit and haul himself over the top.

He missed.

For a paralyzing instant, he was suspended in midair, his body momentarily defying gravity. Then he plummeted like a stone, striking the ground and hurtling downward before he could arrest his momentum.

Straight toward the ants.

He tried to check his descent with his hands and feet, digging them into the earth, stinging his hands. A cloud of dust rose above him as he clutched at the pit wall, vainly endeavoring to stop before it was too late.

The ants had stopped and were waiting near the bottom of the crater.

Geronimo attempted to brake by ramming his tomahawk into the earth, using the handle to gouge a furrow in the dirt. His speed began to taper off.

Would he make it?

Twenty yards remained between the ants' mandibles and his hurtling form.

How would he stave off two ants, even if he did stop in time?

Fifteen yards.

His best bet would be to get under them and slash at their Achilles' heel, their tender bellies.

Ten yards.

His fall was abruptly concluded as he collided with a boulder protruding above the surface of the soil. Totally unexpected, the violent impact jarred his entire body and almost knocked the breath from him. He struck the boulder with his chest, and an excruciating pain lanced through his left side. His senses swam; he wasn't able to focus, to concentrate on the danger in front of him.

One of the ants shuffled toward him.

Geronimo could vaguely detect the approaching giant. He shook his head, wanting his balance to return.

The ant was almost on him when it did.

Geronimo glanced up, saw the jaws coming at him, and rolled to his right, out of harm's way.

The ant closed in, unhurried, seemingly over-confident in its ability.

Geronimo rolled again, dodging a second swing of those huge jaws.

The other ant started to circle below him.

They were going to box him in!

Geronimo hesitated, debating his next move. He'd never reach the rim of the crater, and more ants would be pouring from the tunnel any second. The odds of escaping were practically nonexistent. He grinned.

If his dying time had arrived, if it was time for the journey to the mansions on the other side, he would show the Great Spirit how nobly and bravely a true son could go out.

The ants were now in position, one on either side of their prey.

Geronimo stood, hefting his tomahawk.

Slowly, deliberately, the insects closed in.

Geronimo looked from one to the other. It didn't matter which one he went up against, now. He raised his eyes to the blue sky and vented his war whoop.

Then he attacked, making for the first antagonist,

determined to fight with his dying breath. He swept the tomahawk at the ant's face, but the insect parried the blow with its mandibles. The hair on the nape of his neck rose. He could feel the other ant bearing down on him from the rear.

Geronimo crouched and swung at one of the ant's front legs. The tomahawk sliced in deep, and the ant uttered a strange cry and stepped back several steps.

Geronimo whirled to confront the second ant, but as he did something hard smashed his head. He felt himself losing consciousness, and the next instant something pressed both of his arms together and he was lifted into the air.

I tried my best, he thought, as the darkness closed in. The pity of it, the irony of his passing, was that no one would ever know. The Family, and especially Hickok, would always wonder if he were still alive. They might think he deserted them.

What person in their right mind would desert those who loved them?

And poor Hickok! Who would be around to babysit him from now on? Who would burp him. . . .

The night engulfed him.

# 18

Ferret pivoted, facing the newcomer.

He stood at the edge of the clearing, his hands hanging loosely at his sides. His hair and moustache were blond. He wore buckskins and moccasins, and draped around his waist was a cartridge belt and two holsters containing pearl-handled revolvers, one on either hip. His blue eyes were focused on the fallen Warrior, a frown creasing his lips.

Ferret recognized him from the dossier on the Family maintained by the Doktor. "The gunfighter!" he hissed.

The gunman glanced up. "Did you say something, furball?"

"I know who you are," Ferret stated.

"Then I reckon you know what I'm going to do," the blond man said.

"What you will try to do," Ferret amended. He'd read about this particular Warrior, about his renowned reputation with those revolvers. The gunfighter was supposed to be lightning with those guns, but Ferret doubted any man could be fast enough to counter their speed, their genetically conditioned swiftness.

"Who are you?" Ox demanded.

The Warrior glared at Ox. "You shouldn't have

done that to my pard," he said harshly, nodding at Blade. "And I'm also kind of fond of that critter too." He indicated Gremlin.

"Then you can join them in my stomach!" Ox arrogantly snapped, annoyed this puny man was interfering with his meal.

The gunman's features changed, shifting and hardening.

Ox looked at Ferret.

Ferret nodded his head to the left, and Ox immediately began edging in that direction. His body tense, prepared for a leap, Ferret moved to the right.

The gunfighter chuckled. "You boys ain't none too subtle, are you?"

"Ox is going to rip your head off!" Ox promised.

The Warrior shook his head. "You've got it backwards, you walking pile of horse manure."

"Drop your guns!" Ferret ordered, still inching toward the gunman.

The man laughed. "You've got to be kidding, runt."

Ferret bristled at the slur. Hickok was only four feet away, within range of his powerful leg muscles.

"Any last requests?" the gunfighter asked.

Ox bellowed and sprang at the Warrior.

Over the years, Ferret had observed many men draw their guns. Some of these men were considered quick on the draw, but none of them had prepared him for the speed of this gunman. The man's hands were a blur, his revolvers up and pointed in less than the blink of an eye.

One of the revolvers fired, the left one, and the bullet slammed into Ox's left shoulder.

Ox twisted with the impact, and then whirled,

laughing at the gunman. "You'll have to do better than that!"

"How's this?" the Warrior queried, his right revolver booming.

A small hole suddenly appeared in the center of Ox's forehead; and the grass behind him was sprayed with drops of blood and brains. Ox's eyes crossed as he futilely endeavored to see the source of the pain in his forehead. His mouth opened and closed several times, and his hands clenched and unclenched as he managed to take another step.

Ferret, about to spring, found himself covered by the revolvers.

"I wouldn't, if I were you," the Warrior advised.

Ferret froze.

"I shot your pard in the shoulder because I wanted to take him alive," the gunman said. "He didn't know enough to quit while he was behind. Do you?"

Ferret glanced at Ox, still on his feet, weaving, about to fall.

"Which one of you hurt my lady?" the gunfighter demanded.

Ferret stared at those revolvers.

"Answer me," the Warrior warned.

"I didn't touch her!" Ferret replied.

"Figured as much," the gunman said, nodding. His right gun cracked and the bullet tore into the left nipple on Ox's chest. "That's for Blade," the man announced. The revolver blasted again, and the right nipple vanished. "That's for Gremlin." Twice more he fired, and Ox's eyes became empty sockets. "And that's for my lady." He twirled the right revolver into its holster and pointed the left hand-gun at Ferret's head.

Ox was slowly crumbling, ever so slowly falling to

his knees. He swayed for a moment, then toppled onto his face, his massive body thudding as it struck the ground.

"Now it's your turn, shorty," the Warrior stated. "If you so much as blink, I'll perforate your face and add an additional nostril or two."

Ferret smiled. "I must hand it to you, Hickok," he said in reluctant appreciation, "I've never seen anyone as fast as you. I thought we'd take you out, easy."

"The person or thing who finally takes me out," Hickok predicted, "won't find it easy." He paused. "You know my name. And you're as ugly as they come. So I reckon you're from the same outfit Gremlin is from. You're a G.R.D., right?"

Ferret nodded.

"Gremlin told us all about it," Hickok revealed.

Voices could be heard, not far off, drawing closer.

"Must be tough wearing that brand," Hickok said thoughtfully.

"Brand?" Ferret repeated, puzzled.

Hickok pointed at the collar. "Gremlin says you can't ever take them off, that this Doktor controls you with them."

Ferret nodded, frowning. "We do what we're told or we're killed, electrocuted at the Doktor's convenience. He monitors us using a satellite link. These collars also serve as transmitters, and their range is almost unlimited."

The voices were much nearer.

Ferret took a step toward the gunfighter.

Hickok instantly reacted, thumbing back the hammer on his left Colt Python. "I warned you!"

Ferret grinned impishly.

"You think having your brains blown out is funny?" Hickok asked, perplexed.

"It beats the alternative," Ferret answered.

"I don't follow," Hickok admitted.

"I've failed in my mission," Ferret explained. "The Doktor does not tolerate failures. Any second he will throw a switch on a certain piece of equipment in Cheyenne, and moments later I'll be fried from the neck up. Not a particularly appealing fate. Your way wll be faster and painless."

"You want me to kill you?" Hickok queried incredulously.

"Yes."

"No way! I'm keeping you for Plato to question."

"I won't last that long," Ferret said, his tone pleading. "Please! Finish me now! Before it's too late!"

"Forget it, shrimp."

Ferret growled in frustration. "Don't you see? What happened with Gremlin is a fluke. Hardly none of us ever escape the Doktor's clutches! There's no way to get this damn collar off!"

Hickok shook his head.

"I'll force you to shoot," Ferret stated, crouching. "If you don't, I'll rip you to shreds!"

Hickok stared at the collar, noting the precision of the polished metal. It was a circular band encircling the neck, with a rectangular blue indicator light in the center of the throat. It wasn't lit. Yet. If it did light up, it meant the Doktor had engaged the circuits.

"Do it!" Ferret begged.

"Maybe I should just let this Doktor fry you," Hickok said, "after what you've done to my friends."

"I had to do it!" Ferret snapped, frustrated. "It wasn't anything personal. Gremlin understood that."

"I still don't see why I should oblige you," Hickok commented.

The approaching voices were not more than a dozen yards away, on the other side of some nearby trees.

Ferret glanced at Gremlin, relieved they'd failed in their mission, then at Ox, feeling slightly sorry for the hulking dolt. Any moment he would join Ox in death. What was the Doktor waiting for? Surely he was monitoring an assignment as important as this one had been to him. The Doktor relished revenge, he savored killing and slaughter, the way some people craved sweets. Ferret just knew a tremendous jolt of electricity would zap him at any second, and he couldn't stand the suspense.

He lunged at the gunfighter.

Hickok's response was instantaneous. The left Colt Python boomed and the impact of the hollow-point bullet slammed Ferret backwards several yards. He landed on his back, clutching at his neck.

Ferret twitched a few times, then lay still.

Hickok sighed and slid his left Python into its holster. "I did warn you, didn't I, runt?" he asked the prone form.

Six Family members burst onto the scene, Rikki-Tikki-Tavi in the lead, his katana drawn and ready. He was accompanied by Yama and Teucer, his Triad brothers, and Plato, Jenny, and Joshua.

"Everything all right?" Rikki inquired, scanning the clearing.

"Everything's under control," Hickok replied.

"What was that shooting we just heard?" Plato asked him.

Hickok pointed at Ferret. "The runt there had a vitamin deficiency."

Plato's eyebrows knitted. "He had a what?"

"A vitamin deficiency," Hickok reiterated. "Said he needed more lead in his system."

Jenny was already at Blade's side, cradling his head in her lap. "He's been hurt!" she exclaimed.

"Don't fret none," Hickok advised her. "That blue monstrosity hit him on the head. The thing was lucky it didn't break its hand."

"This isn't funny!" Jenny retorted. "We must get them both to the infirmary right now!"

Plato nodded and motioned at Rikki.

Rikki replaced his katana in its scabbard and, with the assistance of Yama, lifted Blade from the ground, Rikki carrying him by the ankles and Yama carefully supporting his broad shoulders. Teucer and Joshua did likewise with Gremlin.

"Don't trip!" Jenny cautioned them as they departed. She walked ahead, guiding them around obstacles.

Plato watched them go, then faced Hickok. "Did they almost get you too?" He nodded at the two bodies.

"Nope," Hickok said. "It was a piece of cake. Despite their looks, they weren't much more than a couple of amateurs."

"It appears you shot the big one to pieces," Plato commented, mentally counting the five holes in the blue creature.

"I can't abide it when someone drools in public," Hickok remarked. "Shows a pitiful lack of etiquette."

"What about the hairy one?" Plato asked, moving toward it.

"It depends on my aim," Hickok said. He crossed to the furball, knelt, and felt its left wrist for a pulse. At first he couldn't locate any, but then he detected a faint, rhythmic beating. "This one is still kicking."

"You didn't kill him as well?" Plato inquired, sounding surprised.

"Nope. I kind of liked the cute way he twitched his little nose," Hickok answered, grinning.

Plato searched for wounds, but none were visible. He looked at Hickok. "How?"

Hickok reached over and tapped the metal collar the creature wore.

"I don't under . . ." Plato began, then he saw it. Hickok's shot had struck a rectangular component in the middle of the throat. The skin under the collar was broken, but the rectangular part had absorbed the impact of the slug and prevented it from penetrating the neck. "We must get this one to the infirmary. If he lives, he may provide valuable information concerning the Doktor and the Civilized Zone."

"My thoughts exactly," Hickok confirmed.

Plato chuckled. Despite Hickok's reputation as a rash hothead, he frequently displayed logical reasoning of a superior caliber.

Superior caliber?

Plato grinned at his own pun.

"What's so funny?" Hickok asked. He drew his right Colt and began replacing the empty shells.

"Oh, nothing," Plato replied. "If you will lend a hand, we can transport this creature to the infirmary."

Hickok stared at Plato while continuing his reloading. "Just hold your horses, old-timer. I have something to say to you, and it's best I say it now, with no one else around."

"Oh? Why is that?"

"Because you're going to be one mighty ticked hombre after I tell you," Hickok predicted.

Plato smiled. "Well, go ahead, then. Tick me."

"I am going to leave the Home tomorrow," Hickok declared.

Plato promptly frowned. "Again? I wasn't very pleased with you the last time you abruptly departed. . . ."

"I had to go after Shane," Hickok interrupted. He slid his right Colt back into its holster and drew his left.

"Granted, you did save Shane," Plato conceded. "But you also promised me afterwards you wouldn't leave the Home again without informing me first."

"Which is what I'm doing right now," Hickok pointed out.

"I don't like it," Plato said, sighing. "It's Geronimo, isn't it?"

Hickok's eyes narrowed, reflecting his concern. "My pard's been gone way too long. He said he'd be back in a week or so. I think he's in trouble and I'm going to go find him."

"How?" Plato demanded. "You don't have the slightest idea where he is."

"I'll get the Empaths to home in on him," Hickok stated, referring to the Family Empaths, six individuals with exceptional psychic abilities. Several times in the past they had been able to locate others, overdue hunters or lost Family members, at great distances utilizing their psychic capabilities.

"I should never have given my permission for Geronimo to leave the Home," Plato said, "and I'd prefer it if you remained here for the time being. We can't be certain the Watchers won't attack the Home. More of these things might be sent against us. The Family can't spare another Warrior."

"I realize that," Hickok admitted, his left Python reloaded and replaced. "But I took an oath to my fellow Warriors, to my Triad, as well as to the Family and the Home. I won't rest until I know what's happened to him."

Plato absently bit his lower lip and shook his head. "I know better than to attempt to persuade you from doing something you have your mind set on, so I won't waste my breath. But I will make a request of you."

"Shoot."

"Will you at least wait one week?"

"I don't know. . . ." Hickok said reluctantly.

"Just one week," Plato stressed. "If Geronimo hasn't returned in that length of time, you'll have my blessing to go and seek him."

"Why a week?" Hickok inquired.

"I'm gambling," Plato revealed. "I'm hoping Geronimo will return to us within a week and your departure won't be necessary."

"I reckon another week won't much matter," Hickok said. "If my pard is already dead, there's nothing much I can do about it except find the one responsible and plant a bullet between his eyes."

Plato studied Hickok. "Do you mind if I ask you a question?"

"Shoot."

"You're one of the best Warriors the Family has," Plato stated slowly. "You've killed more opponents in the line of duty than all the other Warriors combined, with the notable exception of your peers in Alpha Triad. . . ."

"Yeah? So?" Hickok interjected.

Plato stared into Hickok's eyes. "Don't you ever get tired of all the killing? I honestly can't comprehend how you do it. I could never function as a Warrior. Terminating others would bother me too much. Doesn't it ever bother you?''

A shadow seemed to flit across Hickok's face. ''I don't give the killing much thought. I know all men and women are my brothers and sisters, spiritually speaking. I know if we have a flicker of faith, as Joshua keeps reminding us, we'll pass on to the mansions on high. That goes for the ones I blow away too. I don't get upset about it because I'm not a cold-blooded murderer. I don't go around shooting folks for the fun of it. Usually, it's the enemy or me in a fight, and I don't stop to reflect on whether it's a sin or not. I mean, look at the Bible. We were taught in school about the great warriors in the Old Testament, about Samson and David and the rest. They killed and they were considered highly spiritual. Besides, after it's all done with, what's the use of getting upset? Killing a bad man doesn't get me any more disturbed than, say, killing a rabid dog or a mutate. That make any sense to you?''

''It makes perfect sense,'' Plato admitted.

''Good.'' Hickok nodded. ''The philosophy is far from original. I first came across it in a book in the Family library, a book on the life and times of James Butler Hickok, or Wild Bill Hickok as he was commonly known in his day and time. He once told a newspaper reporter pretty much the same thing. You know how much I admire the man. Heck, I even adopted his name at my Naming.''

''Yes, I know, Nathan,'' Plato said. He glanced at the hairy creature. ''Well, if you will assist me, we'll carry this one to the infirmary and have the Healers examine him.''

''Don't strain yourself,'' Hickok suggested. ''This critter ain't that heavy.'' So saying, he placed his hands under the runt's arms and heaved, lifting the thing up high enough to drape the body over his left shoulder.

"Are you positive you can manage?" Plato asked.

"Piece of cake," Hickok responded, rising.

They started back.

"You'll be happy to know Sherry appears to be fine," Plato mentioned. "She was standing when we reached her, rubbing a bruise on her temple. I ordered her to the infirmary." He paused. "She told us you'd already been by and were after the creatures abducting Blade and Gremlin."

"I was the first one on the scene," Hickok explained. "She was just coming around. Didn't seem like she was hurt very bad. She told me what had happened and I took off after them."

"You should have awaited assistance," Plato quibbled.

"Wasn't time," Hickok countered.

They covered several hundred yards in silence.

"I hope Gremlin's wounds aren't severe," Plato commented as they rounded a boulder.

"You partial to that critter?" Hickok questioned him.

"That critter, as you refer to him," Plato replied, "has been of incalculable benefit in our research into the premature senility. Gremlin is quite knowledge-able in chemistry."

"You're kidding," Hickok said.

"I do not jest," Plato retorted stiffly. "Gremlin evidently spent many hours aiding the Doktor in his laboratory at Cheyenne. With his aid, we may be able to isolate the cause of the senility soon. If we are successful, the next step will be to develop a cure."

Hickok, knowing Plato was one of the half-dozen

or so Elders afflicted with the premature senility, stared at the Family Leader. "How you holding up, old-timer?"

Plato grinned. "Quite well, thank you, Nathan. My arthritis is worsening week by week, but except for unaccountable aches and pains at infrequent intervals, I'm relatively fine."

"We'll find a cure," Hickok predicted.

"We must," Plato stated. "The fate of our Family hangs in the balance."

"Speaking of our fate," Hickok remarked, "what are we going to do about the Doktor and his goons."

"What can we do?" Plato rejoined. "We're vastly outnumbered and outgunned. There are thousands upon thousands of soldiers in the Army of Samuel. The Doktor, according to Gremlin, has around fifteen hundred creatures in his Genetic Research Division. If they should decide to assault the Home en masse we wouldn't stand a chance."

"We've licked them every time so far," Hickok noted.

"True," Plato conceded, "but in our encounters with the Watchers and the genetic deviates we've been extremely lucky. Either we've had the element of surprise on our side, or they simply were not prepared to deal with the proficiency of our Warriors."

"You mean," Hickok elucidated, "they weren't expecting us to be as good as we are."

"Exactly. But our good fortune can't hold forever."

"So what are we going to do?" Hickok queried. "Wait for them to attack us in force?"

"What else can we do?" Plato inquired. "Our vastly inferior number precludes any major offensive move on our part."

"We can't just sit on our butts!" Hickok mumbled.

"I'm open to any viable suggestions," Plato said.

"What about sending one of the Warriors to assassinate the Doktor and Samuel?" Hickok recommended.

Plato gazed at the gunman, half expecting he was joking. "Are you serious?"

"Of course."

"Intriguing concept," Plato acknowledged, "but hardly feasible. Even if we could actualize the logistics, the results aren't necessarily guaranteed to achieve our goals."

"Could you say that again in English?" Hickok wryly requested.

"Even if we did kill Samuel and the Doktor," Plato elaborated, "it wouldn't insure our safety."

"Why not?"

"For all we know, someone else would come along and fill their shoes. We'd be right back where we started." Plato shook his head, his gray beard swaying. "No, that isn't the answer."

"What is?"

"We must amass sufficient strength to effectively repel the Watchers or successfully invade the Civilized Zone."

Hickok chuckled. "Now you're talkin' my kind of language!"

They were abreast of the cabins. A dozen or so Family members were clustered nearby, watching. "Is everything under control?" one of them called to Plato.

The Family Leader waved and smiled. "Everything is fine! Our Warriors have the situation well in hand. Resume your activities."

They walked a little further.

"So how are we going to 'amass sufficient strength'?" Hickok asked, grinning, stressing the last three words.

"We may engage in a treaty with the Moles," Plato said.

Hickok chuckled. He'd encountered the Moles while Blade and Geronimo were in Kalispell, Montana. The Moles lived in a huge earthen mound approximately one hundred miles southeast of the Home. They survived by raiding other communities and stealing whatever they required. He'd offered a pact to the head of the Moles before he'd departed their company. "If you're waiting to hear from them," Hickok said to Plato, "I wouldn't hold my breath!"

"What about the people in the Twin Cities?" Plato asked.

Hickok stopped and scowled at Plato. "What about them?" he demanded, annoyed. "Blade, Geronimo, and I were there months ago. We told those people we'd return in thirty days and look at how long it's been! They wanted to join us, to come here and live, if not in the Home then one of the abandoned towns nearby. They wanted to be our friends and we deserted them."

"We haven't deserted anyone," Plato disagreed. "We couldn't help it if other, more important matters arose. May I remind you we finally retrieved the scientific and medical equipment and supplies we needed in Kalispell?"

"So you're going to allow Alpha Triad to return to the Twin Cities?" Hickok pressed him.

"Yes," Plato stated. "As soon as Geronimo re . . ."

"That could be weeks!" Hickok snapped. "Who knows how long it will take me to find him if he isn't back here in a week?''

"It can't be helped," Plato said. "Can it?"

"No. I reckon not," Hickok ruefully concluded.

"In the meantime," Plato went on, "I have another plan concerning the Doktor and Samuel II."

"Oh?" Hickok's interest piqued. "Like what? I thought my assassin idea was a good one."

"I was thinking more along the lines of a spy," Plato revealed.

"A spy?"

"Affirmative."

"What exactly did you have in mind?" Hickok prodded him.

Plato thoughtfully stroked his beard as they moved toward the Blocks. "I'm considering sending one of the Warriors to infiltrate the Civilized Zone. It wouldn't be an easy task, granted, and would be fraught with risk, but if it's successful, if the Warrior manages to return to the Home, we could learn invaluable information concerning their strengths and, of critical significance, their exploitable weaknesses."

"Just anywhere in the Civilized Zone?" Hickok inquired. "Or do you have a definite destination in mind?"

Plato grinned. "Very astute, Nathan. Yes, I am thinking of sending the Warrior to infiltrate the Citadel at Cheyenne, Wyoming, using one of the vehicles confiscated from the Watcher patrol. Which is another reason I had them ambushed."

Hickok whistled. "That's quite a challenge, Plato. I volunteer."

"Thank you, but that won't be necessary."

"Why?"

"Because this mission is so dangerous, because the odds against its successful completion are so overwhelming, I've decided to have the Warriors draw lots. Short straw wins. Or loses, depending on how you look at it." Plato grimaced, bothered by a painful twinge in his left thigh.

"Sounds fair to me," Hickok commented. "When does this spy mission get off the ground?"

"If we used one of the jeeps we've confiscated from the Watchers, we could send our spy out at the same time Alpha Triad leaves for the Twin Cities," Plato proposed.

"That would leave the Home mighty short of Warriors," the gunman pointed out.

"Not if we select the new Triad and the new Warrior for Gamma," Plato noted.

"As usual, old-timer," Hickok complimented him, "you have this thought out to the smallest detail."

"When you are responsible for the lives of so many people," Plato stated, "you realize how crucial every detail is."

"So when will we hold the swearing in for the new Warriors?" Hickok questioned him.

"The induction ceremonies will be held as soon as Blade makes his final recommendations," Plato replied. "The Elders will review Blade's suggestions and scrutinize the candidates. If Blade makes his selections within the next couple of days, as expected, we'll hold the induction ceremonies within the week."

"Fine by me," Hickok commented, wondering if Sherry would be one of the final candidates.

They were in the center of the cleared space between the Blocks, and they finished their trip to C Block in quite reflection.

Many Family members were gathered in front of the infirmary, engaged in animated conversation, discussing the fight and its implications. A chorus of voices was raised as Plato and Hickok approached.

"What's going on, Plato?"

"What happened to Blade?"

"What was all the shooting about?"

"What's that thing Hickok's carrying?"

Plato stopped and raised his arms aloft.

The crowd grew quiet.

"Brothers and sisters! We have been subjected to another attack from the Civilized Zone. None of the Family has been killed, although several have been injured. In one hour, after I have conversed with those involved and consulted with the Healers concerning the extent of their injuries, we will hold a Family conclave on the commons. Kindly save your questions until then." Plato smiled at them and led Hickok into the infirmary.

Of the four Healers, only three were on duty. Jenny was absent, and there was no sign of Blade. Gremlin was lying on one of the dozen cots in the room, unconscious. Two of the Healers were tending to his wounds. In a far corner of the spacious chamber, on two cots in the corner, were the two captured Watchers guarded by Spartacus and Seiko.

"Here's a present for you, Nightingale," Hickok said to a young woman.

Nightingale glanced up from her treatment of Gremlin and mopped at her sweaty brow with the back of her left hand. Her brown hair was disheveled and her clothes in disarray. "Thanks. Just what we needed! Leave it to you!"

"Any time," Hickok quipped. "Say, did anyone ever tell you you're a mess first thing in the morning?"

If eyes could freeze objects at a glance, Hickok

would have been frozen solid. "You can deposit whatever you're carrying on that cot," Nightingale said icily, pointing at the specified cot.

"Touchy, touchy, touchy!" Hickok playfully commented as he deposited the furball on the designated cot.

"Where is Blade?" Plato asked Nightingale.

She indicated the rear door to the Block. "He wasn't badly hurt. Jenny dragged him outside. Said she had to talk to him."

"Where's Sherry?" Hickok inquired.

"She sustained a bruised temple, was all," Nightingale replied. "She took off out of here on the run. Something about getting back to her man. Didn't you see her on the way here?"

"Nope." Hickok shook his head.

"She may have passed us in the trees," Plato reasoned. "I'm sure she'll be here shortly."

Nightingale was carefully probing Gremlin's legs.

"How extensive are his injuries?" Plato queried her.

"He's taken quite a beating," she answered, "but nothing serious except for his legs."

"His legs?"

"I think the right leg is broken," Nightingale said. "I'm still not sure about the left."

"Continue your examination," Plato directed. "I'll be outside. Inform me when your prognosis is complete." He departed.

"Did you say Blade was out back?" Hickok absently asked.

"Last I knew," Nightingale confirmed, then devoted her full attention to her ministrations.

Hickok ambled toward the rear door.

"What was that thing you just brought in?"

Spartacus wanted to know as the gunman passed them.

"The tooth fairy," Hickok cracked. "Keep your eyes on it in case it comes around. It's one of the Doktor's G.R.D.'s. If it gives you any grief, pard, blow it in two."

Spartacus drew his broadsword, grinning. "Is it okay if I slice it in half instead?"

"Just make sure it doesn't escape or harm the Healers," Hickok ordered.

"If it gives us any trouble," Spartacus promised, "I'll carve it into a nice pair of fur slippers for my girlfriend."

The two soldiers glared at the gunfighter as he strode by.

Hickok ignored them and exited the Block, looking for Blade. He heard voices coming from his right, from behind a large tree. He was about to interrupt, to call Blade's name, when the words being spoken sunk in.

". . . won't put it off any longer!" Jenny was saying. "You gave me your word and I intend to hold you to it!"

"But now's not the right time to get married," Blade protested.

"What are you waiting for?" Jenny bitterly rejoined. "Peace on earth and good will among men? Be realistic! You gave me your word we would marry after you returned from the Twin Cities. Then the run to Kalispell came up. Odds are Plato will be sending you somewhere else before too long. I'm tired of waiting, honey!"

"Wouldn't it be best to wait until we could settle down without . . ." Blade began.

"And when will that be?" Jenny demanded,

cutting him off. "We both know Plato will be sending Alpha Triad on more trips." She paused, and Hickok heard her sigh. "Even if you did settle down, there's no guarantee we'd be left alone to enjoy ourselves in peace and quiet. Look at how many times the Home has been attacked in the past several months! We're not even safe here!"

Jenny's voice broke, and she began crying.

Hickok started to back away, unwilling to intrude on their private discussion. He was almost to the door when her next sentence stopped him in his tracks.

"Didn't you learn anything from Joan's death?" Jenny inquired, sniffling. "Can't you appreciate how important every moment we spend together is? We must love and share while the Spirit provides the opportunity. Who knows when it will come to an end? Look at this morning! You could have been killed! And what about poor Nathan?"

"What about him?" Blade asked, his surging emotion making his tone husky, as if his throat was constricted.

"Joan and Nathan went together for a long time before she was killed," Jenny said. "Don't you think Nathan wonders how much more they could have shared if only they'd married? Don't you think he kicks himself for being so aloof at times, for not taking advantage of her affection while she was still alive and with us? Do you want that to happen to me? To you? To us?"

It seemed like Blade took forever to answer. "No, I don't want that to happen to us. You've made your point." He hesitated. "Will you bind with me in, say, four days? That would give us enough time for the preparations. I want to do this right."

Jenny's shriek of delight was probably heard for miles.

Hickok backed through the doorway, his thoughts troubled.

One of the Watchers, the youngest, the one Yama had smashed on the head with his Wilkinson, saw the gunman enter and snickered, taunting this Warrior as he had the others. Ridiculing his captors was his favorite diversion.

"Hey! What's the matter with you?" the Watcher baited the blond gunfighter. "You look like you've just seen a ghost! Can't you . . ."

The soldier's statement abruptly terminated, his mouth gaping open and his eyes wide in fright, as the barrel of a Colt Python flashed to within an inch of his nose.

The other Watcher, Lieutenant Putnam, his nose heavily bandaged, recoiled, terrified, trying to sink into the cot he was lying on. He knew the identity of this buckskin-clad Warrior with the pearl-handled Colts, and he'd heard stories of how very deadly the gunfighter could be.

Hickok slowly cocked the hammer on his Colt.

Spartacus and Seiko, both surprised by Hickok's reaction, glanced at one another. They were startled by the livid expression on Hickok's face.

"I . . . I . . . I . . . didn't mean anything . . ." the young Watcher managed to babble.

"Hickok!" Spartacus spoke up. "What's the matter? He isn't worth it. Besides, Plato wants them alive for interrogation."

"You're absolutely right, pard," Hickok said softly. "This vulture isn't worth it, isn't worth the grass she walked on. But she's gone, isn't she? Why? Because mangy vermin like this won't leave us alone to live in peace." He paused, his blue eyes dancing with rage. "If Plato needs this one, I reckon I'll let him live, for now."

The gunman holstered the Python and stormed from C Block.

Breathing a sigh of relief, the young Watcher looked at Putnam. "Did you see that? What was eating him? These so-called Warriors sure can't . . ."

His sentence was suddenly cut short, again, by the point of a broadsword appearing where the Python barrel had been just moments before.

Spartacus leaned over and glared at the soldier. "You know, friend, you have a big mouth. Around here we don't like big mouths. In fact, if someone's mouth is too big, if they don't know when to keep it shut, we solve the problem by nipping it in the bud, so to speak. We slice their tongue off. Keeping that in mind, is there anything else you'd like to say today?"

The Watcher vigorously shook his head.

"Didn't think so," Spartacus said, replacing his broadsword. He glanced at Seiko. "What *did* get into him?" he asked.

Seiko, his Oriental features furrowed in contemplation, shrugged.

"Now don't you get inscrutable on me," Spartacus stated. "You were closer to the doorway. Did you hear anything? What got him so upset?"

Seiko stared at the front door, the corners of his mouth turning downward. 'Joan," he answered simply.

Spartacus nodded, understanding completely. "Poor guy. He needs something to take his mind off of her," he commented.

Outside, Hickok was twenty yards from C Block, stalking across the compound, oblivious to the questioning stares of other Family members. His mind whirled, recalling the softness of Joan's lips on his, remembering that horrible instant when she was killed by the Trolls, and reeling from the inadvertent rebuke of Jenny's words to Blade.

Dear Spirit!

How true!

How very true!

He had been aloof, telling Joan he was reluctant to "rush" into anything either of them would regret. And now look at him! His only regret was that Joan was gone.

"Hickok!"

He heard her call his name and turned.

Sherry rushed into his arms and hugged him with all of her strength. Her warm breath was intoxicating as she smothered him with kisses. "Thank God you're alive!" she finally exclaimed. "I was so worried! I was afraid they'd kill you!"

Hickok, his face flushed, held her in his arms. "I felt the same way when I saw you lying on the ground. I thought I'd lost you too."

Her lips lightly touched his own. "Don't worry, lover. I'm sticking around for the duration."

"I hope so," he confided, "because we're getting married in four days and I'd look pretty stupid taking the vows by myself."

Sherry, utterly flabbergasted, stepped back. "We're getting what?"

"Married," Hickok reiterated. "Some of us refer to it as a binding, to bind together in an eternal union. If we . . ."

She gripped him so hard her nails bit into his arms. "You're really serious?"

"Never been more serious about anything in my entire life," he solemnly affirmed.

"But this is so sudden, so unexpected," Sherry noted. "Are you sure?"

"How many times do I have to tell you?" Hickok asked. "Yes, I'm sure."

"I just don't want you to do something you'll regret later," she remarked.

"And why would I do that?"

"Because I might be getting you on the rebound," Sherry observed.

Hickok smiled. "The only thing I'm on the rebound from is stupidity. I don't intend to make the same major mistake twice in one lifetime."

"I don't understand," she admitted.

He kissed her on the right cheek. "The only thing you need to understand is that I care for you. We've been together . . . what? . . . three, four weeks now. If you think you need more time to settle how you feel in your own mind . . ."

"No! I know how I feel," she assured him. "You already know I love you."

"Well, then," Hickok said impatiently, "will you marry me or not?"

Sherry threw her arms around his neck. "Oh, I will! I will! You big dummy! Do you think I'd pass up a chance like this? Of course," she added, "I will feel somewhat guilty."

"Guilty? Why?"

"For taking advantage of you while you're obviously suffering from temporary insanity!" She laughed heartily and kissed him passionately.

"This could get to be a habit," he declared when they came up for air.

"The best habit I've ever found!" Sherry said, giggling. "Hey! Do you realize you've just kissed me in public? In public! I thought you were the one who never makes a display of his affections?"

"Every rule has exceptions," he retorted gruffly, "and this is a special case."

"I'm glad," she sighed.

"But I want you to know," Hickok stated gravely, "that I'm not making any promises. I'm not going to say we'll have a life of ease, because we probably won't. And I won't give up being a Warrior, no matter what. And just because we're gettin' hitched doesn't mean you have a license to nag. Another thing. If I say I don't like a particular food, then I don't want to see it on my dinner table. And if . . ."

Sherry quickly kissed him, aborting the diatribe.

"Perfect timing," someone else remarked, "or he'd have gone on like that until nightfall." The speaker, a woman, chuckled.

Hickok and Sherry turned and found Blade and Jenny only a yard behind them.

"Did we catch the gist of that?" Jenny inquired. "Did he just propose to you?"

"Yes!" Sherry exclaimed. "Do you believe it?"

Jenny looked fondly up at Blade. "Oh, I believe it, all right. Marriage proposals seem to be contagious today."

Blade twisted, thoughtfully staring at C Block for a moment. Then he faced Hickok and nodded. "These women must have drugged our food yesterday. For all we know, the Family could have a marriage epidemic on its hands."

"So when are you two tying the knot?" Sherry questioned Jenny.

"In four days," Jenny replied.

"What?" Sherry gasped, surprised. "Hickok said we're getting married in four days too!"

"Small world, isn't it?" Blade wryly mentioned.

"I know!" Jenny proposed. "Let's have a double

ceremony!''

"Oh! I'd love that!" Sherry said enthusiastically.

Blade moved closer to Hickok and lowered his voice as Jenny and Sherry began discussing the wedding preparations. "Congratulations," he said softly.

"Thanks, pard," Hickok responded in a quiet tone.

"Say, Nathan," Blade commented, curious, "you weren't behind C Block just a bit ago, were you?"

Hickok nodded, then hastily addressed the women. "Say, ladies. I've been thinking."

"About what?" Sherry asked.

"About our getting hitched. It wouldn't seem right without Geronimo here to be our best man." Hickok paused. "Do you reckon we could postpone the ceremony until he gets back?"

Sherry and Jenny glanced at one another, then at Hickok, smiling sweetly.

"*No!*" was their unanimous answer, delivered in forceful unison.

"Just thought I'd ask," Hickok said sheepishly.

"Look at this," Blade interjected. "We haven't even said 'I do' yet, and already they're bossing us around."

Hickok stretched and winked at Blade. "You know, this tends to remind me of something my grandfather used to say a lot."

"What was that?" Blade inquired.

"I recollect my grandpaw telling me that when he first got married," Hickok reminisced with a twinkle in his blue eyes, "he loved my grandmother so much he could have eaten her alive."

Sherry and Jenny, all attention, waited for him to finish.

And waited.

"Yeah? So?" Sherry finally goaded him.

"So in his later years," Hickok said, completing the story, "he used to say he was sorry he didn't!"

# 19

He struggled against the darkness, his own mind balking at the prospect of returning to full consciousness. His head had sustained two severe blows, and the pain was intense, his temples throbbing. He attempted to recall his final memory before he blacked out, but it was indistinct and shrouded in a haze. Slowly, laboriously, his remembrance returned. There was a jumbled picture of a large hole in the ground, of a crater of some sort, of his tomahawk clenched in his right hand, and of . . . of . . . what?

Like a massive tidal wave pounding onto a beach, the final moments before he was rendered unconscious washed over his mind.

Ants!

The ants!

Geronimo came instantly awake, sitting up, perspiration coating his body, his eyes widespread.

The ants!

Where were the ants?

"He's revived," a man's voice commented.

"About damn time!" griped another.

Geronimo gazed around him, still in a daze, uncertain of the reality of what he was observing.

Ten members of the Legion patrol were gathered

nearby, their mounts within a hand's reach for a quick getaway, should the need arise. Kilrane, Cynthia, and Hamlin were also there, Kilrane and Hamlin only feet away, watching him intently, and Cynthia by his side, her left hand on his shoulder.

"How are you feeling?" she asked him.

"Have you ever heard of *deja vu*?" Geronimo replied.

"No," Cynthia said, "can't say as I have. What is it? Sounds like a fancy food."

"Are you up to traveling?" Kilrane interjected.

"I think so," Geronimo answered. "How long was I out?"

"Hours," Hamlin informed him. "It's a little past noon."

Geronimo squinted up at the sun, confirming the hour.

"We have a spare horse for you," Kilrane mentioned. "We've got to get out of here, and fast. We must put as much distance between us and the Dead Zone as we can before nightfall."

"We're still in the Dead Zone?" Geronimo queried, gingerly touching the side of his head with his right hand. There wasn't any sign of blood. It only felt as if his head were split open.

"About a mile from the tunnel we were in," Kilrane elaborated. "Behind a small hill, out of sight of the ants. Very few have emerged from the pit in the past few hours. Apparently you were right about them. They don't like the daylight all that much."

Geronimo spotted his tomahawk on the ground at his feet. He groped under his arm and found the Arminius in its shoulder holster.

"You were still holding that tomahawk when we pulled you from the ant crater," Kilrane remarked. "You wouldn't let go of it for anything."

"How did I escape from that pit?" Geronimo questioned Kilrane.

"We drug you out," Kilrane explained. "I lassoed you from the rim and we all pitched in to pull you to the top. Surprisingly, the ants didn't pursue us. They were occupied with the bodies of the ones you killed, and they left us alone long enough to hightail it out of there."

Geronimo, surveying his surroundings, saw the Palomino behind Kilrane. "Wait a minute! What's going on?" He stared at the Legion captain. "I thought you said you fell into the pit, the same as we did. But your horse is still here."

"I never said that I fell," Kilrane responded. "I saw Cynthia and you go over the edge, reined in, looked down, and saw that ant attacking you. I just had time to yell directions to Hamlin, and then I jumped in to lend you a hand."

"You jumped in? You deliberately leaped in after us?" Geronimo slowly stood, Cynthia rising with him, her concerned eyes never leaving his face.

"I would have done the same for any of my men," Kilrane stated nonchalantly, "or for someone I'd come to consider a friend."

Geronimo placed his right hand on Kilrane's left shoulder and squeezed. "Thank you."

"Yeah," Hamlin was saying, "he told us to wait as close as we could and watch for a signal. We were keeping binoculars trained on that big hole when Kilrane and the woman came out. Naturally, we rode down to help them, and you know the rest."

"Is this all that's left of your patrol?" Geronimo queried, sweeping his left hand in a circle.

Kilrane frowned and nodded. "Don't know what happened to the rest. Maybe they became lost in the dust storm. Maybe the ants got them. No way of knowing. I do know I intend to save the rest of our mangy hides, so we'd better make tracks and vamoose.''

The other riders took that as their cue and promptly mounted.

Cynthia grabbed the reins of a brown stallion. "Here. We can use this one.''

Kilrane swept up onto his Palomino. "We must be out of the Dead Zone by evening,'' he emphasized. "Are you up to some hard riding?''

"We'll soon know,'' Geronimo predicted as he climbed on the stallion. He extended his right arm and Cynthia nimbly deposited herself behind him.

"Give a yell if you get dizzy,'' Kilrane advised. He raised his right arm and motioned for the group to move out.

The patrol rode up the hill and stopped.

The immediate vicinity of the ant tunnel was devoid of life. For the moment, anyway.

"Let's ride!'' Kilrane barked.

They galloped down the hill and onto the plain beyond, bearing to the southwest, casting apprehensive glances over their shoulders, dreading the appearance of those stick-like appendages at the rim of the cavity.

Cynthia placed her lips next to Geronimo's right ear. "It's the hottest part of the day, long about now. If those ants really don't like sunlight or heat we shouldn't see any of them.''

"We hope,'' Geronimo said. He found it difficult to concentrate properly, the motion of his steed causing extreme discomfort in his head. He gritted his teeth and bore the torture, knowing it was unlikely he would survive another night in the Dead Zone. With the descent of darkness, the insects would emerge in force and scour the countryside for food. He didn't intend to become the entree at an ant picnic!

The trip seemed interminable.

The sun beat down mercilessly, draining Geronimo's weary body of what little moisture it had retained. The bouncing of the brown stallion sparked periodic twinges in his head, stabbing, lancing aches and intermittent spasms. Geronimo wondered, again, if he were suffering from a concussion.

The sun climbed higher in the sky.

Geronimo became aware of Cynthia's arms clasped around his waist, of her breath on the back of his neck. He recalled her fiery embrace the night before, and realized he wanted to spend more intimate interludes with her. But how? He contemplated the possibilities and narrowed them down to two. First, he could remain with her, join her on the family farm, or establish a farm or ranch of his own. The prospect was singularly unappealing. He knew working with the soil was exalted labor, but the lifestyle wasn't for him for the same reason he'd declined becoming a Tiller at the Home; watching corn grow, in terms of sheer excitement, had to rate a minus twenty on a scale of one to ten. He wasn't about to resign his status as a Warrior, at least not yet. That left the second scenario. He could take Cynthia with him to the Home. But how would she feel about the idea? Would she be willing to leave her family, give up the existence she knew for a total unknown? Abandon her loved ones for a man she'd only met recently?

"What are you thinking about?" she said in his ear.

"You," he admitted.

"What about me?"

"You sure you want to hear it?"

She laughed. "I don't have anything else to do at the moment."

Geronimo took a deep breath, gathering his courage. "Okay. But you may not like what you're going to hear."

"Why don't you let me be the judge of that?" Cynthia suggested.

Here goes nothing! Geronimo mentally braced himself for rejection and detailed his proposal.

# 20

Plato found Blade and Hickok lounging near the SEAL, sitting in the grass by the transport, relaxing.

"Ahh! Here you are," the Family Leader declared as he walked around the vehicle and saw them. "I've been seeking you."

Hickok looked up. "We're trying to avoid our ladies for a spell," he revealed. "They're driving us nuts with the preparations for our double ceremony."

"I believe I saw them over by A Block," Plato said. "They were looking for you both. Should I go inform them of your location?"

"No!" Hickok almost yelled. "They haven't left us alone since we agreed to tie the knot. Do this. Do that. Make sure this is done before the wedding. If I'd known what I was getting into before I asked her, I might never have asked her!"

Plato smiled. "This is a revelation."

"What do you mean?" Hickok asked, perplexed.

"Perhaps we should hold another Naming for you," Plato suggested, "and change your name from Hickok to Henpecked."

Blade laughed. "Two points for Plato."

"Blade was just telling me about what Star may

have found," Hickok said, adroitly changing the subject. "Why were you looking for us?"

"To show you this," Plato replied, holding up a white sheet of paper.

"What's that?" Blade inquired.

"Read it to Nathan," Plato directed.

Blade took the paper and read the first word. "Hello." He stopped and glanced at his mentor. "You've deciphered the cryptic message Carpenter placed in the Operations Manual?"

"Read on," Plato recommended. "It's self-explanatory."

"Hello," Blade said, resuming his reading. "I must apologize for the devious method I've employed in passing on this information, but the security of my cherished Family is at stake. If someone with political aspirations, a power monger, were to learn of the existence of the SEAL, let alone of its sophisticated armaments, the temptation to exploit this knowledge for personal gain might be too great to resist."

"It's a good thing Napoleon didn't know the buggy is armed," Hickok interrupted, referring to a recently deceased Warrior responsible for the only rebellion in the one-hundred-year history of the Family.

Blade nodded and continued. "I have decided to convey the pertinent details concerning the SEAL by word of mouth, from one Leader to another, from myself to my handpicked successor, and so on down the line. Yes, I recognize the high risk involved, but a safety margin must be maintained."

"So somewhere along the line," Hickok interrupted again, "one of the Leaders told his successor about the transport, but failed to pass on the information about the armanent instructions hidden in the Operations Manual."

"Evidently," Plato agreed. "Will you permit him to finish?"

"What's stopping him?" Hickok countered.

Blade smiled at Plato and went on. "The Operations Manual contains the essential details of the transport's normal operating procedures, but I've purposely excluded the armaments from the Manual. Knowledge of the weaponry should be restricted to the Leader and a few trusted followers."

"This certainly corresponds with the first letter we found," Plato innocently commented. "The one we discovered inside the vehicle after we uncovered the secret chamber."

"Shhhhh!" Hickok placed a finger over his lips. "Can't you see the man is trying to read?"

Blade hurried before Hickok and Plato started up again. "I elected to incorporate certain modifications into the transport, additions intended to preserve the occupants and enable them to defend themselves. There are four toggle switches on the dashboard. These control the armaments. My technicians assure me these weapons are effective, durable, and most importantly, they have a minimal malfunction ratio. The toggle switches are labeled according to their respective function. M. S. F. And an R. The M stands for Machine Guns. Two fifty-caliber machine guns are hidden in recessed compartments directly underneath each front head-light. If the M switch is flicked, these machine guns will be uncovered. A small metal plate will slide upward and the guns will automatically fire. The S stands for Surface-to-Air Missile. It's amazing what you can obtain on the black market nowadays. A miniature missile is mounted in the roof above the driver's seat. If the S toggle is activated, a panel in the roof moves aside and the missile is fired. These particular missiles are called Stingers. They are heat seeking and can down an aircraft at a range of ten miles."

"Incredible!" Hickok declared.

"Sure is," Blade agreed, and returned his attention to the paper. "The F is short for Flame-thrower. This item is positioned at the front of the transport, hidden behind the front fender, in the exact center. If the switch is moved, a portion of the fender will lower and the nozzle of the flamethrower will extend six inches and engage. My experts inform me this is an Army Surplus model, with a range of twenty feet. They also say the SEAL should be immobile when the flamethrower is activated, or the risk of an explosion is dramatically increased."

"I'll never sleep inside there again," Hickok quipped.

"The last toggle switch," Blade was saying, "is marked with an R for Rocket Launcher. The rocket is secreted in the middle of the front grill and will instantly be launched if the toggle switch is thrown. Use extreme caution when near the dashboard; one mistake could have tragic consequences. Concerning ammunition for the machine guns, additional missiles, liquid for the flamethrower, and a con-siderable supply of rockets, you will find them hidden in the same chamber in which you found the SEAL. Examine the north wall. At the base of the wall, in the lower left corner, you will locate a camouflaged latch. Pull on this latch and the wall panel should slide to the right, revealing the Armament Room, as I refer to it. May the Spirit bless all your endeavors. I must hasten this Manual to the underground chamber and cover the chamber before any of my loved ones arrive at this survival site. All my love. Kurt Carpenter."

"This contraption is armed to the teeth," Hickok noted. "Say, Plato, do you suppose we could use the flamethrower at the next Family barbecue? Roasting the deer would be a piece of cake!"

# 21

"How much farther?" Cynthia asked him.

Geronimo shrugged. "I don't know, for sure, but it can't be too much farther."

"What makes you say that?"

Geronimo lifted his left hand and pointed. "See that hawk up ahead?"

Cynthia squinted. "That black speck is a hawk? You must have fantastic eyesight."

"It's a hawk," he assured her. "Searching for prey. I doubt any hawks would bother scouring the Dead Zone. We haven't seen any sign of small game here. No, that hawk is probably circling over a field, looking for a rabbit or a field mouse. If I'm right, we should be out of the Dead Zone in a mile or less."

Three-quarters of a mile later the patrol was perched on the top of a rise.

"I've never been so happy to see green grass in my life!" Hamlin said happily, accurately reflecting the collective sentiment.

"We can't stop yet," Kilrane declared. "Those Cavalry boys might still be in the area."

"I doubt it," Hamlin disagreed. "They must have figured the ants did their dirty work for them and went home."

"Let's hope so," was Kilrane's reply.

They rode down the rise and entered a narrow valley, a verdant patch nestled between two sloping hills.

"We need to find water for the horses," Kilrane stated.

Their small group covered half of the valley when Kilrane abruptly reined in the Palomino. The others immediately did likewise.

"Why'd you do that?" Hamlin queried.

"I heard something," Kilrane responded, his head cocked to one side, listening.

"Like what?" Hamlin wanted to know.

"Like them," Kilrane said, and pointed.

"Son of a bitch!" one of the other riders snapped.

Dozens and dozens of riders were forming on the rims of the two hills. Another line had formed directly in front of the Legion patrol, blocking their path. The only avenue still open was to their rear, back into the Dead Zone.

"They have us boxed in!" one of the men cried.

"How many are there?" Cynthia questioned, attempting to count the Cavalry riders.

"I make eighty or ninety," Kilrane answered.

"What do we do?" Hamlin anxiously inquired. "Head back to the Dead Zone?"

Kilrane shook his head. "No. That's what they want us to do. We wouldn't stand a chance of surviving another night in there."

"Then what do we do?" Hamlin nervously repeated.

"We stay put," Kilrane announced, his blue eyes blazing.

"You're crazy!" Hamlin exclaimed. "What chance do we have against that many men?"

"Better odds than against the ants!" Kilrane rejoined.

The Cavalry unit was closing in, the riders on the hills descending as the line in front of the Legion patrol advanced.

"They'll mow us down!" Hamlin wailed.

Geronimo noticed Kilrane's attention was arrested by someone in the skirmish line. The Legion captain was staring intently at the center of that line of horsemen.

"Who do you see?" the Warrior asked.

"I don't believe it!" Kilrane replied. "We're about to be honored with the royal presence."

"Rory?" Hamlin moaned. "Rory is with them?"

Kilrane nodded. "So is Boone."

"But I thought Rory hardly ever left Redfield," Hamlin said, his fright evident.

"So did I," Kilrane confirmed.

"What's he doing way out here?" Hamlin demanded.

"We'll know in a moment," Kilrane predicted.

"They're closing in behind us!" another Legionnaire shouted.

Geronimo edged the brown stallion alongside the Palomino. "Will Rory shoot you in cold blood?"

"Don't think so," Kilrane opined. "He'll want to gloat, knowing him. He'll want to brag a spell before he does us in. That's good."

"Good?" came from Cynthia. "How can that be good?"

"You'll see," was all Kilrane would answer.

Geronimo kept his eyes on the approaching line of horsemen. Two men in the middle of the line, and slightly in front of it, drew his interest. One of them was a tall, handsome frontiersman in buckskins, the other a stocky man wearing brown pants and a brown shirt, emanating an impression of sheer power. Geronimo guessed the taller man was Rory and the other one Boone.

The Cavalry line stopped five yards from the clustered Legion patrol.

"We meet again, bastard!" Kilrane said to the shorter rider with his blond hair cropped close to his head.

"Is that any way to greet your proper leader?" the stocky man retorted.

Geronimo sighed. So much for his deductive insights! The one in the buckskins must be Boone.

"Howdy, Boone," Kilrane greeted the tall rider. "Long time no see."

Boone nodded. "It's been too long."

"Well, isn't this touching?" Rory sarcastically snarled. He glanced at Boone. "You sure you're on the right side?"

Boone stared at Rory until the latter, uneasy, turned away.

"Take a good look, men!" Rory shouted to his followers. "Take a good look at the mighty Kilrane! He's nothing more than a common traitor and deserves a traitor's fate!"

"What fate might that be?" Kilrane calmly inquired.

"Oh," Rory said shyly, "I was thinking along the lines of death by hanging."

"You planning to put the noose around my neck yourself?" Kilrane questioned him.

"I'd love to!" Rory shouted.

"Rolf wouldn't like it," Kilrane casually remarked.

At the mention of his brother's name, Rory became livid with rage. His hands dropped to his automatic pistols.

Geronimo caught a flicker of motion out of the corner of his eye.

Kilrane held his revolver in his right hand, pointed at Rory's chest.

Rory blanched, his hands on the pistol grips.

No one else moved. The riders on both sides glanced nervously at one another, some with their hands near their weapons.

"You should have shot me on sight," Kilrane said to Rory, and then he raised his voice so everyone could hear. "Don't anyone interfere! This is between Rory and me!" He paused. "But it involves all of you, so listen up!"

All parties were focused on Kilrane.

"You all know me!" Kilrane shouted. "You know my word is true. If there's anyone who thinks I'm a liar, speak up now."

There was a murmur among the Cavalry men, but none of them spoke up.

Kilrane took their silence as agreement. "All right. Then you know what I'm about to tell you is true." He hesitated, grinning at Rory, taunting him. "Most of us are tired of the split! We're sick of the separation, of the two camps, of being called the Cavalry and the Legion. We want to be one people again! We want to be nothing but the Cavalry! Am I right?"

Geronimo watched the Cavalry men, noting the look in their eyes as many of them nodded their heads in assent. A chorus of cries rose from the ranks.

"You know we do!" yelled one man.

"You got it!"

"Of course!"

"Long live the Cavalry!"

Kilrane patiently waited for the hubbub to subside. "Okay, then! If you want the two sides united again, you may be like me and wonder why we're staying apart. Does anyone know?"

None of the men responded.

"Does anyone even know why we split up in the first place?"

Again, no one replied.

"Well, I'll tell you!" Kilrane shouted.

Rory's face was beet red, his veins bulging on his beefy neck.

"I was there when it happened," Kilrane told them, "so I know what I'm talking about!" He stopped and scanned the riders. "But first I want to tell you the reason I'm telling you all this. I had a chance to do a lot of thinking in the past day or so, thinking about how stupid we've been. Stupid! Why? Because we allowed a bitter feud between two brothers to separate us, to draw us apart, to cause us to fight each other, although our hearts aren't in it. We don't want to kill each other! Because we know that being part of the Cavalry or the Legion is all the same! We're still brothers! It's like being part of one big family!" Kilrane pointed at Geronimo. "Do you see this man here? He's a stranger. You don't know him. But he said something to me that started me thinking. He said that his people would worry about him, and I got the impression they would send someone looking for him. Think about that! I did! It reminded me of how it used to be, how it was before the break. Do you remember? In the old days, if anyone attacked even one of us, they faced the wrath of all of us. We were the Cavalry, by damn, and we stuck together through thick and thin! Do you remember?"

The uproar was deafening.

Kilrane sat quietly until the din tapered off. "And now look at us! Brother fighting brother! Cousin against cousin! And why? I'll tell you why!" Kilrane

gestured toward the furious Rory, "Because of him!
Because of that . . . slime . . . we grew apart! Ten
years ago Rolf announced he was leaving, and many
of us volunteered to go with him, not understanding
what was going on. At the time, I was pledged to
silence. But what's a promise compared to the
welfare of our entire people?" Kilrane sighed, his
baleful gaze locked on Rory. "The reason Rolf
stepped down, the reason he left and started the rift
in our people, was because *Rory raped Adrian!*" The
last three words exploded from his lips.

Geronimo saw all eyes turn toward Rory,
studying him, measuring him, testing the validity of
Kilrane's revelation.

"Raped Adrian?" one man said skeptically. "Why
didn't Rolf kill Rory then?"

"You know Rolf," Kilrane answered. "Remember
how he always let Rory get away with almost anything? He always was soft on his brother. Maybe it
had something to do with them being twins. I don't
know. I do know he allowed Adrian to talk him out
of killing Rory."

"And that's it?" another Cavalry rider asked.
"That's the real reason we've been subjected to a
decade of grief? That's why we've endured ten years
of alienation and separation?"

Kilrane nodded.

Geronimo observed the men talking amongst
themselves, many casting expressions of loathing
and hostility at Rory.

"And that's it," Kilrane concluded. "Frankly, I'm
tired of it. I want us reunited! I want us as one
people again! Are you with me?"

Their response was a clamorous affirmative.

"Who's going to lead us if we get back together?"
one man demanded when it was quiet again.

Hamlin suddenly cupped his hands to his mouth. "Who else should lead us but Kilrane? Kilrane! Kilrane!"

The chant was taken up by the others, and soon it became a swelling litany.

Kilrane held his left hand aloft for silence. "I appreciate the honor," he stated, "but this time we'll do it right. This time we'll put it to a vote of all our people."

"But what about Rolf?" someone inquired.

"Rolf can run for leader the same as anyone else," Kilrane replied.

"More to the point," questioned an elderly rider, "what about Rory?"

"Hang the bastard!" a rider screamed.

"How about a firing squad?" suggested another.

"Geld the son of a bitch!"

Geronimo, amused, watched Rory squirm. He was looking around in stark fear, vainly searching for support.

"Maybe we should send him into the Dead Zone," Kilrane recommended, "on foot."

Rory gulped and finally found his voice. "It isn't true!" he feebly protested. "How can you believe him? I never raped Adrian! You believe me, don't you?"

His appeal was useless. He realized that. The faces confronting him were as hard as granite.

"No one is going to back you up," Kilrane said quietly. "So let's get this over with. How do you want to go out? A bullet in the brain? I'd love to do it!" he said, mimicking Rory's earlier statement.

Rory licked his thick lips, his mind racing, trying to find a way out. Suddenly an idea occurred to him and he smiled. "I demand a trial by combat!"

Geronimo detected a stirring, an unrest, in the

horsemen. Snatches of conversation drifted his way, and he overheard enough to learn the men did not like the idea.

Kilrane was frowning. "Trial by combat?"

"It's my right!" Rory exclaimed. "You know it is! It's been the law since the Cavalry was formed."

Geronimo saw Kilrane glance at Boone.

Boone, clearly displeased, nodded. "The bastard has a point. He does have the right."

Kilrane surveyed the other riders. "Rory has requested a trial by combat! We have no choice! His request must be granted."

Mutterings and mumblings arose from the men.

"Okay, Rory," Kilrane addressed him. "If we denied you a trial by combat, we'd set a bad precedent for the others. According to the law, if you survive the combat, you will be permitted to leave here unmolested."

"Why do you think I picked it?" Rory asked, mocking his nemesis.

Kilrane's lips tightened. "Also according to the law, you are allowed two choices. First, your choice of weapons."

"I pick the lance," Rory stated.

"He's crafty, that Rory," Hamlin whispered to Geronimo and Cynthia. "He's good with the lance, and he knows it."

"The lance, then," Kilrane declared. "All that remains is for you to pick your opponent."

Rory twisted his neck, examining the men, hunting for the ideal foe.

"We haven't got all day," Kilrane snapped after some time had elapsed.

Rory, unexpectedly, smiled, seeming to relax, to suddenly become surprisingly confident. "I've made my decision."

"So who is it?" Kilrane demanded. "Who gets the honor of doing you in?"

Rory, grinning, slowly raised his right hand. Everyone watched with bated breath, awaiting his selection. Rory extended his pudgy index finger, smirking. "I have a right to trial by combat!" he yelled. "I also have the right to select the man I will fight, and that man . . . is . . . *him*!" Rory abruptly leveled his arm, indicating his intended adversary.

It took Geronimo several seconds before he realized who the antagonist would be.

Rory was pointing at him!

# 22

It was late afternoon. The sun was high overhead in a clear blue sky. Except for Beta Triad on guard duty on the walls, and Spartacus and Seiko watching the prisoners in the infirmary, the entire Family was gathered on the commons between the Blocks to hear a special announcement from Plato. Men, women, and children were packed into a tight circle, their faces directed toward Plato and several of the Elders. Blade stood off to one side, about eight feet from Plato, in the center of the encircling Family.

"I will make this as brief as possible," Plato began. "For the benefit of those who might have been outside the Home wrestling mutates all day, two couples have declared their intention to bind in four days. I know how much we love to gossip, so I imagine everyone already is aware of the fact, but for the few still ignorant of the news, Blade and Jenny and Hickok and Sherry are going to marry in a double ceremony."

There was a spattering of applause, laced with expressions of delight from several of the women, and one or two suggestions from the men on the proper wedding night activities.

"That's only part of the news," Plato continued. "We are all painfully cognizant of the shortage of

Warriors, a deficiency made glaringly obvious by
the Troll raid on our Home some time back. Con-
sequently, the Elders have decided to add another
Triad to the four already in existence. Joining
Alpha, Beta, Gamma, and Omega Triads will be
Zulu Triad. Additionally, we must fill the vacancy in
Gamma Triad created by the demise of its leader."

Some of the Family began conversing in muted
tones, discussing the fate of Napoleon, the late
powermonger and former leader of Gamma Triad.

"The Elders have also reached the conclusion
Alpha Triad should return to the Twin Cities soon.
That being the case, and in order to assure adequate
time to provide minimal training, we have elected to
announce the final candidates for Warrior status.
I'm afraid we're rushing into this. I'd prefer more
time to devote to training the new Warriors before
Alpha Triad departs, but for reasons I will elaborate
upon later, it is imperative Alpha Triad hasten to
the Twin Cities and establish a friendly pact with
the inhabitants. So . . ." He paused and surveyed
the dozens of faces surrounding him. "If there are no
objections, we will proceed with the induction of the
new Warriors."

None of the Family lodged a protest.

"Excellent," Plato resumed. "We were honored
this time to have ten candidates for Warriorhood.
Unfortunately, we only require four at this point.
Regrettably, this means six had to be eliminated. I
want to stress, for the benefit of those six, that
being dropped from current consideration does not
adversely reflect on their personality or quali-
fications for the post. It simply means the four
chosen embraced certain factors or experience
essential for becoming a seasoned Warrior, factors
predicated on incidental circumstances and not

deliberate design.''

Hickok, who was standing two feet from Blade, Sherry at his side, leaned forward. "You know, pard," he whispered, "you're always saying how funny I talk sometimes, but at least folks can understand me!"

"First I will announce the replacement for Gamma Triad," Plato stated. "Because he displayed considerable courage during his confrontation with the Moles, and because Hickok vouches for his potential, and overlooking his insubordination when he left the Home without permission and was later captured, the Elders have chosen Shane as . . ."

Plato's comments were loudly punctuated by a shout of delight from the chosen one.

Others laughed at Shane's reaction.

". . . the new Gamma Warrior. While on the subject of Gamma Triad, you all know they require a new leader. So, because of his loyalty in the face of deliberate rebellion, and with Blade's highest recommendation, the Elders have picked Spartacus as the new head of Gamma Triad."

A young woman, Spartucus's girlfriend, broke away from the Family and ran toward the infirmary, her long black hair flying, as she raced to convey the good news.

"As for the new Triad, Zulu Triad," Plato continued, "we have selected the following three individuals to comprise it. The first is Crockett, in light of his exceptional marksmanship and confirmed bravery. We all recall how he saved several of the children from that mutated wolf. Our second pick is Samson, for his undisputed allegiance to the Family, and for being one of the few who can boast a physique almost as mighty as Blade's."

Plato stopped and cleared his throat.

"Before I reveal the third new Zulu Warrior, an explanation is called for. Some of you might question the wisdom of our next candidate, but hopefully you will understand after I supply a bit of background. As all of you are aware, a number of outsiders have come to dwell among us in recent months. We have, of course, embraced them with open arms, and been delighted at the ease with which they have found a niche in the Family culture. One of them has impressed us with her integrity and her devotion to our ideals. This morning, when our Home was invaded by a pair of genetic deviates sent by the nefarious Doktor, she displayed considerable courage in opposing a creature of formidable power and savagery. . . ."

Hickok flinched as Sherry's fingernails dug into his right forearm.

". . . and was slightly injured in the process. And, in a rare formal appeal, three of our most skilled, accomplished Warriors petitioned the Elders to suspend normal procedure and hear their request for her induction. Usually, as you know, we permit one Warrior to sponsor a new candidate for Warrior status. In this case we made an exception. When the likes of Blade, Rikki-Tikki-Tavi, and even Yama come to the Elders and urge acceptance of their unique nomination, believe me, the Elders listen. . . ."

Sherry placed her lips near Hickok's right ear. "All three of them? I hardly know Yama! Why would all three vote for me?"

"Because I begged them to," Hickok quietly replied.

"Really?"

"No. I threatened to tell everyone they like to

wear dresses to bed."

". . . so without further ado, I am proud to announce that Sherry, the woman from Canada, has been selected as a new Warrior."

Before Hickok could grab her, Sherry released his arm and ran to Plato, startling the Leader by hugging him and kissing him on the left cheek. "Thank you!" she happily blurted. "Thank you! This is the best wedding present I could have received!" She released him and darted to Hickok's side.

Plato, flustered by her display of affection and gratitude, managed a lopsided grin. "Thank the Spirit all of our Warriors aren't women," he quipped, "or my wife might become extremely jealous!"

There was a spontaneous outpouring of mirth from the assembled Family.

"In summation," Plato eventually went on, "we feel the Family will be well served by the additional Warriors. We can increase the number of patrols on the walls, and afford the Warriors more leisure and recreation time. An overworked, fatigued Warrior does not function at peak effectiveness, and might actually endanger the Family by an inadvertent mistake. Does anyone have any comment to make concerning the selections?"

No one raised a hand.

"Fine. Then let's review our Warrior organization. Blade is still the chief Family Warrior, and leads the Warriors in all operations. Our Triads will be constituted as follows. Alpha Triad will include Blade, Hickok, and Geronimo. Beta . . ."

"Where is Geronimo?" one of the men shouted.

"Yeah," echoed another. "We haven't seen him around for a while."

Plato frowned, the lines around his eyes deepening. "Geronimo requested a temporary leave of absence, which was granted. He has been gone much longer than initially expected, however. We do not know where he is at the moment, but plans have been made, should he not return within a week, to try and locate him."

"I hope he's okay," said a young girl in the crowd.

Plato recognized Star's voice. She was quite attached to Geronimo, perhaps based on the mutual bond they shared; they were the only Family members with Indian blood. He hastily forged ahead. "Beta Triad will be comprised of Rikki-Tikki-Tavi, Teucer, and Yama, with Rikki as the head. Gamma will be made up of Spartacus, the leader, and Seiko and Shane. Omega Triad will still include Carter, Gideon, and Ares, and Carter will serve as their chief. . . ."

"Do we have to memorize all of this?" one of the men asked, and others laughed.

". . . and finally we come to the newest Triad, Zulu, consisting of Crockett, Samson, and Sherry. There you have it. Fifteen Warriors responsible for the defense of the Home. May the Spirit grant them the strength and bravery to fulfill their duty admirably. Will the inductees please step forward?"

Blade strode to Plato's side and watched as Sherry, Shane, Crockett, and Samson emerged from the gathering.

Sherry waved to Hickok and blew him a kiss. Someone behind the gunman tittered and he whirled, glaring at those to his rear.

Suppressing a grin, Blade addressed the four candidates. "You will raise your right hand and repeat after me."

All four complied.

Blade studied their faces as he recited the Warrior's pledge. "I promise to preserve the Home and defend the Family at all costs. I will give my life, if necessary, to protect the lives of every Family member. I will obey all orders at all times. I will faithfully discharge my duties and obligations. . . ."

The four inductees repeated the pledge, word by word, their serious expressions reflecting their sense of commitment.

". . . . I will be steadfast and loyal to my Family, my fellow Warriors, and my Triad. In the sight of the Almighty Spirit, as witnessed by this assemblage, I hereby vow to live, and die, being the best Warrior I can possibly be." Blade paused and swept them with his intense gaze. "So do I swear," he concluded.

"So do I swear!" they chorused.

"Congratulations." Blade smiled. "You are now Warriors."

Crockett, a lean, dark-haired man in buckskins, nodded. Samson, a muscular powerhouse of a figure attired in ill-fitting jeans, grinned. Sherry screeched and spun around in her tracks. Shane, surprisingly, simply stood there, slack jawed.

Blade stepped closer to him. "Are you okay?"

"It just occurred to me," Shane said.

"What did?"

"I'm really a Warrior!" the youth exclaimed.

"Yes," Blade nodded, "you're really a Warrior. Just do us both a favor and don't get yourself needlessly killed. We expect only your best at all times."

"You don't have to worry," Shane assured him.

"I don't? Why not?"

"Because," Shane beamed, "I'm going to be one of the best Warriors the Family has ever seen. I'll be just like my hero."

"Your hero?" Blade repeated.

"Yep."

"Who's your hero?" Blade inquired.

"Who else?" Shane seemed surprised at Blade's ignorance. "Hickok!"

"Let me get this straight," Blade said slowly. "You plan to become just like Hickok?"

"Sure do."

"Exactly like him in every respect?"

"Absolutely," Shane stated, nodding.

Blade made a show of placing his right hand on his forehead and groaning.

"What's wrong?" Shane immediately queried him.

"It just boggles the brain!" Blade replied.

"What does?"

"Two Hickoks on the same planet! I don't know if we can survive it!"

# 23

"You don't have to do this!"

"You're crazy if you go through with it!"

"Don't do it! Please? For me?"

Geronimo glanced at the trio of speakers in the order in which they'd spoken: Kilrane, Hamlin, and Cynthia. Boone stood nearby, shaking his head.

"I still don't get it," Geronimo admitted. "Why did he pick me? I'm not with the Cavalry or the Legion."

"He's well aware of that fact," Kilrane responded. "But you were riding with us, so technically he could choose you."

"But you said I was a stranger," Geronimo pointed out. "He can still do it? Select a stranger?"

Kilrane glared at the distant Rory, fifty yards away, seated on his horse and holding a metal-tipped lance in his right hand. "The bastard is clutching at straws. He picked you hoping we would say no. You see, the majority of us can't stand his guts, but there are some who would become mighty upset if we did anything unfair, if there was the slightest hint of a frame or a setup."

"Even after what he did to Adrian?" Cynthia interjected.

"They'd still want his fate to be decided justly,"

Kilrane declared. "We never kill anyone without a reason. You know that. And we always give the accused the chance to defend himself. Or herself. We believe in fair play."

"What happens if I refuse to fight him?" Geronimo asked.

"Then the son of a bitch will claim a forfeit," Kilrane detailed, "and skip out, free as a bird."

"But you can't honestly expect Geronimo to do it?" Cynthia asked.

"It's up to him," Kilrane said. "Hell, I'd challenge Rory myself, but I know he'd refuse, and where would that leave us? If I gun him down in cold blood, I'd be a marked man."

"But just a while ago the men were clamoring for his death," Cynthia reminded them.

"And they want him dead," Kilrane stressed. "But he's demanded a trial by combat and we can't say no."

"Let me get this straight," Geronimo interrupted. "If you tell Rory I'm not one of the Cavalry and won't fight him, then he goes free?"

"On a technicality, yes," Kilrane confirmed.

"And if I personally say I won't do it," Geronimo said, "then he claims a forfeit and can go?"

"That's about the size of it."

"So the only way of preventing his departure," Geronimo concluded, "is if I kill him in this duel with lances?"

"You got it," Kilrane stated. "Unless one of us wants to shoot him on the spot."

Geronimo sighed. "I wish my friend Hickok *was* here."

"Why's that?" Cynthia asked.

"Because he'd walk right up to Rory, give him to the count of three to draw, and then shoot him in the head whether he drew or not," Geronimo explained.

"This Hickok would do that?" Kilrane inquired, impressed.

"Without hesitation," Geronimo affirmed.

"I sure would like to meet this hombre some day," Kilrane said wistfully. "He sounds like my kind of man."

"So what are you going to do?" Cynthia addressed Geronimo.

"I guess some of Hickok has rubbed off on me," Geronimo remarked. "Someone get me a lance."

"No!" Cynthia protested. "Don't do it!"

"She's right," Hamlin joined the conversation. "There's another reason why you shouldn't do it."

"What is it?" Geronimo asked.

"Have you ever used a lance before?" Hamlin questioned.

"No," Geronimo admitted. "Never have."

Hamlin looked at Rory. "He's good with a lance. Real good. He's had lots of practice and killed a number of good men with a lance. Not many use the lance on a regular basis. He probably figured you'd be no good at it."

"We don't have any choice," Boone said, speaking up. "We can't allow this man to fight Rory."

"As much as I hate to admit it," Kilrane said, "I have to agree. It would be suicide."

"Good," Cynthia smiled. "It's settled."

"No, it isn't," Geronimo disagreed. "I'm going to do it."

"What? Why?"

"Because," Geronimo told her, "I owe Kilrane for saving my life. Because I can't stomach the idea of Rory getting off the hook. Because he challenged me, counting on my cowardice. And finally, because I'm a Warrior. I don't care whether it's my Family or someone I don't even know; if they're threatened, then I'll eliminate that threat. A long time ago I gave my word. I promised I'd be the best Warrior I could possibly be, and no Warrior worth his pledge would allow the Rorys of this world to run loose, to go free to probably kill or rape someone else. I've met men like Rory before. They don't deserve to live."

Kilrane was smiling. "Hickok isn't the only one who's my kind of man. This Family of yours must be tough. I'd sure hate to tangle with them."

"After this is over," Geronimo offered, "I'll take you to meet them, if you'd like. We'd like to consider you as our friends."

"Sounds fine to me," Kilrane declared. "We'll hold the election and escort you home."

"Aren't we getting ahead of ourselves?" Hamlin asked, nodding toward Rory.

As if on cue, Rory suddenly shouted to them. "Let's get on with it! Is he going to fight or not? I haven't got all day!"

"Cocky turd!" Hamlin spat.

"If you're set on doing this," Kilrane said, "you're going to do it right. Forget that brown stallion."

"Then what horse will I use?"

Kilrane turned and grabbed the reins of his Palomino. "Here. Use my horse. It's been trained to handle lance fighting. Use your knees to guide it. I trained this animal myself. It will do everything for you except plant the lance in his gut."

"Are you sure?" Geronimo queried. "It's a fine horse. I'd hate to damage it."

"Be serious," Kilrane replied. "What's more important? Your life or a horse?"

Boone motioned, and one of the Cavalry riders approached with a lance. He gave it to Boone, who then presented the weapon to Geronimo.

Geronimo hefted the lance. It was ten feet long, as thick as a man's arm, and tipped with a metal point. Despite its size, the weapon was surprisingly light.

"Geronimo!" Cynthia exclaimed, abruptly grabbing him by the shoulders.

"I'll be all right," he promised her.

"Take care," she said, and kissed him on the lips.

Geronimo nodded and mounted the Palomino.

"Extend about two-thirds of the lance in front of your body," Kilrane advised. "Keep your grip firm, but don't lock your elbow in case you have to turn fast."

"Keep your body as close to the horse as you can," Boone suggested. "Present as small a target as you can."

"Watch that prick," Hamlin joined in. "Rory likes to twist as he's passing and jab the other guy in the back."

"If you knock him from his horse," Kilrane detailed, "you can finish him any way you want. It's the rules."

"I've got it," Geronimo told them.

"Take care," Cynthia repeated, her lovely eyes brimming with worry.

"Give him one for me!" Hamlin urged.

"Ride out until about twenty-five yards are between you," Kilrane directed. "When you hear me fire my gun, that's the signal. Remember, this Palomino knows what to do. Rely on its instincts."

Geronimo nodded, gazed fondly at his newfound friends, and rode forward.

Rory saw him coming and tightened his grip on his lance, raising it to chest level.

Geronimo felt an adrenaline surge rush through his body.

Rory's black horse was prancing in place, apparently accustomed to the duel and ready to begin.

It figured. Rory would own a well-trained horse too.

The Cavalry and Legion men were lined up to the east and the west of the duelists, about half on each side.

Geronimo glanced over his left shoulder and noted Kilrane was holding his revolver in his right hand.

Any second now!

He recalled every word of advice they'd given him, going over it again and again. Stay low, close to the Palomino. Keep two-thirds of the lance in front of him. Don't lock the elbow. It all sounded easy enough, but one mistake could cost him his life. His best bet might be to knock Rory off his horse. According to Kilrane, if he succeeded, he could end the conflict any way he desired. He'd use the Arminius to . . .

Hold it!

Had he reloaded the revolver after the fight with the ants?

No!

Geronimo debated whether to attempt to load the gun before Kilrane fired the starting shot, but decided against it. Too risky. Besides, he still had the tomahawk tucked in his belt. If worse came to worst, he'd use the tomahawk against his foe.

Rory was eyeing his opponent with a smug expression on his rotund face.

Hamlin was right. Rory was a cocky turd, to say the least!

The blast of Kilrane's revolver behind him was the signal for the contest to begin.

Rory immediately goaded his mount forward into

a gallop, leveling his lance as the horse gained speed.

Geronimo barely applied pressure to the Palomino and it was off, charging at Rory. He found it difficult to hold the long lance steady as the horse moved; the point kept bouncing up and down. The two animals were eating up the distance at an astounding rate. He realized he'd never impale Rory on the initial pass, so he opted to concentrate on avoiding Rory's first strike.

Rory came in fast and strong, his lance aimed for Geronimo's midsection. He leaned forward, adding momentum to his lunge, as the two horses came abreast of one another.

Geronimo saw that gleaming metal tip sweeping toward his stomach, and he instinctively adjusted, using his lower legs and knees to retain his hold on the Palomino as he lowered his upper torso over the side of his steed, away from Rory's thrust.

The lance missed, and the two horses were past each other and already circling.

Geronimo sat up, trying to hold his lance steady. He heard an outburst of applause from the assembled horsemen.

Rory, his features a mask of intensity, was coming in for the second strike.

Geronimo hunched over, keeping his eyes locked on the tip of Rory's lance.

The horses were only feet apart when Rory made his move, ramming his lance at his enemy.

Geronimo was scarcely able to twist aside. He felt Rory's lance scrape his right side, and knew his own weapon was held too wide to be of any use.

In an instant, the mounts were circling again for the next strike.

Geronimo changed his grip on his lance, extending more of it in front of him, hoping the additional length would compensate for his inexperience.

Rory was bearing down, grinning, confident in his superior ability.

Geronimo gauged the space between them, prepared to attempt a new tactic.

Fifteen yards.

Ten.

He tensed his body, his fingers holding the lance so hard the knuckles turned white.

Five yards!

Now!

Geronimo swung to his left as Rory jabbed with his lance. The tip passed to Geronimo's right, just missing his chest. In that split second, Geronimo had swung his own lance outward. He caught Rory in the side, smashing the wooden section against his ribs, but missed with the metal point.

A rousing cheer arose from the men as the two steeds geared for the fourth run.

What were those idiots cheering about? Geronimo wondered. He'd missed, hadn't he?

He suddenly realized Rory had reined in.

Why?

Geronimo did likewise, confused. What was Rory up to now? He was just sitting there, staring. What for?

"You're better than I thought!" Rory called out.

What was this act? Reverse psychology?

Geronimo smiled and raised his lance. "I'm getting the hang of it! Let's try it one more time!"

Rory frowned. "You're awful eager to die!"

"No," Geronimo yelled. "I'm eager to kill you!"

"You don't even know me!"

"True," Geronimo conceded. "And from what I've heard, I wouldn't want to know you!"

Rory, insulted, started his next charge.

So much for Mr. Nice Guy!

Geronimo leaned forward as the Palomino galloped ahead. He had to try something new this time, something unexpected. He couldn't expect Rory to miss forever. So far, only dumb luck and his quick reflexes had prevented disaster.

Twenty yards to go.

Let's see. What would be completely different? Something Rory wouldn't expect in a million years?

Fifteen yards.

What could he possibly . . . ?

They were ten yards apart when the inspiration struck Geronimo, and he put his idea into operation instantaneously with the thought. He wrenched on the reins, the Palomino responding magnificently, the horse slewing to an abrupt stop, even as Geronimo rose to his full height, the lance clenched in his right fist. He elevated his arm and swung the lance back, gathering his strength.

Rory, startled by the unorthodox maneuver, vainly endeavored to turn the black aside before it was too late.

He failed.

Geronimo swept the lance forward, throwing this weapon as he had a spear many times in the past. Among the many weapons Kurt Carpenter included in the Family armory were several spears, enclosed in a rack labeled "Miscellaneous." Under a section headed "Early North American" were several genuine Indian spears, and Geronimo had become proficient in their use by his tenth birthday. He'd spent hours upon hours developing his skill, and it had finally paid off.

The lance left Geronimo's hand and arced through the air, the shining tip tearing into Rory's body, entering at the right shoulder and exiting near the shoulder blade.

Rory shrieked in agony and released his hold on the black's reins, toppling off the horse, falling to his left, still holding his lance as he fell.

Geronimo wheeled the Palomino clear of the still running black, then slid from his steed and dropped to the grass, drawing his tomahawk as he landed.

Rory was on his knees, his right hand clutching the lance in his shoulder, his own lance on the ground in front of him.

Geronimo charged.

Rory saw him coming. He gripped the shaft of the lance in his shoulder with both hands. His face turned red as he exerted himself in a herculean effort and tore the lance from his body. Blood flowed down his brown shirt as he frantically clawed for the automatic pistol in his left holster.

Geronimo realized he'd never reach his foe before he managed to draw his pistol. The Arminius was empty, so there was only one thing to do.

He threw the tomahawk.

Rory was already bringing the pistol up.

All action seemed to revert to slow motion, as Geronimo watched the tomahawk flip end over end. He plainly saw the sweat on Rory's strained face; he could see the stark fear in Rory's wide eyes as he pointed the pistol; he observed, as if from a distance, the keen edge of the tomahawk bite into Rory's forehead, splitting the skin and penetrating the bone, crimson spurting over Rory's face, blood covering his eyes, as Rory's head jerked backwards from the impact.

The pistol discharged, the shot plowing into the ground at Geronimo's feet, and suddenly the world was operating at normal speed again.

Rory opened his mouth to scream, but nothing

came out except for a dribble of red over the right corner. He gasped, a vastly protracted sound, seemingly striving to inhale all the air in the atmosphere. Then his entire form quivered violently for several seconds before falling to one side. He landed on his left shoulder, rolled slightly forward, and lay still.

Dead.

Geronimo sighed and wiped the perspiration from his brow with the back of his right hand. He felt so weary, so tired of all the conflict. All he wanted was to get to the Home, to see those he loved, to relax and enjoy life again.

What was that noise?

The horsemen were giving him a thunderous ovation.

Geronimo slowly walked to Rory's body. He bent over, placed his right hand on the tomahawk handle, and pulled. There was a sucking sound and the blade popped free of the forehead, dripping blood on Geronimo's pants.

Footsteps pounded on the ground behind him and arms encircled his waist.

"You did it! You're alive!"

"How about letting me turn around?" he proposed.

She released her hold on him, and he twisted and smiled, delighted at the affection reflected in her admiring eyes.

"I thought I'd have a heart attack!" Cynthia exclaimed.

"You?" Geronimo laughed. "I did have one!"

"You did all right," stated the deep voice of Kilrane.

Geronimo glanced around.

Kilrane, Boone, and Hamlin were standing behind

him, Hamlin gaping at Rory's body.

"I never would of believed it!" Hamlin said in awe. "If I hadn't of seen it with my own eyes, I'd never believe it was possible!"

"Remember the technique in case you're ever in a lance duel," Geronimo suggested.

"I'll remember it, all right," Hamlin promised. "It's something I'll tell my grandkids about."

"How's your side?" Boone inquired.

Geronimo looked down, surprised to observe a rip in his green shirt and blood trickling over his pants.

"You're hurt!" Cynthia cried.

"Just a scratch," Geronimo remarked.

"You let me be the judge of that," Cynthia said. "Sit down," she ordered him.

Geronimo complied, grinning.

Cynthia looked at Kilrane. "Can you get me some cloth and a canteen?"

"You got it." Kilrane strode toward the horsemen.

"Take your shirt off," Cynthia directed, crouching next to Geronimo.

"You seem to enjoy bossing me around," Geronimo observed wryly.

Cynthia stared fondly into his eyes. "You better get used to it."

"I'll try."

Boone stepped closer. "I've never seen anyone use a hatchet like you."

Geronimo held the tomahawk aloft. "It's not a hatchet," he informed Boone. "It's called a tomahawk."

"You reckon you could teach me how to toss that thing sometime?" Boone asked. "A talent like that could come in mighty handy."

"Whenever you want," Geronimo told him.

"Well, it sure isn't going to be right this minute," Cynthia let them know. "He's not tossing anything for a while. Not until he heals."

Boone winked at Geronimo. "Ain't true love wonderful?"

Cynthia smacked Boone on the left shin. "Don't you have something else you can do besides bother an injured man?"

"I can take a hint," Boone stated, smiling. He nodded at Geronimo and departed, just as Kilrane arrived with a canteen and a blanket. Hamlin waved and strolled off too.

"Here," Kilrane said, offering the items to Cynthia. "You can cut the blanket into strips if need be."

"Thank you," Cynthia responded as she took the blanket and the canteen. "Now why don't you run off and water your horse or something?"

Kilrane grinned. "Will do. But first I have something to say to Geronimo."

"It's not necessary," Geronimo informed him.

"Yes, it is. By taking care of Rory for me, you've evened up the score. You've also given my people a new lease on life, for which I can't thank you enough. We'll be able to unite the two factions again, and it will be just like in the old days. The Cavalry rides again!"

"I'm glad I could help," Geronimo mentioned.

"You're pretty anxious to get home, aren't you?" Kilrane asked.

Geronimo nodded.

"Well, I'll see what I can do. I'm going to dispatch riders to Pierre. If they ride all night, and borrow mounts as they need them from the farms and ranches they'll pass along the way, they should deliver my message to Rolf sometime tomorrow.

I'll tell him to come to Redfield on the double. The election won't take that long, and once that's over I'll get you to your family safe and sound. Okay by you?" Kilrane concluded.

Geronimo glanced at Cynthia and she nodded.

"If it's not an imposition," Geronimo said, "there is one more thing you could do for me."

"True friends will do anything for each other," Kilrane stated. "What do you need?"

"I need you to send out some riders," Geronimo revealed.

"Where to? Your family?"

"No." Geronimo looked at Cynthia. "You tell him."

So she did.

Kilrane smiled, his eyes twinkling. "Hot damn! Are we gonna have one whopper of a wingding! I may have a hangover for a week!"

"Me too," Geronimo commented.

"Over my dead body," Cynthia vowed.

"Oh. Why not?"

"Because you'll be too busy doing something else."

Kilrane's laughter filled the valley.

# 24

"Can I tell you something, pard?"

"Of course."

"You promise not to tell anyone?"

"I promise."

"Are you sure you won't tell anyone?"

Blade sighed. "Nathan, if you're that worried about it, then don't tell me."

Hickok was nervously rubbing his hands together. "But I've got to tell someone."

"Then tell me."

Hickok scanned their immediate vicinity to insure they were alone. The two Warriors were standing near one of the few trees in the commons area, attired in their best clothes. Hickok wore a new set of buckskins and new moccasins, his Pythons were polished, the pearl handles gleaming in the afternoon sunlight, and his hair was neatly combed. Blade wore clean fatigue pants confiscated from the Watchers, a white shirt stitched together from the remnants of an old sheet, and his black vest. His Bowies were strapped around his waist.

The Family was assembled twenty yards from the Warriors, every member wearing their finest clothes. Omega Triad was on duty on the walls, but Spartacus and Seiko were temporarily relieved from guarding the prisoners for this special occasion after first binding the two soldiers and Ferret with so many loops of rope only their faces and feet were visible.

"Don't let this get around," Hickok said quietly, "but for the first time in my entire life, the very first time, I am so scared I could pee my pants!"

"You'd better not," Blade advised. "Sherry made those for you herself, and I don't think she'd like it too much if you put a stain in them."

"Aren't you just a mite edgy?" Hickok asked.

"What's to be edgy about?"

"You're binding, pard! You're getting married! You're giving up bachelorhood for an anchor and chain!"

Blade chuckled. "Is that how you view it?"

Hickok pondered a moment. "No, I reckon not. I guess I've been listening to Spartacus too much."

"He's a fine one to talk," Blade snorted. "I'll bet you anything he's the next one to tie the knot."

"I almost wish he was doing it now instead of me," Hickok mumbled.

"Sherry's a fine woman," Blade stated. "You're a lucky man."

"But what if I ruin her life?" Hickok inquired in a plaintive tone.

"What are you babbling about?"

"What if I ruin her life?" Hickok gravely repeated. "I'm a Warrior, plain and simple. I can't promise her a fancy spread or ritzy clothes, because I know I couldn't deliver. . . ."

"So who in the Family has a fancy spead or ritzy clothes?" Blade interrupted.

"I mean," Hickok went on, ignoring Blade's comment, "we could starve to death, couldn't we? If we're ever out in the world, on our own, what happens if I can't deliver? What happens if I can't do my job as a man, as the provider for my family?"

"Are you planning to leave the Home soon?" Blade interjected.

"Well, no," Hickok admitted.

"Then you won't need to worry about providing, will you? The Tillers take care of our needs here, as far as food is concerned. All you have to do is your job as a Warrior. The rest will take care of itself."

"But what if I get shot?" Hickok queried, his face a study in self-torment. "What if we have kids and I get killed? Who's going to look after Sherry and the kids? Who's going to stare into their cute little faces and tell them their papa was blown away in the line of duty and won't be home that night to tuck them in or read them a bedtime story?"

"More to the point," Blade stated, "who's going to look into their cute little faces and inform them their dad was a dimwit?"

"I'm serious about this," Hickok snapped.

Blade gazed skyward and shook his head. He placed his right arm around Hickok's shoulders. "Nathan, listen to me. You're working yourself up over nothing. Sherry knows you're a Warrior and I doubt she'd want you to change. We've had Warriors in the Family for a century, and many of them have married and reared children. Sherry knows the best she can expect is a cabin in the Home and the security it provides. At least, in here, she'll have a safe haven, somewhere she can raise her offspring with confidence."

"But . . ." Hickok started to speak.

"Let me finish," Blade cut him off. "As far as you're being killed is concerned, every parent faces that prospect. You should talk to Yama sometime. He has an interesting philosophy about dying. He says death is inevitable. Everyone and everything dies. So why in the world do so many people get upset about dying? Death is merely the method for getting from where we are right now, from this planet, to where we're going from here. Plato and Joshua say we pass on from here to the mansions on high. So . . ."

"But . . ." Hickok tried to interrupt.

"Will you let me finish?" Blade demanded. "So it's useless for you to become so upset over death. Besides, Sherry is a Warrior now, and it could happen to her as easily as to you. Your children will understand, and they'll have everyone in the Family here to look after them. I personally guarantee Jenny and I will treat your kids as our very own if something ever happens to Sherry and you. What more . . ."

"But . . ."

Blade, annoyed, removed his arm from Hickok's shoulder. "Here I am, trying to have a heart-to-heart talk with you, and all you can do is interrupt. But! But! But! But what?"

Hickok's face was decidedly pale. "I appreciate what you're saying, pard," he said, "but the whole matter is moot."

"Why's that?"

"Because binding time is here." Hickok pointed.

Blade turned and saw several of the Family beckoning for them to approach.

"They've been wavin' at us ever since you started yapping," Hickok mentioned.

"Why didn't you tell me?"

"I tried," Hickok replied. "But you were on a roll."

They walked toward the Family, which was divided into two groups of comparable size, standing with their backs towards the two Warriors. The entire Family was facing due south, their eyes on the man presiding over this most meaningful of ceremonies, the Family member viewed as the most intensely spiritual man ever to arise in Family history.

"I hope old Josh doesn't flub his lines," Hickok whispered as they neared the clustered Family.

"Joshua is the same age you are," Blade absently remarked, his mind on the impending ceremony.

As was Family tradition, the two Warriors stood at the rear of the narrow aisle between the two waiting groups. Standing alone in front of the Family, at the end of the cleared pathway, was Joshua, his long brown hair blowing in the cool breeze, his beard and moustache meticulously groomed, his large Latin cross visible in the center of his chest, suspended from a golden chain draped around his neck. He wore a faded but clean black suit and a white shirt with a ruffled front.

"Josh looks like a sissy," Hickok quibbled.

Blade turned toward B Block, wondering what was keeping the women. That's when he saw them, already half the distance to the gathered Family.

"Maybe I should give Sherry more time to think about this," Hickok was thinking to himself. "After all, you don't want to rush into anything as important as marriage. I'll bet . . ."

Blade smacked Hickok on the left shoulder and nodded toward the women.

Hickok swiveled, his mouth dropping. "Dear Spirit! Aren't they a sight!"

Blade was experiencing similar emotions. In all his days, he could recall nothing as beautiful as the vision of Jenny coming toward him, dressed in a replica of the typical wedding garment worn by women in the pre-war society. She'd taken a photograph from one of the books in the library and, with the aid of several of her friends, after sewing and cutting and experimenting with crude patterns for two days, produced a marvelous reproduction of a wedding dress.

Sherry had opted for a white pants suit, remarkable because white clothing was at a premium. One of the older women owned a swatch of white material preserved from the pre-war times, and she generously gave it as a gift, after bleaching it to remove the discoloration.

Smiling, the two women reached their intendeds.

"You're beautiful!" Hickok whispered to Sherry.

Blade stared down the long path to Joshua, then at Hickok. "You can go first," he graciously offered.

Hickok gazed along the rows of expectant faces, then grinned at Blade. "Thanks, pard, but you can go first."

"No, you go first."

Hickok politely shook his head. "No, you go first. You're bigger than me."

"What's that got to do with anything?"

Joshua was watching them in bewilderment, perplexed by the delay.

Jenny glanced at Sherry, rolled her eyes heavenward, and took Blade's right hand, forcefully pulling him the first few feet down the aisle.

Hickok leaned toward Sherry. "Listen," he said softly, "if you'd like to postpone this for a year or so, I'd under . . ."

He nearly lost his footing when she unceremoniously yanked him along the pathway.

Joshua, hoping his beard and moustache hid his grin, stood solemnly until the couples reached him, Blade and Jenny standing to his right, Hickok and Sherry to his left.

Plato and his wife, Nadine, were in the front row of the Family, Nadine with tears in her eyes.

Joshua raised his hands over his head.

"Brothers and sisters," he began, "fellow children of our loving Creator, we are gathered here today for a very special ceremony, for the eternal binding of these two couples. As the Spirit is our witness, we pray for their happiness together as husband and wife."

Joshua lowered his arms and stared at the four people in front of him.

"Binding," he continued, "is a serious responsibility. A union of a man and a woman should be an equal partnership, a mutual sharing predicated on love and loyalty. The woman agrees to go through life with her man, to assist the man in dealing with the hardships of life, and to diligently shoulder the burden of bearing and rearing children."

Joshua glanced at Hickok and Blade.

"The man must appreciate the sacrifice the woman makes in carrying, bearing, and usually assuming the far-greater share of responsibility in raising the children. The man must be willing to offer not only protection from the evils of this world, but also the loving companionship and consideration the woman deserves."

Joshua's voice rose in volume.

"The man and the woman have not only joined in partnership with one another, they have also joined in partnership with the Spirit as co-directors of their destiny and as procreators of a new life, new eternal souls, for the bringing of innocent infants into the world."

He gazed at the women.

"Do you, Jenny and Sherry, take these men as your respective mates, to love and cherish through-out all eternity?"

"I do," Jenny stated.

"I do," Sherry concurred.

"And do you, Blade and Hickok, take these women as your respective mates, to love and honor throughout time without end?"

"I do," Blade promptly replied.

"I . . ." Hickok began, and then coughed, his throat congested.

Sherry glared at her beloved.

"I do!" Hickok hastily exclaimed, so loudly they heard him in the infirmary.

Star, standing in the front row alongside Plato and Nadine, giggled.

"Remember your vows to one another," Joshua resumed. "When the storm clouds gather overhead, in times of sickness or danger, ever bear in mind the supernal affection you share, the unbreakable bond of love, cemented by this ceremony."

He paused.

"I now declare you to be husband and wife. You may kiss as a symbol of this union."

Many Family members were clapping as Blade took Jenny in his arms.

Hickok hesitated.

"You'd better kiss me," Sherry warned.

"In front of all these people?"

"Would you rather have a kiss or a fat lip?"

Hickok reluctantly complied, embracing Sherry and gingerly kissing her on the lips.

"Oh, good grief!" she declared, and grabbed him by his hair, planting a kiss on him, her tongue boring into his mouth, that he'd never forget.

A strident horn suddenly sounded from the west wall, and the gunman stiffened and pushed Sherry away.

"Hey! Something wrong with my kiss?" she demanded.

"Shhhh!" he shushed her.

The horn blasted twice more in quick succession.

Instantly, the Family members were in motion, running every which way.

"What's going on?" Sherry asked, alarmed.

"The danger signal," Hickok answered. He pecked her on the cheek. "You get inside until I see what it is."

"I will not," she defied him. "I'm a Warrior now, and where you go, I go!"

Blade and Jenny were racing toward the west wall.

"All right," Hickok agreed. "But stay close to me." He jogged after Blade, noting the drawbridge was up, relieved because any attackers would experience supreme difficulty in gaining entrance to the Home otherwise.

Hickok reached the stairs, Sherry on his heels. Blade and Jenny were already at the top.

"I make it about forty horsemen," Blade stated as Hickok reached his side.

"Any idea who they are?" Hickok asked.

The line of riders was poised at the edge of the forest, one hundred and fifty yards from the compound walls. The fields surrounding the Home were kept cleared of all vegetation as a security precaution.

"They're not Watchers," Blade deduced, "and they don't look like scavengers. The Moles don't own horses, and neither do the people in the Twin Cities. I don't know who they are."

Three of the riders detached themselves from the rest and rode slowly toward the wall.

"Is one of them a woman?" Sherry inquired, squinting to see better.

Rikki joined them, binoculars in his left hand, his katana in his right. "Here," he said, offering the binoculars to Blade. "You'd better take a look."

Blade did, and grinned. "Well, I'll be damned!"

"What is it?" Hickok pressed him.

"See for yourself."

Hickok took one look and spun, bellowing at several men standing near the massive mechanism utilized for lowering and raising the drawbridge. "What are you yokels waiting for? Lower the blasted drawbridge!"

The men exchanged puzzled looks as they obeyed the order.

Hickok tossed the binoculars to Blade and bolted down the stairs. He impatiently waited for the drawbridge to fully lower, then casually sauntered across it to the field.

"I don't understand. . . ." Sherry said to Blade.

"You will in a minute," he predicted.

The three riders reined in when they reached the gunman.

Hickok, all smiles, strolled over to one of the horsemen, his thumbs hooked in his gunbelt. "Howdy there, pard. Long time no see."

"Did you miss me?" Geronimo asked.

Hickok feigned a yawn. "Naw. I never even noticed you were still gone until this morning."

"Oh." Geronimo sounded disappointed. "Anything happen while I was away?"

"Nope. Nothing much. How about you? Run into any trouble out there in the big, bad world?"

"A very boring trip," Geronimo answered. "Nothing much happened."

The lovely woman on the horse next to Geronimo glanced at him, her black hair waving in the wind. "Oh? Is that right?" She wore black pants and a yellow blouse, both in reasonably good shape.

Geronimo cleared his throat. "One event of some significance did occur," he sheepishly admitted.

"What's that, pard?"

"I got married."

Hickok's astonishment showed. "You did what?"

"Her parents wouldn't allow her to come here if we weren't married," Geronimo explained. "Otherwise, I'd have invited you to the wedding."

"Don't feel bad," Hickok said.

"Why not?"

"Because," Hickok smiled, "Blade and I got hitched too."

"What? When?"

"You're interrupting the ceremony right now," Hickok informed him.

"We pushed it as fast as we could," commented the third rider, a tall man with blue eyes and light brown hair, wearing buckskins and mounted on a fine Palomino.

"Hickok," Geronimo introduced them, "this is Kilrane, the leader of the Cavalry."

"The what?"

"I'll explain after we're inside," Geronimo said.

"I'm right pleased to make your acquaintance," Kilrane declared, extending his right hand.

Hickok reached up and shook.

"I've heard a lot about you," Kilrane mentioned.

"So have I," Cynthia stated, offering her own hand.

"You must be the lucky lady," Hickok commented as he turned and shook with her.

"The name is Cynthia," she revealed.

Hickok faced Geronimo and raised his right hand. "Let me be the first in the Family to offer congratulations."

"Thank you," Geronimo said, leaning down, completely unprepared for what transpired next.

Hickok gripped Geronimo's wrist and hauled him from the horse. Before Geronimo could resist, Hickok had him by the front of his shirt and was shaking the tar out of him.

"Don't you ever do this to me again!" Hickok shouted. "Do you have any idea how worried I was? I was all set to come after you, you lousy Injun! Ruin my honeymoon and everything! And all because you can't find your way back here without help!"

Geronimo was beaming in unrestrained delight.

"So," Hickok went on, his voice lowering several octaves, "why don't you come in and meet the missus?"

"It is Sherry, I assume," Geronimo remarked.

"Well, I wouldn't be marrying Yama, now would I?"

They started to stroll across the drawbridge.

"Hey!" Cynthia shouted. "What about me?"

"You and the others are free to enter in peace," said a deep voice above them.

Cynthia and Kilrane looked up. A huge man with bulging muscles was perched on the edge of the rampart, standing behind the strands of barbed wire placed all along the top of the wall.

"You sure it's all right?" Kilrane asked, gazing at the Bowies on the man's hips.

"You have my word," the man assured them. "You and your men will not be harmed. The Family welcomes you in peace and friendship. Any friends of Geronimo's are friends of ours."

"You can't have too many friends in this world," Kilrane said.

Blade glanced behind him, watching Hickok and Geronimo enter the compound, exchanging lively banter. "Ain't it the truth?" he stated quietly. He faced Kilrane and Cynthia, smiling, speaking louder for their benefit.

"Ain't it the truth!"